Norman Dale was simply not the charming father he'd presented in his letters. What other surprises did he have in store for her? Did he imagine her so besotted she wouldn't mind?

No matter. She'd signed that register pure and simple. He'd made her his wife, and she'd willingly taken him as her husband. For better or worse.

"Sit yourself down. I'll go get Silly and the rest of the kids," he said through slitted lips. He raised his brows at the blonde woman and she nodded, leaving them in private.

"The rest of what kids?" Minda's skin prickled. Deciding to obey him for the first and only time, she sat down.

"Our kids. Yours and mine."

"Our kids? What in the world do you mean, Norman Dale? You wrote that you've got one daughter. Fourteen years old." Minda's voice rose and despite the heat, her shoulders tensed with a sudden chill as if a clump of snow had just fallen from the treetops. "What kids? What on earth are you saying, Norman Dale? Your letters didn't say one single words about *kids*."

He glared down at her. "You must've misread my brother." The last two words slid from his tongue in slow deliberation.

His brother? She sat helpless, hopeless, paralyzed against the back of the hard little chair. For a moment, she had no air to speak.

"Your brother? *Your brother*? What do you mean?"

He leaned close to her, like he had during their kiss, but at her ear he growled, low, "You promised to wed a Haynes today. Well, I'm the only one left. Your Norman Dale, my brother—" His fingers, calloused and hot, held her chin still so he could glare into her eyes, "—is dead."

Kudos and Reviews for Author Tanya Hanson

MARRYING MINDA placed first with perfect scores in the "Ignite The Flame" contest, historical division, sponsored by Central Ohio Fiction Writers, 2007.

MARRYING MINDA placed first in the Merritt "Magic Moment" Contest, historical division, sponsored by San Antonio Romance Authors 2008.

And for MIDNIGHT BRIDE:

"If you like the writings of Diana Palmer, then you will definitely want to pick up MIDNIGHT BRIDE."

~Joyfully Reviewed

"Ms. Hanson has a distinctive voice and a wonderful turn of phrase...making this a book to curl up with."

~Love Western Romance, Four Spurs

"...a book you won't be able to put down."

~Romance Junkies, Blue Ribbon Rating 4.5

"Tanya Hanson creates a great plot with a well-developed cast that keeps the pages turning."

~Coffee Time Romance, a Four Cup Outstanding Read

Marrying Minda

by

Tanya Hanson

Marrying Minda

Contact Information: info@thewildrosepress.com

Cover Art by *Nicola Martinez*

The Wild Rose Press
PO Box 706
Adams Basin, NY 14410-0706
Visit us at www.thewildrosepress.com

Publishing History
First Cactus Rose Edition, 2009
Print ISBN 1-60154-469-3

Published in the United States of America

Dedication

With love to my sister and brother-in-law,
Roberta and Tim Pelton.
I couldn't have made it without you.

Chapter One

Paradise, Nebraska, July 1878

Where is Norman Dale?

Minda's heart thumped. The noon stage had run late, so he had plenty of time to get here. Unless he had backed out.

She swallowed hard. Nowhere on the empty street did she see a bridegroom bearing a bouquet of her favorite white roses. The gulp turned into a sob. They had signed a legal contract fair and square, and the dry official document hadn't stopped them from falling a little bit in love with each other. His letters had been full of compliments and promises and excitement, too, about meeting face-to-face.

And today was the day.

Even in the stuffy interior of the stagecoach, Minda shivered with a chill of unease. After tossing her valises on the boardinghouse steps, the driver lifted her down. Minda shrugged out of the long linen duster she'd worn as protection against the grime of travel, for underneath she wore her wedding gown. Norman Dale's last letter had sweetly insisted they wed the minute she arrived.

Trying to impart a radiant smile, she paid no heed to the reactions of her fellow travelers. The woman wearing an old-style coal-scuttle bonnet of green gingham had chatted pleasantly for the last five miles, but upon seeing Minda's silk and lace, her mouth turned wide and silent as a full moon. And a grubby codger leered while showing off his two brown teeth.

She ignored them just as she'd paid no heed to her younger sisters' claims that a spinster didn't need a lovely white wedding gown. Well, Minda Becker might be a spinster and a mail-order bride on top of it. But she *was* a bride, and she was going to do it right.

In the hot dust of the departing stage, she drooped in disillusion at the hard-luck little town. Norman Dale's letters had glorified Paradise. Truth to tell, her new hometown was one brick building and a dozen false-front wooden structures with miles of cornfields and prairie grass billowing around the edges. Her bridegroom's own farm and fine wooden house must lie quite a ways outside of town.

She caught sight of a trim white church down the street and the slew of horses and wagons hitched to rough-hewn posts along its side. Relief as sweet as her silk dress flooded her. Of course. Norman Dale must be busy greeting wedding guests who waited on a bride delayed by a stage running late. Of course, he'd be along in a minute to fetch her. They'd already agreed to march up the aisle together. A widower had no reason to wait at the altar for a mail-order bride who had no one to give her away.

Past the church, tables piled with platters and baskets sat in the shade of big cottonwoods along the riverbank. Her wedding dinner. Goodness, she was about to become Mrs. Norman Dale Haynes. With a quiver of delight, she shook dust and wrinkles from her skirts and walked up the boardinghouse steps to seek a mirror and a bowl of cool water for freshening.

But a *closed* sign hung on the lopsided door. Minda smiled at her reflection in the grimy window anyway. Likely the innkeeper was a wedding guest already at church. After digging through a valise, she brought out the veil she'd fashioned from odds and ends at the millinery back home. Just touching the beautiful headpiece set a new flock of butterflies aflutter inside her belly. The froth of netting cascaded from a wreath of roses she'd crafted from scraps of ivory velvet.

As she arranged the veil, she heard her name. However, the angle of reflection didn't let her see the speaker.

"Miz Becker? You are Minda Becker, right?"

She turned to see a man approaching, tall and lean in his Sunday best, awkwardly carrying her bridal bouquet.

Mr. Norman Dale Haynes. She couldn't stop the outtake of breath. He was much younger and far more handsome than the daguerreotype he had sent her. Hair dark as midnight brushed each side of his neck, and tall as he was, her head wouldn't reach his shoulder. Her face warmed. It wouldn't take long at all to give him her whole heart.

Or her body.

Her heart hammered beneath her whalebone corset. Heat that had nothing to do with the weather poured over her like new milk. Merciful heavens, he must have wed young the first time around to have the teenage daughter he needed her to raise.

This man didn't appear to have any flaws at all. She tingled from top to toe, recalling how her three married sisters, with many blushes, had explained the delights of the marriage bed. She wanted the same for herself.

Her eye for style had designed quality hats in Gleesburg, so the poor fit of his dark coat stumped her. She'd expected better attire from a well-off farmer on his wedding day. More important, his grim countenance and the black moustache over his unsmiling lip started the blood in her veins to run cold. But a second later she warmed a little. Likely he had some jitters himself. His masculine handsomeness made her proud. She'd chosen well.

Although she was almost twenty-five, she quivered like a flighty schoolgirl. Gathering up her dignity, she walked toward him, eager for a welcoming embrace. In truth, his letters had indicated he'd fallen for her as well.

"Yes, yes, of course, I'm Minda Becker." She smiled big and bright to keep her words from shaking. "Is there another bride arriving this afternoon?"

"Nope. Just you. Let's get you married up." He still didn't smile or offer a hand or an introduction. Or even remove his hat. Heart sinking, she shut her lids tight to hold back tears.

Had she come a thousand miles to get her heart broken?

A wisp of the veil fluttered across her face in the hot wind and she grabbed the edge to have something to do. Had that interminable trek from Pennsylvania been a powerful mistake?

Folks in Gleesburg had considered her a spinster after she gave up her girlhood to raise her three little sisters when Mama died. But at least her hometown had cobbled streets and brick houses, decent businesses including the hat shop where she'd made her living. Neighbors close by, too. Every homestead she'd seen around here seemed miles away from the next one.

She still had time to change her mind. But no, she'd signed that contract. She'd given her word. More than anything, she wanted a husband and a home of her own. As she forced herself to return her bridegroom's unyielding gaze, her skin prickled a little at his dark eyes that didn't blink.

"I regret the late start to our wedding, Norman Dale. My train arrived in Columbus on time, but I truly had no control over the stagecoach getting me to Paradise." She tried to laugh lightly. No thinking person could hold her responsible.

Her face burned. Unless he thought she'd delayed the stage's departure by taking time to change into her wedding dress. His correspondence had complimented her plenty on her common sense. She couldn't bear him thinking her frivolous and vain.

"A late stage isn't your fault. But hurry up now. Folks are waiting."

Minda's spirits plummeted once again at his abrupt tone. Was this the man she'd spend the rest of her life with? Worry and doubt turned her cold in spite of July. But as he handed her the flowers, he took her hand.

At his touch, she barely found enough air. Her bosoms shivered beneath the lace and silk of her gown, and the bones of her corset seemed strangely tight. Silent, he led her toward the church. Stepping away from some horse dung, she leaned hard against him. He pulled away.

Her heart sank. Maybe Norman Dale hadn't written those wonderful letters himself. Maybe he wasn't eager to meet her like he'd claimed. Maybe all he wanted was a new mother for his teenaged girl.

Or maybe he was dissatisfied with her looks. She bowed her head in a sudden petition. The daguerreotype she'd sent showed her flaws as well as her graces. Although her sisters had declared her lovely enough to steal any man's heart, Minda gulped disappointment along with the hot summer air.

Fully intending to honor her promises and her vows, she tightened her fingers in determination. She wanted a family all her own. There was nothing left for her back home where bachelors sought younger belles, and the sisters she'd raised were busy newlyweds. No matter what, she'd take on Norman Dale Haynes and his child and his household, make it all her own. And get him to love her like he'd hinted.

At the church steps, he at least found enough manners to hold her skirts and help her inside. A pump organ faltered over the wedding march.

Unwavering, Minda walked into her future. The wide-eyed interest of the wedding guests didn't surprise her much. After all, she'd traveled a long way to marry a man she'd never actually met. For a half-second, she recalled the amused and dubious eyes of the folks back home when she left. No, she'd never go back. Not ever. Resolute, she gripped Norman Dale's arm.

A few female voices cooed as her bridegroom tossed away his hat with his free hand, then straightened her veil that the wind had rustled. Pride burst inside her.

For a delicious moment, Minda enjoyed the view of his shoulder muscles moving underneath his tight black coat. Of course, she'd expected a hard working man of the land to be strong and hale, but this man looked like he could lift her with just one arm. And she wanted his touch, pure and simple. No, it wouldn't be hard at all to be his loving wife.

She walked beside her bridegroom on steady feet up an aisle that seemed a mile long. The organ faded as the reverend started the vows without delay.

"Miss Becker, do you take this man to be your lawful husband?"

She stared at the young reverend who didn't look at her. He hadn't used her full christened name, Melinda Susanna, and his knuckles whitened around his prayer book. She peeked at her husband, but he didn't catch her eye either. Perhaps this was the minister's first time officiating at a wedding and he'd forgotten her name.

Norman Dale's hand tightened around hers as if expecting her to say no.

"Yes, I do," she said, eager for her new future.

"Do you, Mr. Haynes, take this woman for better worse?"Her bridegroom growled his response as he slid a ring on her finger. Minda trembled at the sound and the touch.

The ring fit perfectly.

"Now if there be anyone present who objects to this union, let him speak now, or ever after hold his peace." Her bridegroom's hand tightened again during the silent moment. When no one said anything, Minda heard sighs of relief from a hundred throats.

"Then I now pronounce you man and wife."

There. It was done. She was married. Her husband bent down and touched her lips with his own. Gentle but somehow insistent, his mouth closed around hers, and his warmth settled all the way to the ends of her toes. At the deliciousness of it, she reached up to hold him close.

Yes indeed. He tasted like peppermint with a hint of cherry. Tobacco maybe. Oh, it wouldn't take long at all to fall in love the whole rest of the way.

****

Brix stepped back from his bride, hating himself for liking the kiss.

But damn, she was a pretty thing. Likely untouched, too. Those sweet but tight lips made him think no man had kissed her before. For a split instant, he leaned down to brush his face over the top of her head, drinking in one last whiff of her warm, rose scent. His poor brother had missed out on one hell of a wedding night.

So would he.

Something had stirred his heart deep inside during that kiss, and he didn't much like the feeling. Not at all. Hadn't felt it since the rancher's daughter in West Texas had stomped on his love so hard he still felt the pain.

Brixton Haynes knew how dark a woman's heart could be. This one was no different. Something she'd written in her damn letters had made his brother work himself to death for her. Why had she allowed Norman Dale to think the man he was, and what he had to give her, wasn't good enough?

Anger snarled his gut. Yes, indeed. Brix had duped her, but he'd had no choice. He'd promised Norman Dale. With his last breath, his brother had made Brixton swear to take his place, marry Minda, and make the kids his own. Keep everybody together, one family. Already folks hereabouts had started laying claim to the kids, one at a time. Like they were abandoned puppies needing homes.

The congregation started warbling a hymn, and his bride pulled away in a maidenly manner. He felt that tug on his heart again that spread down to the notch of his trousers. Damn indeed, she was the prettiest thing he'd seen in a month of Mondays.

Her big pansy eyes twinkled and her cheeks bloomed bright red from the kiss. And hidden beneath that veil was hair the colors of every precious metal he'd ever seen. She was far younger and daintier than that little brown portrait his brother had loved to show off.

Jaw tight, he looked away from her, out the little window next to the organ. Shutting his eyes to hold off a tear, he regarded the fresh mound of dirt that made Norman Dale's last bed. He fingered a fresh blister on his right hand. He'd helped fill up that grave just an hour ago. His heart hardened against Minda Becker. Minda *Haynes*.

His back teeth ground together. Damn it. Norman Dale had pulled wheat from the ground for fifteen summers and never died. It was the whitewashing, the trimming, the gussying to impress this *outsider* after harvesting twelve hours a day that had done him in two days ago. Resentment built like a thunderhead and pounded behind Brixton's eyes.

Before turning back to his bride, he rubbed his hand over his eyebrow. Past the graveyard, the prairie rolled like a golden ocean, running into sandy hills on its way to the Shining Mountains. He'd been there, seen Pike's Peak. Right now Brixton Haynes wished he was sitting right on top of it. Instead, he was pa to a passel of kids and married to boot, something he'd sworn he'd never do.

Married to a woman he didn't want.

****

The kiss had shaken Minda and made her more eager than ever for the night to come. When she pulled him close, for that single proper instant, his chest had felt rock-hard against the softness underneath her corset. And for a most improper moment, church or not, she'd imagined how they'd feel skin to skin, without all the layers of clothes.

"Let's get that register signed," her husband said harsh and low during the song. He tightened his grip on her hand.

At his touch, every inch of her shivered. He led her to the big book where she signed the name Melinda Susanna Becker for the last time. Her shaky fingers could hardly manage the inkwell. Then he grabbed the pen from her, scribbled something, and led her from the sanctuary, all the way down the aisle. Once in a while he reached out to clasp the outstretched hands of wedding guests.

Minda found herself smiling at her new friends and neighbors, glad they couldn't see her trembles or read her fiery thoughts. While her husband's behavior seemed a bit gruff, she relaxed somewhat at his firm grip on her fingers. Surely it was a sign that he never wanted to let her go.

Outside, she started some polite conversation as he headed toward the wedding dinner. The tables set up under the trees, she realized, were old barn doors on sawhorses, scattered once in a while with bed sheets.

"I'd hoped Priscilla might stand up for me," she said, holding back the disappointment at the absence of the stepdaughter she longed to love.

"Who?"

"Priscilla? Your daughter?" She had spoken clearly enough. "I'd suggested her as my bridal attendant in my last letter."

"Ah. You mean little Silly." Her husband grinned. "She doesn't have the faculty to do any such thing. All she cares about is a full belly and clean britches."

"Silly? *Little Silly?*" Minda stumbled in shock, but he forced her onward toward the tables.

"Be still and hush now," he said. "Don't make a scene."

As she passed folks full of congratulations, Minda decided not to embarrass herself by pulling away from her husband, but she tossed him a quick mutter. "What's this about *Silly?*"

"I said not now."

Fuming, Minda plastered a fake smile on her face. She would speak her mind later in private. How could her husband have failed to mention that his daughter was feeble-minded?

And how could anybody, much less a father, ridicule a backward young girl with such an offensive nickname? His own blood? By now, he'd hauled her over to a table under a trio of box elder trees. A young, yellow-headed woman was draping a garland of meadow flowers along two slatback chairs.

Minda wanted to appreciate the attempt to prettify the plain chairs, but she pondered more and more on a wedding that might be a mistake. Norman Dale was simply not the charming father he'd presented in his letters. What other surprises did he have in store for her? Did he imagine her so besotted she wouldn't mind?

No matter. She'd signed that register pure and simple. He'd made her his wife, and she'd willingly taken him as her husband. For better or worse.

"Sit yourself down. I'll go get Silly and the rest of the kids," he said through slitted lips. He raised his brows at the blonde woman and she nodded, leaving them in private.

"The rest of what kids?" Minda's skin prickled. Deciding to obey him for the first and only time, she sat down.

"Our kids. Yours and mine."

"Our kids? What in the world do you mean, Norman Dale? You wrote that you've got one daughter. Fourteen years old." Minda's voice rose and despite the heat, her shoulders tensed with a sudden chill as if a clump of snow had just fallen from the treetops. "What kids? What on earth are you saying, Norman Dale? Your letters didn't say one single word about *kids*."

He glared down at her. "You must've misread my brother." The last two words slid from his tongue in slow deliberation.

His brother? She sat helpless, hopeless, paralyzed against the back of the hard little chair. For a moment, she had no air to speak.

"Your brother? *Your brother?* What do you mean?"

He leaned close to her, like he had during their kiss, but at her ear he growled, low, "You promised to wed a Haynes today. Well, I'm the only one left. Your Norman Dale, my brother—" His fingers, calloused and hot, held her chin still so he could glare into her eyes, "—is dead."

Minda gasped and grabbed the flower-covered chair so she didn't fall out of it. Her Norman Dale, dead? The handsome widower of thirty-nine who had promised her a new life?

"Yep, Miz *Haynes*." His voice was dry as August dust. "I come all the way back home to stand up for my brother at his wedding, and instead I get to lower him into the ground. And it's all your fault." Eyes as black as Pennsylvania coal bore into her. "You killed him, sure enough."

Chapter Two

"What?" The word came from her in a soundless puff.

"You heard me." Of course she'd deny it, but it was her fault. Here he stood before her, hemmed in with a wife and kids. Freedom forever gone, his brother dead. Shaking his head at the turn of his life, he held back his feelings of chastisement against Norman Dale and turned his resentment to Minda. His brother had died trying to impress her, and her arrival made things worse.

Her face turned white as her veil, and he figured she was about to swoon. Cold water for her and a long hard swig for him sounded mighty good about now.

She shut her eyes tight and he looked away from them, away from those eyelashes lying on her cheeks like butterfly wings. He wanted to touch that cheek, reckoning it was even softer than it looked, and anger rose in his gut. He didn't need her, not one single bit. But even with the chitchat around them, he felt like they were the only two people in the world.

Just as he thought the words, she stood up angrily and pulled off the veil. She must've loosened her hair pins, too. Copper, silver, and gold tumbled past the sash around her waist. His fingers twitched, longing to touch the gleaming cascade.

Something more, something worse, tightened his manhood.

Her lips flapped same as a fish needing air, but

still he longed to kiss them. He remembered their sweetness and warmth, like wild strawberries in spring sunshine. She took a deep breath, stared back at him and spoke.

"My fault? What can you possibly mean?"

As he straightened up beside her, the hot afternoon gusts whipped her hair across his cheeks. It smelled like roses. He grabbed the calm control that had gotten him out of many a stampede. Sure as hell he could wrangle one small woman.

"My brother's done nothing but work his fingers to the bone getting ready for your arrival, Miz Haynes. In this ruthless heat. Two days ago, his heart plumb gave out."

"But…he claimed he was in the best of health."

Brixton shrugged. "Doc Viessman said even a hale man can see his heart give up during overwork." He looked away from Minda's wide eyes. "He lingered half a day."

"Well, I am sorry for your loss. But I lost somebody, too." Her voice rose. "Didn't you think to ask me? What on earth possessed you to imagine I'd want you?"

He shrugged again, not letting her words sting. It didn't matter at all, her not wanting him. Even if he figured she did, deep down. Her kiss had been timid, but real. But she did owe Norman Dale the honor of his last request. His brother had out and out planned for her future, a stranger in a strange town, in his dying moments.

"You ought to be grateful Norman Dale picked somebody to take care of you."

"But...it's…"

"It's the right thing to do." He pushed her back down on the chair. "Calm down. Folks are watching. You traipsed hundreds of miles to wed up with a stranger. Don't matter which one of us now, does it?"

"This is unimaginable," she muttered.

Brixton Haynes disliked her big uppity word, disliked her more and more. She was the reason for all his problems. He couldn't very well resent his own brother, but he damn sure could resent Minda. "Don't like it any better than you, but you owe it to my brother. It was his dying wish. You and I hitching together fixes everything."

And it did. He liked Norman Dale's brood just fine, but had no idea what the hell to do with them. He knew all about calves, fillies, and johnny mules but not one damn thing about kids. His life in Texas gratified every inch of him. The open sky and endless miles. Hearth, home, and young'uns were the farthest things from his mind.

The rich rancher's daughter who'd betrayed him had taught him that lesson and taught him well. He shot Minda a hot, angry glance. She was worse. This one hadn't just *broken* a man's heart. She'd managed to stop it.

Yes, indeed. She owed Norman Dale. She owed Brix, too, as well as the kids. From the moment she stepped off that stage, she'd planned to take on a husband and family. And the kids sure as hell expected a new ma. This marriage was the answer. If she was smart as Norman Dale had claimed, she'd have sense enough to see it.

With nothing to worry about now, Brix would be back in Texas outside of a week's time. His trail boss was an impatient man.

"This fixes nothing, Mr. Haynes," she stormed. "You've tricked me."

"Reverend Satterburg himself and all these fine folks heard you promise to be my wife today," he said.

"I did no such thing. Not exactly, I mean. Not *you*. I thought you were Norman Dale." Then she nodded slowly. "Oh, I see. Even the preacher was in on it. That's why he didn't say our Christian names.

Because if he'd said—what is your name anyway? I'd have refused on the spot. And what about—?" She waved her arms about the tables of people watching them from the corners of their eyes. "—all of these folks? They're all tricksters too? *This whole town?"*

"Most thought it a fine change of plan. Better than you come all this way and not find a husband." He wouldn't mention the few that hadn't agreed. Truth was, he had expected them to protest during the ceremony. The schoolmaster, and Norman Dale's nearest neighbor, even the reverend's wife had been against it. But clearly, they'd changed their way of thinking.

"What a ridiculous notion. Well, Mr. Haynes, this is not at all why I came to Paradise. I had nothing to do with Norman Dale's death, and I don't owe him a thing. Dying wish, my foot. You and your preacher have committed serious sins of omission. I won't stand for this. I...I..." She looked around, helpless-like, and turned from him.

"Where you going?"

"That's his grave over there?" She pointed to the fresh mound.

He nodded.

"I'm going to, how shall I put it? Pay my respects." She stood up with her wedding bouquet and tossed him one last scowl.

Damn roses. That bouquet had cost his brother a small fortune.

"Hold up a minute," he said to his wife, who halted and stared. "You forgot your bridal veil."

As he rose, he leaned toward her, almost wishing he could kiss her again. He placed the veil back on her head, fluffed the edges around that lovely face. He couldn't help touching her cheek while he did so. His bride.

His fingers met her soft warm flesh, and she let them remain for a moment that was almost magical.

Then both of them flinched at the same precise second.

****

Minda could hardly breathe. The corset had suddenly gotten too rigid, and in the heat, her inexpressibles clung to her skin like wet paint. For an unseemly second, she imagined that warm calloused hand running across her body.

What on earth was happening? Her life in Gleesburg was over by choice, but this was not what she'd chosen in its stead. Not this man. And what had he, her *husband*, said about kids? Norman Dale had seen fit to mention only one, and a simple-minded one at that. Silly. At least she'd do what she could to prevent that horrid nickname.

Her husband? Shutting her eyes, she tried to hold the nightmare back. Mercy, she'd come to Paradise to have her dreams come true for a change.

Resolute, she nodded firm. Sadly, Norman Dale had passed on before his prime, but neither Haynes brother, living or dead, would get by with tricking her into raising more children. That was a thing of the past. She'd done her share.

As proud as she was of how well her younger sisters had turned out, now was *her* time. Of course, she'd agreed to tend Priscilla who, at fourteen, would be married off herself in just a few years' time. And if she and Norman Dale had been blessed with children of their own, she would have raised them willingly, but out of love, not duty.

But Norman Dale wasn't here any more.

Likely she should feel some grief at his passing, but Norman Dale had been dishonest with her and deserved no tears. He and his scoundrel of a brother had made plans for the only life she would ever have without considering her thoughts and wishes. And now she had no money and nowhere else to go.

As she stomped over to Norman Dale's grave,

she grumbled out an angry prayer and heard someone come up behind her. An idiotic disappointment simmered when it wasn't her husband.

Holding a baby in her arms, the yellow-haired young woman who'd decorated their chairs smiled shyly.

"I'm Gracey, the preacher's wife," she said, eyes and voice soft. "What a tragedy, meeting Norman Dale the first time from beyond the grave."

"Well, it appears he made other arrangements." Minda tried to keep a sweet tone. This healthy, sun-kissed young woman seemed pleasant enough. Maybe they could be friends. Minda sent her a bright smile.

For a flash, Gracey's smile and golden hair reminded Minda of her youngest sister. She recalled the lovely Easter bonnet she'd made for Libby. The low-crowned straw "flat" topped with silk cornflowers and tied with blue satin would sit just as fine atop Gracey's braids, the wide brim an umbrella against the bright Nebraska sun. The poor dear needed a new hat badly.

"This is little Silly," Gracey said, with shy but troubled eyes. "Jake—the reverend—is yonder, dishing up for the rest."

Silly? Priscilla? Minda's smile vanished. "Little Silly" was an infant? So that's why she was content with a full belly and clean britches. And *the rest?* Her husband had mentioned other kids, too. Just how many more were there? Her eyes narrowed.

What other lies had Norman Dale told her?

"Now, sugarplum," Gracey crooned, "it seems this nice lady's your new ma, and your uncle Brixton's your new pa."

Brixton. So that was her scoundrel-husband's name. As furious as she was, she liked the silent ripple his name made against her tongue. But new ma? New pa? Things would need to change and quick.

The baby was beyond precious, but Minda didn't dare humiliate herself by inquiring about the rest. She'd seem a simpleton, expecting one nearly-grown girl when there was a slew of little ones underfoot. No one would insult a dead man by believing he'd lied to her.

"There's been a lot to think about on this day, Gracey," Minda said instead.

"Truth to tell, Brix's a fine man to take you on."

Minda harrumphed to herself and tossed the wedding bouquet on the grave. She caught the scent of her husband—Brixton—before she heard his footsteps. In spite of the heat, he smelled wonderful, clean and outdoorsy both.

He nodded at them. "Afternoon, Gracey. Miz Haynes, you sure look like you could use a long tall drink..."

"Why, how dare you, Mr. Haynes?" Minda said with an aggrieved sputter. "I need no such thing!"

"Of *lemonade*," he finished.

She hoped the big trees hid her blush. "Of course."

For a moment, Brixton Haynes stood tall as a tree and still as a pond like he had something more to say. Then Gracey thrust Priscilla in Brixton's stiff arms. He acted like the baby burned him, and Minda hid a smile.

The child wore a beautiful white linsey dress trimmed with tatted lace, pin tucks, and delicate satin ribbons. Her tiny black leather boots gleamed. Minda knew quality. It was indeed the proper outfit for the daughter of a successful farmer. About thirteen, fourteen months of age, she guessed, stifling new ire against the dead man.

This girl was supposed to be fourteen *years* old.

"Silly," Gracey cooed, "Uncle Brix's your new

pa."

In the hot wind, tree branches rasped against each other like ripping silk. A meadowlark sang, but to Minda, it sounded like squawking. New pa? Minda snuck a peek at Brixton.

Her husband moved his face awkwardly from the searching fingers of the baby's left hand. Priscilla's dark eyes matched her uncle's, and curls as black as his tufted her little skull. It was a charming sight, until Minda reminded herself just how this man had tricked her.

Just then, Priscilla squirmed and stretched restlessly, knocking Brixton's big-brimmed black hat to the mercy of the wind.

"Damn!"

Gracey's eyes widened in horror, and little Silly's face crinkled with oncoming tears.

Instantly, Minda took the baby from him and soothed the chubby face into a bright pink smile. Priscilla laughed outright as she grabbed a lock of Minda's loosened hair.

Minda couldn't resist kissing the tiny hand, then turned to Brixton as he bent to retrieve his hat.

"Watch your mouth, Mr. Haynes. Even little ones have ears."

"Don't you tell me what to do," he growled, but conceded, "I do beg pardon, ladies."

She tried to return the glower he gave her on his way back to standing upright, tried to ignore her confusion, the unsuitable attraction for a husband she hadn't chosen. At least he returned her scowl. She needed a firm reason to forget that gentle touch upon her cheek. Sighing, Minda wanted Gracey to leave. Then she and Brixton could discuss the outrageous situation in which they found themselves.

In which she found herself, that is. He'd plotted it all along, all the while blaming her for his brother's death.

His accusations pounded again in her mind and she frowned at the unfairness. In front of them, Gracey's shoes shifted under her pink calico skirts, somewhat awkwardly, like she didn't really want to leave. "Um...Minda? Brix?"

The reverend's wife looked down at her toes for another moment.

"Yes, Gracey? What is it?" Minda said.

"Well, Brix, you always said you're no family man. And you two being newlyweds, well, it'd be hard taking on a baby right away. Jake and I, well, we'd like to take little Silly home. Raise her as our own." She glanced at Minda, and just as quickly, looked away. Sadness softened her words. "Our baby girl, Ruthie, why, she became an angel last fall from that scarlet fever. We miss her something awful."

Minda felt a stab in her heart as Gracey's eyes filled with tears.

"Just Silly?" Brixton said. "Not the others?"

"With our own three boys, we got no room for more than a baby, Brix. You know that already." Gracey looked away. "Much as I love 'em all, other folks will take 'em off your hands. There's already talk."

"I heard some talk, but it don't seem right, Grace. You know my brother would never stand for it." Brixton straightened, taller than ever.

"Well, he's dead and gone. But you and Minda might as well think about it. Less things to worry about."

"Children aren't things, Gracey," Brixton said, his voice a growl, "and it won't happen."

Without saying another word, Gracey grabbed little Priscilla from Minda's arms, held her tight, and ran off.

Take Priscilla from her siblings? An old pain filled Minda's heart. She had spent her girlhood keeping her sisters together. Whatever Minda had expected, it hadn't been the break-up of a family. She peered at her husband who stood grim and stalwart, his jaw clenched, staring at Norman Dale's grave. Not a family man? He'd come all the way home for a wedding? Come from where? Who and what was he?

He must have borrowed that poor-fitting coat. Any decent man possessed his own Sunday best. And that vest of many pockets. Hmm. He probably had a Peacemaker or other weapon hidden inside, and a flask of whiskey, too. She'd read a dime novel on the long train ride.

A bounty hunter? Or…her eyes narrowed. Or worse, an outlaw. How could any feeling person leave a man like that in charge of innocent children?

Once again she heard her mama's dying request that Minda keep her sisters all together, under one roof, no matter what the cost. At not quite fourteen, she'd taken the commitment to heart. Of course it had been difficult, sometimes downright backbreaking, but she had learned first-hand what family meant.

But this wasn't her family, was it? Not if she'd been tricked into it.

"Who are the others, Brixton?" It was the first time she said his name aloud.

"Katie and Neddie-boy. And you can call me Brix. Little Paul's over there." His voice slowed as he pointed near Norman Dale's grave. "Asleep in his ma's arms. Six years old he was. They both died from the scarlet fever last fall." His gravel voice softened. "I best see to some gravestones now. My brother didn't get to it."

Minda held her hand against her throbbing throat. Both parents dead, and a small brother, too. The surviving youngsters had suffered terrible loss, and their hurts seeped into her. The wind moved eerily through the cottonwoods.

"Your brother never mentioned them," she said, lips stiff with shock. She grabbed handfuls of her white silken skirts to keep them from brushing into Norman Dale's dirt.

"Letter must have gone astray." Her husband shrugged.

"He sent six letters, and I received and answered every one. He kept the children from me on purpose, didn't he? Why might he do that, Brixton?" Minda knew why, in her heart and in her brain. She'd made it clear she was done with child-rearing.

Brixton's eyebrows rose. "I claim you misunderstood him."

"Balderdash. I can read just fine."

"The kids are right over there." He pointed toward the tables where Gracey Satterburg tended to them.

Minda's mouth dropped open. Norman Dale hadn't left a teenaged daughter to care for the little ones. His oldest—what was her name, Katie?—looked no more than ten. Raising younger siblings was an impossible task for such a little girl.

She closed her eyes, but it didn't matter. Inside her head, the faces of Norman Dale's children hung like a wall of portraits. Six helpless eyes watched while grown-ups ransacked their lives.

"Let's go greet our guests." Brixton took her arm, stiff and polite. Even still, her skin sizzled at his touch.

Minda didn't move. She'd married off all three sisters in the last two years, Mattie just in April, and she knew well what was expected. A bridal couple mingled. The bride giggled amid secret sniggers about the night ahead. The bridegroom swaggered at the delights to come. They danced, cheek to cheek.

Her heart thundered.

"They're not wedding guests," she said, as nerves jumped across her skin like summer bugs. "They came here for a funeral."

"Truth to tell, the funeral today saved them two trips. Folks have been planning to make merry today at a Haynes wedding for nigh onto three months."

"Norman Dale's funeral and wedding. None of this is for me."

"Oh, it's for you, all right, Miz Haynes. You signed that register fair and square."

And she had. Glumly, she wondered if he figured that entitled him to a wedding night. He might consider himself her husband, and he might make her heart pitter, but if he had such a thought, he had half a minute to think something else. Despite the riots in her heart.

He must have read her mind. "Save your worry, Miz Haynes. You get Norman Dale's bed all to yourself. I sleep outside. Too crowded inside with that litter of whelps. Now get some food inside you. There's nothing much back at the homestead."

"Homestead? There's no room and no food at Norman Dale's fine white farmhouse?"

Brixton squinted at her, forehead furrowing like a plowed field. But he said nothing.

"All right, Mr. Haynes." She placed her hands on her hips. "Before we *greet* our guests, I want some straight talk."

****

Fine white farmhouse?

Brixton Haynes's fingers tied up into knots. Was that whitewash one of her mail-order demands? Or...his squint narrowed even more than the years in the sun on the trail.

Or was she believing another of his brother's lies?

"My brother built Ida Louise a wood house a

while back," Brixton said in a flat voice, "a fine one for hereabouts. And I helped. Some folks live in soddies and dugouts." Even still, he'd seen *fine* wooden homes in San Antone and Denver, and Norman Dale's sure wasn't one.

"But there's no room for you?"

"My choice. I like life under the stars. My brother was the homesteader, not me. I was going on eleven when he claimed his quarter section in '62. President Lincoln's Homestead Act, you may recall. I helped Norman Dale carve a farm from one-hundred sixty acres of bluestem and prairie grass. It's a right fine place."

But at seventeen, Brixton had accepted the call to ride the cattle trails and never looked back. Still, not even ten years of cow towns and trail dust had rubbed manners completely from his bones. As he clicked his heels together, he offered Minda his arm, intending to act like a true bridegroom. Damn, what he wouldn't do for the brother who'd raised him.

His skin twitched with downright pleasure beneath the cloth of Norman Dale's coat when she touched him. He hated the feeling, and hated himself more.

"Hurry up," he said into her bright blue eyes.

The eyes turned hard. "Perhaps I need to let *you* know, Mr. Haynes, that you do not tell *me* what to do."

"Well, Miz Haynes. As for this wedding of ours, would you be happier today wailing at Norman Dale's grave? Leastways now you got what you come here for, a husband and a home."

"Not the husband I came for." Her voice shook.

"Well, no worry. I won't be around." Across his shoulders, his brother's second-best coat pinched his muscles, trapped the clammy air against his skin. His flask pressed hard against his heart. Damn, he'd been itching for a swig all day, more than ever since

Minda arrived. If things had gone right, he'd be off carousing with his boyhood chums about now, planning a shivaree and certain amounts of mischief upon Norman Dale's person.

Norman Dale who hadn't lived long enough to love his beautiful bride. As if losing little Paul and his sweet sister-in-law hadn't been enough, Brixton's gut churned with another gush of grief for his brother. Minda's eyes widened and he saw himself in them.

"You won't be around? Why, you intend for me to rear those children by myself?"

"Come on, Miz Haynes." Brixton frowned with a guilty peek at the grave. Norman Dale had explained how she'd tended three sisters from childhood to bride. Hell, that was the main reason he picked her. "You took to Silly like a cocklebur to a wool sock."

And he'd seen it for himself. Her reaching for Silly like that, stopping the tears. Getting her to smile, kissing the tiny hand. Not minding that pulled hair a bit. "You know how to tend a little one. You even chided me for cussing."

"This isn't fair, Mr. Haynes."

"My brother was right, holding me to such a pledge. The kids belong together." And now Minda was responsible for all of them. He had no time to spare nurse-maiding a clutch of hatchlings.

He'd ride half a day in muck and rain to rescue a calf stuck in a creek bed, he'd give up his last drop of water to a sick filly, but kids were another whole species. Long ago, his own pa had run off, leaving him and his brother abandoned and alone. Fatherhood wasn't part of his nature. But motherhood sure was in Minda's. A blind man could see that.

Her mouth hung open like she either had no words or no air. It was that mouth he'd tasted after she promised to be his wife. He wanted it. He wanted her. He couldn't help it. So it was good he was leaving.

"And you'll have help," he said. "I got enough cash money saved to hire hands. They'll harvest the last of the wheat and tend the corn."

"Why, where will you be?" Her face had turned white again, lips moving like she was recalling other things he'd said to her. He figured he knew the trail of her thoughts.

"Ah, I get it, Miz Haynes. You think I'm something of an outlaw or stage robber, don't you, because I can't hang around. Not so. I just happen to like dirt under my horse's hooves better than dirt under my fingernails. I ride point along the Goodnight."

"But that's…that's Texas."

Brixton nodded, lips firm and silent. In three days time, he'd set out for Kansas, meet up with the trail boss and other drovers at the railhead town of Ellsworth. Then they'd all head back to Butter Creek to start the next drive. "Yep. That's my job. It's what I do and who I am. But I'll send you my salary. Much as I can, that is."

He owed his brother that. But it wouldn't be much, not at first, not until he took care of Norman Dale's debts.

"Come on," he said in a bit nicer voice. "Let's go greet the kids."

They walked over to the tables.

At least she acted polite and friendly. He held his breath for a while, waiting to see if she'd make a ruckus. But she crouched gently next to Katie and Neddie-boy. And watched Gracey's face grow red and mad. Hmm. Now he knew why she'd threatened to complain when her husband asked the congregation.

She must want Silly bad.

Five years old, Ned looked up at Minda with big

eyes like blueberries growing ripe in the sun. Katie fingered the wedding veil, and Minda took it from her head and handed it to his little niece.

"I think I see a piece of chocolate cake over there that's waiting for a nice big boy like you," she told Neddie.

Neddie's eyes turned soft with tears. "Miss Gracey says I don't get more."

At that, Minda give Gracey a long measuring glare, and a stir of pride niggled in Brixton.

"Well, Neddie, of course you can have another piece," Minda said. "*I* say so."

"Are you my new mama?" the little boy asked.

Brixton Haynes watched his wife's throat muscles catch beneath the lace at her neck.

Chapter Three

"How far to the farm?" Minda asked warily. Her wedding day was over, and all her dreams had died along with Norman Dale. Staring her in the face was a wedding night unlike the one she'd longed for with a loving bridegroom. And she had no choice but to go to the homestead with a husband who found her so unattractive he'd sleep elsewhere.

And not just any elsewhere. Outdoors with the chickens.

"Not far," he said, as he guided the buckboard over a rickety bridge. In the twilight, fireflies danced along the banks of the Loup River below.

She managed a quick peek at him underneath the brim of the bonnet she'd made herself in the high-crowned French style. Before leaving town, she'd shed her wedding finery and now wore an everyday calico dress.

Gazing at his strong profile, she saw a man to be reckoned with, a man who kept his word, a man who was accustomed to getting his way, even through trickery. Wouldn't a man like that demand his husbandly rights no matter what? And would the bride of such a powerful man really want to sleep alone? After all, at first sight of him, she'd accepted that he'd be a mail-order husband easy to love.

Except, she reminded herself, he wasn't her mail-order husband at all. Anger flared again at his tricking her. Truth to tell, Brixton had made it clear he didn't want any kind of life with her. She had to find a way out.

"We'll get there soon enough. And by the way, Miz Haynes—" Brix's eyes narrowed. "I resent the insult of my bride choosing to sleep her wedding night alone in that boardinghouse. I already told you I sleep outside. Did you really think I'd pay for your lodging?"

"It was a good idea, and you know it," Minda said, not revealing that she'd intended to bribe a room with a pretty black velvet cap she'd not yet worn. Ladies back home had quickly taken to her modernized version of the old Huntley style.

"Well, I won't lose face in front of this town. At least the boardinghouse is booked solid with wedding guests tonight."

A little smile of victory twitched around her husband's mouth.

Without meaning to, she remembered kissing that mouth and hoped the dusk hid her blush. He'd promised her a room at the homestead to herself, but would he comply? Her heart fluttered at the thought of lying beside him in bed. After all, they were legally wed. But it wasn't a true wedding at all.

"Besides, it's no wedding night," she said, her voice terse but soft, so as not to wake the children napping in the wagon bed. "All I am is a nursemaid. Because you tricked me."

"You owe my brother."

"Don't start that. I had nothing to do with his death. Why, he might have keeled over last Tuesday whether he planned to remarry or not. You can't know."

He bent his face toward her and glared at her beneath his black Stetson. "It's a fact he died getting ready for you. His heart didn't give out getting dressed for a barn dance. And like I say, you owe him. You owe me. And the kids."

"Yes, Mr. Haynes," she said wearily, "and I have agreed. Of course, I'll hire my care of the children to pay back the travel expenses Norman Dale sent me. But you'll have to make other arrangements after that. I think a quiet annulment might be possible." The last sentence caught in her throat as she blinked away unexpected tears. She'd come for a home and husband.

Just not this one. But in the meantime, she had nowhere else to go and no money to get there anyway. He'd have to do for now.

For better or for worse.

"Not so fast, Miz Haynes. That isn't all Norman Dale spent on you. The whitewash, the rose bushes. Those fancy new duds for the kids. He had that bouquet of yours sent all the way from Monroe. And that was a brand new wedding suit he was buried in." Brixton Haynes stopped at a crossroads and raised his eyebrows at her in the last ray of setting sun. A wagon more decrepit than their own passed by, and surprisingly, the couple inside didn't wave or call a hello.

"Mr. Haynes, none of those decisions were mine. By the way, who are those snoots?" Minda pointed at the unfriendly people. Since most folks today had greeted her with honest welcome, she was rightfully confused, even a little hurt.

"That's Tom Holden and his woman, but don't change the subject on me." Brixton threw her a warning look, and his voice turned low and harsh. "You weren't here for my brother's laying out, now, were you? You weren't there when he breathed his last. Were you?"

"No." Minda swallowed hard. Grief rimmed his dark deep-set eyes. For an instant, she wished he were her true husband and she could have a night of his love and give him the comfort he craved.

Then she fought the unruly thought, and blame assailed her. She ought to be mourning Norman Dale. Not for a second did she believe she'd caused his death, but some guilt couldn't help rankle. No matter his frauds, he had *died* getting ready for her.

And she and Brixton Haynes certainly didn't belong together. He might have thrilled her heart at first sight of him in the dusty street, but their marriage was a complete sham. Her marriage to Norman Dale had been carefully planned, but not this masquerade.

"But you're wrong, Mr. Haynes, if you think marrying a stranger doesn't matter to me." She fought away a sob. "I picked Norman Dale fair and square. He was my first and only choice."

"How's that? You and him never even met."

"Oh, you don't understand," she said, then grabbed hold of her temper to continue politely, "After subscribing to Miss Viola's Heart and Hand newsletter, I received correspondence from many gentlemen. But only Norman Dale's letters touched my heart."

But those dreams were over, and Brixton was returning to the Goodnight, leaving her alone as before, only in a strange town this time. Worry and weariness sagged her shoulder blades, and she grabbed the edge of the wagon seat for support. She might be more nursemaid than wife, but no matter his claims otherwise, a manly man like him was sure to want a wedding night before he took off. Suddenly breathless at the thought, she swallowed hard and saw that he did the same. Her heart softened just a little. Once she, too, had felt the hopelessness of grief.

"And what's that about an annulment?" Brixton said after a long silence, ending her brief compassion. "You agreed the kids belong together. They're a family."

"Yes indeed, they belong together, Mr. Haynes. And they are a family. Just not mine."

"Beg to differ, Miz Haynes. I won't see those

kids shamed by divorce. Myself neither. Everybody in Platte County heard you say those vows."

The harsh truth set Minda's skin prickling, but she'd never let him suspect her despair. Sitting up as straight as she could in the jostling wagon, she hissed into his ear. "But surely I get some say in all this. No judge would hold me to this vow. I never married a family, Mr. Haynes. And I never intended to marry *you*."

He exhaled deep. "Homestead's just ahead."

Like a prim little ghost, Norman Dale's white farmhouse glistened through the nightfall. The infamous rosebushes bloomed along the porch, and Minda groaned. Tending roses was almost as much work as tending children. What else was she going to find at the end of this ride? Already her wedding day had been fraught with the unexpected.

"I'll tend the livestock," Brixton said gruffly, but she noticed how gently he lifted the children from the wagon. He tossed her one final stare while he unhitched the horse.

Maybe she'd feel good slamming the door on him.

Holding Priscilla, she stepped inside. The house was neat as a pin, but humble and spare. In spite of clues all day long, she couldn't help the disappointment that whittled away the last of her dreams. Then guilt prickled again and weighed hard. Maybe she'd just been greedy, wanting a successful husband and a fine house after all those years of scrimping and saving. Maybe she was getting just what she deserved now.

"I can wash up Ned and change Silly's britches for you, ma'am, if you want me to," Katie said soberly. The child's calling her ma'am nearly broke Minda's heart. Young children deserved a mother.

"Do you often care for your brother and sister?" Minda asked, remembering Norman Dale's doubtful mention of a housekeeper, "or did your papa have some help?"

"I'm a big girl. I help since Mama passed."

Since Mama passed? Goodness, that had been last autumn. Had this small girl been burdened with grown-up chores and responsibilities all this time? Minda caressed the thin little shoulder. "But what about neighbors? And school?"

"Well, Miss Marylaura next place over does the wash, and Miss Gracey sees to us sometimes," Katie said, then started to grin. "But these days Uncle Brix cleans us up just fine. He braids my hair and doesn't pull a bit."

"Braids?" Minda said aloud, unable to hold off her surprise. Did that hard-hearted rogue have a soft spot somewhere? But Minda needed another answer. "School?"

"I couldn't get there much. The schoolmaster says I have a fine brain. But with Papa out in the fields, Silly needed me."

Little Ned looked up at Minda. "Uncle Brix sings me a lullaby. And I can wash my face all by myself."

The little boy's big blue eyes bore holes into her soul. He and his sisters deserved a family. But their uncle, her husband, made no bones about leaving. Was he such a scoundrel that he didn't care?

Yet, what sort of villain braided a little girl's hair and sang lullabies to a motherless boy?

"I'm happy you're here," Katie said softly, and Minda's breath caught in her throat. Was she herself a scoundrel who didn't care? She pondered over the sight of her husband outside.

He leaned against the barn in the dusk with a flask to his lips, sipping whiskey like he held the weight of the world on his shoulders. For a moment, she hated that he drew comfort from a cold, hard flask, longing instead to hold him close with womanly warmth and hope. But then he stood up tall and strong, like he needed nobody at all.

Other than someone to tend the kids.

A thought irritated her mind, like a rash she couldn't stop scratching. Dreams she had come here to make real lay unfulfilled in a fresh-dug grave. All she'd done now was start a new chapter of an old theme, caretaker with no one to take care of her or give her love. She wanted something more.

Right now she had a debt to pay, but she was smart and resolute. Brixton might be handsome and the children endearing, but this was a husband and household she didn't want. Someday she'd find someone to cherish her.

She sighed. It just wouldn't be today.

****

Night fell soft and silent, and the snuffles of Norman Dale's livestock comforted Brixton with memories of the trail. Lord, he couldn't wait to get back.

Habit had him walk as quietly as he could from the barn to the house. Even the tiniest noise sparked stampedes on the trail, so his footsteps were cautious wherever he went.

At the back porch, he set down Minda's valises and paused to peek in the back window. Her lush curves swayed beneath the simple dress as she readied the children for bed, and he couldn't fill his vision fast enough. The memory of her soft, sweet cheek brushed his fingertips once more, and his heart raced and his groin throbbed. It was the heartbeat he didn't like; a man desiring a beautiful woman was just what a man did. But a galloping heart might mean a man felt something deep inside.

Even worse, night after night alone on the trail, he'd keep seeing her shining hair sweep across Ned's shoulders while she kissed the top of the lad's head. So he pulled out his flask and drank deeper. It was too much like having a family of his own, something he swore he never needed. Suddenly, he missed his brother more than he'd missed anything.

Until this minute, he had never felt shy about coming through this door without a knock. His wife's current disposition gave him pause, but he had goods to deliver, and damn, the kids just might like one of his good-night songs. His tongue clicked. Truth to tell, his bride would think him nothing but a rowdy bridegroom wanting a tumble between the sheets. Already she'd tried to disgrace him by letting a room at the boardinghouse just for herself.

Another long, hard swig consoled his throat as it emptied his flask. Damn woman. Anger, not desire, flared in his gut now. To calm down, Brixton ran his arm up the smooth window casement. In his mind, it was a fine white house no matter what his bride thought. While Ida Lou was breeding little Paul, he'd helped Norman Dale construct this very house. He loved the feel of well-lathed wood underneath his fingertips almost as much as he loved the feel of a woman's skin.

Then his heart darkened as a lightning bolt of bad memories crashed into his mind. He'd built Esperanza Eames a house much like this one, on the six-hundred acres her rich pa had deeded them in Butter Creek, Texas. Built every inch with dreams. Pounded each nail with hope. Carved her a bedstead worthy of a queen.

The week before their wedding last fall, he'd come home early from round-up and found her in the arms of Rawley Snate, a cowboy who'd come by the ranch for a couple days' work.

With a passion she'd never shown Brixton, she kissed her lover, letting Snate's hands roam where they had no business. She was barely clothed, nipples bright as rose buds atop snowy breasts. A pain both old and new darkened his mood even now. Since Brixton respected a bride's right to wear white, Esperanza's womanhood had been a mystery to him. He'd looked toward their bridal night with lust as well as love.

The scene played itself again behind his eyelids, killing another piece of his spirit.

In disbelief, he'd hauled Snate away from his bride and bloodied the man's nose, watched the lies gleam in her eyes while she dressed, explaining Rawley away as an old flame who meant nothing, nothing at all.

His belly ached one more time, and it wasn't the whiskey. That had been the worst of it, her ruining what they'd had for something that meant nothing at all.

No matter how Esperanza touted her wiles on him and begged his forgiveness, Brixton Haynes bid his bride a bitter good-bye and turned his back. Still, there'd been a time when she'd been his world and his future.

Right now, he watched another bride who didn't want him. He shook his head, took another swig to drown his feelings. But his flask had emptied, and he needed a refill from Norman Dale's supply. The decision stumped him though, whether to knock or go right in.

After a couple of half-hearted taps, he walked into the house. Minda's eyebrows rose.

"Been tucking the kids in these last days," he said. "Thought you might like some help."

"Oh. You do, do you? I think I know how to put children to bed. Besides, isn't this my new job?" She stuck her pretty nose high in the air, but he saw the sparkle of tears first. Then she ruffled Ned's hair while she put a cup of milk in front of him.

Damn, why couldn't his wife attend to him like that? Milk wasn't as good as whiskey, but her soft hand would sure improve his mood. His body heated like flame and tornado combined, just imagining those slender fingers traveling over him. He changed the subject and his train of thought fast.

"I brought your valises. And Gracey packed up a hamper of food."

"That's kind of her, considering."

Little Ned looked up at Minda. "More chocolate cake?"

Brixton rejoiced at the chuckle escaping from her lips.

"No more cake tonight, sweetheart." She tossed Brixton a half-smile. "Now you go clean your teeth and hop to bed. And be quiet. Katie's already asleep."

Now, Ned peered hopefully at Brixton. "A lullaby?"

"Not tonight." He grinned. "You heard Minda. Your sisters are asleep. Now hop to."

The boy stopped for a brief hug, then headed to the alcove in the corner, hidden by a calico curtain, where Katie already slept. A protective sensation surged through Brixton at that hug. Back teeth grinding, his humor fled as he recalled the threat coming from Norman Dale's neighbor, Tom Holden. Tom had made no bones yesterday about wanting to take Neddie-boy on as a field hand. The five-year old would nest in the barn at night with the hogs after blistering his fingers all day. Brixton could hardly stop up his wrath. At least Jake and Gracey had thought to make Silly their daughter.

Of course, Brixton had already tossed out an angry *no*, but how could he keep the kids from such vultures if Minda left?

He figured her caressing Ned was a sort of victory. Minda had to be feeling something deep down for the kids to touch them like that. She'd hold off Tom Holden.

"Actually, Priscilla is having a hard time going to sleep." Minda said, not looking at Brixton. She moved toward the little trundle where Silly slept. The baby appeared to doze now, but her covers were tangled with restlessness.

"Well, it's been a busy day," Brixton said.

"It's more than that. And she hasn't eaten much." Minda tossed him a look and got up to wash Ned's dishes. Even performing such an everyday task, she moved like she had magic and music in her bones. For a moment, Brixton imagined the sweet warmth of her lips on his once again. That short kiss at the altar hadn't been near enough.

But the moment passed quickly when he considered it likely she'd slap him away like a Texas tick. After all, she'd talked of annulment, and the shameful notion bothered him. Folks around here knew the truth, though. She was bound to find sympathy for getting tricked, an annulment forgiven and her reputation saved.

How could he hold on to Minda once she'd done her payback? He'd have to. Nothing could break up the kids. He'd given Norman Dale his solemn oath.

"Well, I ought to turn in myself," he said, saving these considerations for a time his brain wasn't so tired. "But thought to fill my flask from Norman Dale's stash."

"Indeed. I've moved things around. The children don't need to see that. The bottle's here now." She came with him to the kitchen shelves. That rose scent traveled with her, pleasuring his nose. And a sense of satisfaction pleased him, too. If she was rearranging things, she must already consider this her home. "And I do thank you for retrieving my valises," she said, soft as snow.

"You're very welcome, Miz Haynes."

"The whiskey's top shelf now, behind that basket of onions. Out of sight."

He reached at the same time she pointed, and their hands met by accident. How her fingers could be so soft and supple after an evening of everyday chores baffled him.

She stood still, bright eyes watching him, like she might be waiting for something. Well, here he was, a man with a beautiful bride, and no wedding night in sight. Might as well take a chance.

"Don't think it's out of line to give my wife a good-night kiss," he murmured, leaning down, hand on her shoulder, eyes closing as her warmth enfolded his entire self.

"That's just the whiskey talking, Mr. Haynes."

He halted and frowned, speaking the truth. "I never imbibe more than I should, Miz Haynes. And never in front of the kids. This is an honest kiss. And I don't think you'd mind."

She looked down at the rag rug. "I don't deny I wanted more after our bridal kiss. But that was before, Mr. Haynes." Without meeting his gaze, she reached up and handed him a cold bottle, then stepped far out of reach. "You're leaving me. What kind of husband does that?"

Her eyes filled with tears and her voice shook. With no other answer than a polite nod, he headed without a word toward the backdoor, something he couldn't define weighing heavy on his shoulders. "Good night, Minda."

"Good night yourself," she said, without glancing at him. In the lone upholstered chair, she sat down with a sheaf of papers.

Norman Dale's letters, to be sure. Even though the dead deserved respect, Brixton shook his head at his brother's lies and the trap they had set. Sighing, he left out the backdoor, took off his shirt, and washed up at the well, letting the ice-cold spring water cool his heat. Then he bunked down against the barn. The stones underneath his bedroll comforted his spine like goose feathers did anybody else. As he licked a drop from the grooved mouth of his flask, he wished he could drink from Minda's lips one more time.

As stars blinked overhead, she doused the lantern in the house to sleep all alone in a big bed on her wedding night. By all rights, Brixton should be climbing in beside her.

Even alone, lying on a dusty farmyard, he grew hard as hell, imagining a time he might have the right to explore those womanly curves. Like an answer to prayer, sometime during the night the scent of roses crept up his nose. A woman's warmth filled the darkness, and lantern-light fell like rain.

The dream-woman knelt at his side, but she seemed so real, so soft and fragrant. Her hair brushed his cheek. Did his bride want him after all?

Was she just a dream? Or a dream come true?

"I need you..." she said.

"And I need you, darlin'," he muttered into the night and pulled her down against his bare chest, his fingers reaching deep into her hair, as he kissed his bride long and good.

****

"Mr. Haynes, how dare you? Leave me be." Minda pushed away from him as she shrieked softly. Urgency pumped in her veins, but she knew horses and didn't want to unnerve the livestock. "What are you about? I thought we made this clear."

Despite her protests, her lips had opened for a split second, and she raised her fingers to hold onto his kiss just a bit longer. It was her wedding night. If only this were real. Even with dread damping her flesh, she remembered his offer of a good-night kiss, and how truly difficult it had been to refuse him.

"Minda?" Sleep glazed his half-lidded eyes, his dark hair rustled against his bare shoulders. In the soft lantern light his chest showed chiseled shadows of muscle, and she feasted on the tantalizing sight. "What are you out here for?"

"I do need you." Heat rushed to her toes as she found her voice. "But not in that way. It's Priscilla"

He moved inside his bedroll uncomfortably. "What? What about Silly?"

"She woke me up an hour ago with a fever that's rising too fast. I know sickness. Brixton, I need you to go fetch that doctor."

As he scrambled to his feet, gracefully for a man so big, she shut her eyes tight against the tempting vision of him. After the trick he'd played, she wasn't supposed to want him at all. Annulment was the only recourse, disgraceful though it might prove. When she dared a glance at his face, he turned his back to her, as if he were embarrassed, too, and quickly pulled on his shirt.

He loped toward the house as he set his buttons.

"Wait, Mr. Haynes! Saddle a horse and be off. I said I need you to go get the doctor." Maybe if she used his formal name, the rioting feelings would stop. But no. It just reminded her that she'd willingly married "Mr. Haynes." Desperately, she tried to resume their prior animosity. Then panic, rather than anger, tore at her. "Hurry."

"Thought I told you once. Do not tell me what to do." Her husband's voice was dark as the sky overhead, his eyes bright in the lantern light. His breath still came hard. "And I can't oblige you anyway. Doc Viessman left town yesterday for David City. His eldest gal wed up with a farmer there. She's birthing their first any day now."

Minda's face flamed at his mention of such a womanly topic. He went on, "I want to check Silly myself."

"Gracey claims you're no family man," Minda said, wishing like anything she wore something other than just the bridal nightclothes she'd bought for Norman Dale. She still hadn't cooled down and her breasts breathed underneath the silk, loose and taut at the same time. Most likely her husband had read invitation in her attire when she came to him. Or had the kiss been just a man's uncontrollable lusts? She moaned in some disgust. How could she consider such selfish thoughts during this time of crisis?

"I'm no family man. Gracey's right about that," he said into her thoughts. "But I learned some medicine from a Kiowa guide. Saved Timmy Jacobson's leg one time."

"Heathen medicine? I think not," she said, as Brixton reached for the door, all but tearing it off its hinges. "This isn't some buckaroo's leg, but a baby girl."

Hanging up the lantern, he threw her a scowl. "Heathen medicine?"

"Please be quiet," Minda hissed, though his footsteps had barely made a sound. "Don't wake up the others."

"Miz Haynes, I know how to keep quiet around sleeping things." His low voice was hot gravel again, and his gaze would have scratched if such a thing were possible.

The inside of the little house was still and stuffy from the hot day, and the odor of sick hugged the air. Piled wildly in a corner were Priscilla's fouled garments and bed linens. Minda waved her hands at the awful turn of events.

Listless in her trundle bed with eyes bright from fever, the baby whimpered.

"We'd best keep both doors open," Minda said, somewhat embarrassed at the disorder, "You know, let the fresh night draft flow from one end to the other."

"Smells worse than this on the trail." Brixton met her gaze then, and his eyes were softer now, almost kind. He bent down to the child, and Minda marveled at the big hardened hand touching

Priscilla's forehead so gently. He cringed a little at the temperature. "She's on fire."

"I know. Why do you think I'm so frightened?"

Concern creased his face. "Now, the Kiowa think to sweat a fever out..."

"Absolutely not," Minda said. "She'd explode into flames if we heated her up more."

"Didn't say I agree."

"We need ice. She needs to cool. Do they harvest the river ice in the winter? Is there an ice storehouse in town?"

"It's after midnight, Miz Haynes. That'd wait until morning. Besides, I reckon ice is just as bad. Gets a body to shiver and shake, brings on conniptions."

"I'm sure you mean convulsions, Mr. Haynes." She picked up the lethargic little one. No ice? No doctor? What on earth were they to do?

"Better not tell me how to speak, either." He headed toward the kitchen and got the big washtub. "Water not hot or cold will do just fine. I'll get us a scoop of well water. Pump's too noisy for the kids. You go heat up the kettle. Then we'll mix the two. *Please*, Miz Haynes? Soon as it's daylight, I'll get some bark from the willow trees along the river. Helps bring down a fever."

"Rough bark on that baby's tender skin? I think not!"

"Ground up, it makes a tea. I'll find some yarrow, too. In between, sassafras tea or aconite might help."

"I know those last remedies perfectly well," Minda said, irritated that this unruly cowboy knew healing methods when she was the one who had raised children. "But there aren't any such ingredients in your brother's supplies."

"Probably got all used up during the scarlet fever," Brixton mumbled, his voice growing taut.

Minda's body chilled and her face flamed at the same time. This man had suffered unthinkable loss in the course of the past four seasons, and now his niece—and adopted daughter—was stricken.

And, Minda acknowledged with a tremble, it might be her own fault. She'd cuddled the baby most of the afternoon. Who knew what contagion she'd brought with her on her long journey from Pennsylvania?

She met her husband's bleak gaze.

What if little Silly died? Minda could already hear Brixton's angry words of blame at her causing the death of someone else he loved.

He came to stand close to her. "Now you go get some water heated up." Then of all things, he took her hand and held it to his lips just for a second. She didn't know men, but she did know comfort. That's all this gesture meant. "She'll be all right," he said. The soft, sad tone of his voice crept into Minda's heart, as it had when they'd stood by little Paul's grave.

"Yes, of course," Minda whispered, then repeated Mama's words. "The Good Book says we don't get handed more than we can bear."

"Wouldn't know," Brixton murmured, holding onto her hand a second longer. "Never read it."

Chapter Four

"Fever's down a bit, I think," Brixton said an hour later. Little Silly seemed content enough, ready to drop off to sleep in the washtub between Minda's supporting arms. "Let's get her dried off and back to bed."

It had taken this full hour for his own panic to subside. When scarlet fever struck Paradise, he'd been on the trail. Jake's letter had caught up with him at the Cheyenne General Delivery, three weeks after the Satterburg's baby daughter had died, many others too. Including Norman Dale's own wife, Ida Louise, and young Paul. Norman Dale had been taken ill himself, never to recover completely. Truth to tell, Norman Dale had known he hadn't but months to live. He needed a new wife fast.

Brixton tightened his jaw. On top of his other lies, Norman Dale had known full well his damaged heart would have widowed Minda soon after their wedding day. Maybe even in their bridal bed. But Minda must never know. She'd hightail it out of here fast, and the kids needed a ma. Brixton had no wish to knot up his life with fatherhood.

Or with a wife. What the hell had he been thinking, gathering her in his arms like that when she'd come to his bedroll? Tasting her lips, holding her close? Who knew what might have happened next if common sense hadn't prevailed? He needed to leave Paradise fast. Even now, remembering the heat and scent of her, the sight of her in white lace in the lantern glow had his manhood twitching in forbidden joy.

But he stopped those runaway thoughts and feelings. Instead, his heart tugged to see little Silly suffering. Any creature in misery had him longing to help, but this was his own kin. Likely the fever had tuckered her out, but she wasn't well yet. Who knew what the morning would bring? What if… A nightmarish question fizzled in his brain. What if he didn't get to leave?

Worse, what if Silly died?

Without a word, Minda lifted the baby, pinned on new britches and laid her gently in the trundle. The child moved listlessly, but seemed to be sleeping. Minda moved to Brixton, eyes wide and troubled.

"We've got to get Neddie-boy and Katie off safely in the morning," she said. "I'm sure Jake and Gracey will take them in for a time."

In spite of his uneasy thoughts and her outlandish announcement, Brix couldn't help noticing how cuddling the baby's wet flesh had dampened his wife's nightdress. Her nipples stood out like rosebuds from beneath the thin white fabric.

He fought the hardening in his groin and forced his mind to the matter at hand. "What the dickens are you saying?"

"Priscilla might be infectious. We need to get the others away."

"That's foolish talk, Miz Haynes. I promised my brother I'd keep the kids together. No matter what."

"This isn't foolishness, Mr. Haynes. It's the one thing that kept the diphtheria from my sisters and me when Mama was stricken. She sent us away."

"Seen diphtheria. This isn't it. Likely Silly ate some corrupted food at our wedding dinner. Hot sun spoils food quick. Wouldn't take but a bite to sicken somebody so small."

It sounded strange to talk about his wedding.

Minda shook her head almost wildly, eyes bright with something like fear. "No, no. We can't take any chances. Besides, Gracey and I fed Priscilla some nibbles from Neddie's plate. He's sleeping fine."

"Well, like I say, Miz Haynes. The kids stick together."

"How can you be so irresponsible?" Her voice rose, and she stiffened away from the baby's bed.

He remembered her chiding him to be quiet and reminded her of the same. "Keep still, Miz Haynes. We got them all sleeping soundly. You ought to get some rest yourself. It's been quite a day."

And it had. A sudden weariness clamped around him like the cloying heat. Lighting the stove hadn't helped. He longed for his bedroll, for a long sleep under a cool night sky even though, by now, morning wasn't far away. But that bedroll only brought Minda to mind again, and her warm body kneeling there, kissing him like she meant it for that split second.

In front of his eyes, her shoulders slumped. "I couldn't possibly sleep with all this on my mind."

She said *my* like he wasn't caring as much, and his irritation flamed. Of course, she'd been good with Silly just now, and with all the kids all day long, but was she suggesting he wasn't doing his share? That he didn't have worry on his mind? He wasn't even over Norman Dale, and now he had to think of possibly laying this baby girl in the dark earth, too.

His skin crawled like fleas on a mutt. He might not be a family man, but these kids were his last flesh and blood.

In his own way, he cared one hell of a lot. Else he wouldn't have stuck himself with Minda Becker.

Minda *Haynes*.

But he held his tongue. "Then at least sit yourself down, get a load off your feet." The lone upholstered chair was the damnedest uncomfortable thing, but Ida Lou had been proud of it. For a flash, he wondered if Minda minded moving into another woman's home. Then he squelched the thought. Didn't matter if she did. She was here now, and he'd make sure she stayed.

Rather than fuss, she did as he said, but perched at the edge of the cushion like she wanted to flee. Or like she had something else to say. He might as well let her speak up now, or he'd likely never hear the end of it.

"Brixton," she said, looking about the kitchen instead of in his eyes. It struck him that she used his christened name for once. And he realized that something like terror colored her face. "Brixton, I think this might all be my fault."

"Your fault? What on earth are you saying?" He pulled up a simple X-shaped chair he'd made from two flat boards when he was nothing but a tad of twelve. As he sat, he peeked over at the sleeping baby. She seemed peaceful.

"I think I brought the contagion," Minda whispered. "It has to be me, something so sudden. With all the filthy air and dirty towns and unwashed passengers on that long journey, I'm certain I carried the sickness here."

Whether she was right or wrong, he didn't like the fear in her eyes. For an odd moment, he touched her hand. "I'm telling you, it's corrupted food. Happens sometimes after a potluck."

"How could you know? You don't live here anymore." Her beautiful white neck tensed as she swallowed hard. She stayed silent, though, like she might be considering what to say next.

"I remember things." He moved his hand back to his thigh. "And whatever you might think, my brother and I were close. We kept in touch. I got here three, four times every year."

Yet those three unknowing weeks still caused

him some troubled dreams. He hadn't had the smallest hunch things had gone so wrong in Paradise.

"Then you need to do the best for his children."

Brix bristled at her words. Hadn't he done just that, taken them on, and worse yet, taken a wife, for better or worse? He'd done the impossible—gotten himself married. But he'd wrangle with her about that some other time. The edges of her eye sockets were gray from lack of sleep, and he grudgingly allowed that she was caring right well for a family not even her own. "I do, Miz Haynes."

"Then listen to me! A newcomer changes everything."

Damn right, he said to himself, holding his tongue tight so he didn't speak the words out loud.

"After Papa died at Gettysburg, my mama sewed and mended for a living," Minda said in a drained voice. "A troupe of traveling players came to Gleesburg and hired her to stitch up some damaged costumes. Mama came down with the diphtheria right after those intruders left. I know they brought the illness into our house. I know of what I'm speaking, Mr. Haynes."

He swallowed hard himself, figuring she had a right to feel some dread. For a strange reason, he sought to disavow her notion.

"Well, I come just as far as you," he said. "If what you say is true, I'm guilty myself. Now, I'll get you some tea."

He headed for the stove, mostly to lose sight of those wide, hurt eyes. He'd rather make some Arbuckle's but knew that would keep them awake for whatever was left of the night. The tea was weak, so he added some color with a dash from his brother's whiskey bottle. That'd sure get her to sleep. But when he got back to the ugly stuffed chair, he found her fast asleep already. The real thing, too—her mouth hung open a bit. For an unwise second, he longed to kiss it, stroke her tongue with his. Then he remembered his vow to her that she'd have Norman Dale's room all to herself.

Well, hell, this wasn't any bedroom. He leaned over and closed her mouth with his. Took him about a minute to calm his raging cock, but giving into that second of temptation had been worth it.

She was lighter than a bag of dried beans. Gently, he carried her to the bedroom. Norman Dale had gotten the new bed-tick filled with feathers for his bridal night. Across the pillow, her hair splayed around her head like a gold and silver wagon wheel touched with gentle rust, and Brix couldn't resist touching it. Like he'd watched her do with Silly, he drew the cover gently up to her neck and took one last guilty peek at her bosom while he did so.

Then he looked out the lone window. It wasn't long until morning, and for a beguiling second, he wished he could climb in beside her until the sun rose. She was his wife.

And it was his wedding night.

But he remembered the vow again.

Instead, he sighed and pulled the X-shaped chair next to Silly's bed, to keep watch.

****

Minda woke to a blare of sun shining in her eyes. Her heart pounded. Where in God's heaven was she?

Then she remembered. She was *married.* She had a husband. The bed was soft and smelled clean but had Brixton kept his word?

Of course. He had promised not to take advantage. And truth to tell, she knew she'd remember if he had… If they had… No woman would forget her first time, not with a man like Brixton Haynes in charge. Relief mixed with regret flooded her body and mind, until she remembered

Priscilla's violent illness. How had she come to be in this bed?

Her husband, of course. Had he touched or seen something he shouldn't? Embarrassment flared.

Rising quickly, she grimaced at yesterday's calico dress. It was the gown she'd worn before washing up from Priscilla's sickness. But to her relief, she saw the valises her husband had brought in from the wagon. She scrambled through her meager collection of clothes and pulled out her most serviceable, well-worn frock. After all, if she were a nursemaid, she might as well look the part.

The scent of coffee hit her nose when she left the small sleeping chamber, and her stomach growled. Yesterday had been so tumultuous that she hadn't eaten much at her wedding dinner.

Her wedding dinner. Her jaws clenched tight around her teeth. What in the world was going to happen next? Her anger, for one thing. Where on earth was her husband? Had he left Priscilla all alone? She found Katie at the rough-hewn dining table, stirring some kind of mush for Neddie-boy, who looked glumly at the pasty mess in the bowl.

In her little trundle, Priscilla at least appeared to be sleeping soundly. Minda breathed deep in relief.

Or had she died in the night? Minda's skin danced with dread, and her bile rose. Where was Brixton? And how in heaven had she allowed herself to fall asleep? She ran to the child's bed and barely heard Katie's good morning.

Thank God. Priscilla's body gave off normal heat, and her little chest rose and fell naturally. Brixton's washtub remedy had worked. Then it hit her. He'd gone like he said he would.

Of course. If the baby was well, he had no reason to stay. He had that trail boss to meet up with in Kansas somewhere. Yesterday, he had explained leaving his horse in Ellsworth and would catch a train to get there. Now that he'd made her his wife and the children's mother, he could go on with his life. Like he'd said right off, what did it matter? She'd come to Paradise to become Mrs. Haynes, and she had.

Disconsolate, she poured a cup of coffee. His leaving wasn't a surprise, yet she was staggered at how bereft she felt. But he'd surprised her last night, too. His worry for Priscilla had seemed genuine. So how could he leave his own kin? As she forced her mind to recall all his disagreeable qualities, she reminded herself that she didn't want him either.

"Where's your uncle? Why has he left you alone?" she asked dully, not sure what she felt or why.

Katie shrugged as she shoved a spoon in her brother's mouth. "I don't know. I found these grits hot on the stove. And a fresh pail of milk."

"I can eat all by myself." Ned wiped the gray goop from his mouth with his sleeve.

"Then do it." Katie said.

Minda almost smiled. The children bantered in just the way she remembered her little sisters doing all those years ago. Even with Minda standing here for the first time, the children behaved like the morning was a normal one. Obviously, they had no idea their baby sister had taken desperately ill in the night. And she wouldn't tell them, not just now. Not ever, if Priscilla was on the mend. She couldn't worry their little hearts so soon so soon after they'd lost their father.

And their wayward uncle. If he had even a tiny bit of concern for them, why didn't he stay at least a little while?

Or at least say good-bye?

She picked up Priscilla, who cuddled for a moment, then seemed to writhe against Minda's body heat. Maybe she ought to try giving the baby something to eat, although memories of that little rebellious stomach last night didn't encourage her.

Still, it would give her something to do instead of thinking about Brixton's abandonment. She had a ton of fouled laundry to keep her occupied as well. But after a peek in the corner, she realized the pile was missing.

"Oh, there he is. There's Uncle Brix," Neddie pointed out the window. "He's been out using the privy."

Minda warmed at the thought, and she didn't know why. She had a lot to get used to, living with a man. For a breathless minute, she watched him from behind, the bare muscles of his back bronzed and sculpted. Then he hunkered over a tinny mirror on a fence post to shave. At his feet, Priscilla's washtub foamed with suds.

At least Brixton hadn't left her. Yet.

After he wiped his face with a towel, she went out to him. Katie had found a loaf of bread sent home from the wedding, and a pot of some kind of jam. That would keep her and Ned busy while Minda had words with Brixton.

"Morning, Miz Haynes," Brixton said without turning around. "Looks like little Silly cooled right down."

Minda rolled her eyes at the triumph in his voice, but let her ire pass. Thankfully, his idea had worked. "Yes, thank God, but it's *Priscilla,* thank you."

"I left some coffee and grits for you. I'll be off soon's I get my jacket."

Be off? So he was leaving. She kept her face as immobile as possible. And why not? They'd both agreed the baby was fine.

"Well," she said, unable to think of a proper good-bye.

He straightened up from the mirror and turned around to her, coming as close as when they'd kissed at the altar. Other than the white towel hanging around his neck, his sun-browned chest was bare, carved hard like his back, dark swirls of hair here and there tickling nipples as round and copper as coins. Minda knew her face flushed purple. She'd thought of that bare chest touching her own even at the altar, and that dream had come true last night, in those few breathless moments on his bedroll. His heat would stick in her memory for a lifetime.

For surely it wouldn't happen again. He was leaving. But in time, she reminded herself, so was she.

"Just taking care of business, Miz Haynes. All the kids seem right as rain. No infection." His eyes, too, gleamed with triumph.

"You can't know that," she said, unwilling to discard her initial suspicions, but thankful Priscilla was well, and the others hale and healthy. In fact, she owed him thanks as well. "I must thank you for last night." Shyly she turned from that magnificent chest. Good heavens, what if he assumed she meant their bedroll kiss? "Your help with Priscilla, I mean."

By the time she dared look at him, he'd buttoned up a shirt, not appearing ruffled at all. She felt a foolish dash of disappointment, but quickly knocked the thought from her head. He wasn't a real husband, and he was leaving anyway. Why shouldn't he have helped in the health concerns of his own niece? Why was it Minda's responsibility? Just because Norman Dale had paid for a travel ticket?

The reminder of the reasons for her predicament started hackles of anger. "You've no right to leave me alone with a sick child. The fever's down but that's no guarantee."

"I admit that, Miz Haynes. But I think you'll be fine on your own for a few hours."

Just a few hours? Relief tickled her skin. "Why, what do you mean?"

"Fever's down, but I'm still going after that willow bark and yarrow. You need some on hand. And I'll get into town for aconite, and some ice."

"I thought you said that was a bad idea," Minda said, feeling her own sense of triumph. "'Brings on conniptions.'"

His familiar glare was back. "I'm checking at the ice house. Your ice box's near out. I milked the cow. Don't want it to go bad."

A flush warmed her cheeks. Milking the cow was likely a chore she'd need to learn. A glance at the wheat field showed her the hands he'd hired already at work. No doubt she was responsible for some kind of noon meal for them. And her husband had clearly implied just now that the ice box was hers, not theirs. So he wouldn't be staying or helping to work the land.

The thought shouldn't bother her as much as it did. He was annoying and rude and had played a mighty trick on her.

"And since you asked," Brixton said, "yep, they harvest ice from the Loup. But if it don't last through July, Paradise hauls it from the Missouri. I'll go and get you a block."

He picked up the washtub as easily as a drinking cup and dumped the water in the rose garden Norman Dale had planted for her.

"Silly's pukey clothes are all boiled clean, over there on the line," he said, as he reached for his hat and gave her a long look from top to toe. "And don't you worry, Miz Haynes. When it's time for me to go, you'll know it. I won't leave without kissing you good-bye."

Chapter Five

Right away he found the herbs he needed along the river and headed for town. Of anybody around here, Jake Satterburg would know if Silly's sickness was something that had spread to other folks. Folks turned to the preacher first in times of trouble.

Damn, Brix wished he had time to cool down his heated body in the river. What the hell had he done, stealing a kiss from Minda like that at midnight? Now, with Silly recovered, he couldn't get the taste of her lips out of his mind, or the feel of her breasts underneath that nightgown. True, he was her husband, but he was a husband who didn't want a wife. Just a man who wanted a woman.

A woman he didn't dare take.

Being outdoors contented him, like it always did, even with Minda on his mind and the bugs tangling in his eyelashes. All around him, meadows and prairie grass and homesteads spread out, split here and there with creeks. It wasn't much like the miles of sagebrush and mesquite in Texas, but the sky was high and the horizon long. No roof or walls for Brixton Haynes.

And with the baby seeming all but well this morning, he could be on his way in two days, like he'd planned.

As he rode into Paradise, he looked longingly at Skinny Hank's saloon, but didn't stop until the church. There he found Jake, sweeping the aisles clean of the footprints from yesterday's wedding guests. It was a strange activity for the preacherman.

"Doing woman's work now, are you?" Brix grinned.

"How's the bridegroom?" Jake said with a cheeky smile that set Brix to scowling. It might be the house of God and Jake a man of the cloth, but they'd been chums since their boyhood. Anybody else would have his nose bloodied.

"One of the kids took sick," Brix said, without answering Jake's question, and without saying Silly's name directly. Jake's face darkened anyway. "Recovered now. I'm just wondering if you heard of an ague or somesuch going around?"

"Which kid?"

"Don't matter. Just wondering."

Jake shook his head. "So far, it seems like just another day in Paradise. But I'll let you know if I get wind of anything. And—" He leaned on the broom like he did his pulpit. "I'll wire Chester in David City if he's needed."

"Figured you'd do that."

"It's Silly, isn't it," Jake said, never moving the broom.

"Yep. But like I say, things seem better now." A rush of relief cooled Brix's body.

"I won't say a word to Gracey," Jake said, but his eyes looked away.

"You better not. I admire Gracey, Jake, but Silly's my child. And Minda's now, too." Just saying his wife's name made him peek around the church where their wedding had been. Her face outlined by that white fancy veil had been as beautiful as any man could imagine. And that kiss at the altar…

Despite his holy surroundings, Brix's trousers tightened around his swelling erection. But even with Minda inside his head, he cooled his thoughts and body by remembering the facts. Minda was greedy and had driven his brother to his death.

Esperanza had been fickle, breaking his heart just as he'd been ready to give it to her forever.

"Brix..." Jake hesitated a bit. "Making Silly our own was never my idea. I had no part in Gracey cooking up such a scheme."

"I figured that. But sometimes folks keep secrets. We did it to Minda. You, me, and Norman Dale agreeing I should wed up with her right off."

"We did the right thing, Brix," Jake said, drawing breath deep inside, then blowing it right out. "Your deathbed vow to Norman Dale is a sacred trust. You aren't regretting it, are you?"

Well, he didn't want a wife, but the memory of her sweet kiss and hot body sure made him imagine possible delights.

"Hell, no," he said. "The kids need her, and I won't be around. Minda's got what she came for, a house and family. But she said you and I committed a sin of omission. I remember catechism class. That wasn't a good thing back then."

"Since when did any kind of sin fret you?"

"Never. I'm bound for hellfire, to be sure."

Jake's friendly snort interrupted Brix's dark thoughts. "You're a good man, Brixton Haynes."

"Try telling my wife," he said. "She's already yapping at me to call the baby Priscilla, not Silly. Don't approve of me at all, I can tell."

"Minda's a good woman to take you on."

"What?" Brix looked sideways at Jake, disbelieving. She hadn't done any such thing. It was him who'd done all the sacrificing. She had wanted to get married. He hadn't.

"Well, think about it. The noon's stage has come and gone. And she wasn't on it."

Brix opened his mouth then shut it quick, afraid he might let a cuss slip. Of course Minda wasn't on the stage. But she wasn't staying because of any goodness in her dark heart. She *owed* him. He couldn't confess their unholy alliance to Jake. Not in the house of God at least.

Both men turned toward a commotion at the tall entry doors. From the gun belt and star, Brixton knew the newcomer was a lawman.

"Brixton Haynes, here's the new county sheriff, Robert Pelton," Jake said.

The sheriff tipped his hat. "Call me Bob. Sorry to miss your nuptials, Brixton. Had a ruckus over in Monroe yesterday." He stared Brixton up and down like he was a new mutt in town who needed to be sniffed up, then tipped his hat again. "I just got word the Perkins Gang's been sighted in Norfolk. Preacher, me and you can pass the news along in town. Brixton, maybe you can let the out-of-towners know on your way home."

"The Perkins Gang? Whew." Brix exhaled. He knew of the real-life troublemakers who'd become heroes in dime store novels. He hated folks thinking such antics were nothing but boyish larks. These were grown men who took what wasn't theirs. "Thought they worked Missouri and Kansas."

Sheriff Pelton grunted. "Must have run out of horses to steal down there. Thanks, fellas." He gave a short wave and left.

For a second, the sheriff's words stayed on Brixton's mind. Was the family he'd taken on in any kind of danger? So far, the men in the Perkins gang weren't killers, but Norman Dale had two fine geldings and a good draft horse. And no money left behind to buy more.

Then there was Minda, a citified female who likely didn't have the faintest idea how to protect herself.

He sighed aloud, thinking of the kids, too. He grabbed Jake's broom. He needed a few minutes to settle his thoughts, maybe to hear some Gospel to save his sorry soul. Besides, the Perkins gang didn't have gumption enough to strike during daylight. "Go on, go practice your preaching. I'll get this finished up."

"What? Brix Haynes doing women's work?"

Brixton gave a snort. Already today he'd milked a cow, scoured a pot, cooked up grits and coffee, and washed a batch of reeking laundry. He'd done every womanly thing but change the baby's sopping britches.

And, of course, do one's spousal duty.

"If you only knew," he said dryly. "Anyways, I'm leaving before sun-up on Sunday, and I'll miss your oration. Might as well let me hear it now."

Jake held tight to the broom handle. "You sure?"

"About what? Hearing your sermon? Not so much. About leaving? I'm sure as hell. That was the bargain. Remember?"

Jake's mouth opened, but Brixton tipped an uncouth salute and left. Suddenly he wasn't in the mood for any kind of Gospel about Jake's second thoughts. Brixton sure as hell wasn't having any. No matter that Minda was beautiful and his lawful wife. When he mounted Norman Dale's horse, his manhood swelled at his thoughts of her. Truth to tell, the pressure of the saddle made him wish he was riding his bride.

Yep. His thoughts were crude. Add another sin to his list. That icehouse better have a nice big block to cool him down. Smacking at a mosquito, he cussed a streak, but at himself, not the bug.

Before he left this town, he had to warn his neighbors and teach his wife to use a gun.

Storm clouds collected overhead but passed by on a high wind. There'd be more, though. Weather in Nebraska changed every five minutes. And he hoped Ahab Perkins and his renegades passed by just as soon.

Brixton Haynes had a train to catch.

****

"Can you shoot? You keep a knife in your boot?" Brixton stomped through the backdoor and stored the ice. All the warnings he'd passed out along the way home had made him nervous. After all, thugs changing their territory might be changing their tactics.

Brixton had half-expected an empty corral and a battered family and felt a stab of relief. But even though things seemed peaceful enough today, he had to do what he could before he left to make sure Minda could keep the kids and herself from trouble.

"What are you on about, Mr. Haynes? And please keep your voice down. You'll wake the baby." She got up from shelling peas to frown like a regular wife. Looked like she wore a prettier gown than he'd seen that morning. Her hair hung loose, almost to her waist, and like yesterday, he wanted to gather it in his hands like a thirsty man chugged water to his dying mouth.

"She feeling better?" He noticed a pretty posy of wildflowers smack dab in the middle of the eating table. Damn, had she gone wandering about picking flowers instead of doing her duties?

"She's sleeping now, and I think much better. I took her for a little stroll along the road." She gave him a glare as though daring him to disagree. "I don't hold with sick folk being cooped inside in dank, stale air. Whether or not Priscilla has caught an infection, the outdoors is sure to have some sort of healing effect on her."

He tightened his teeth. Would she ever stop preaching? Sounded worse than Jake. Brixton was a man who spent most every living minute in the outdoors. He of all people knew of its powers. Fine then, that she'd taken a few moments to brighten her day with some of nature's floral bounty.

"And I don't care whether or not you agree," she

said, sniffing. "You'll no doubt carp at me whatever I do."

"Not so, Miz Haynes," he said. He hated feeling charitable, but he figured she had a right to be peevish, her life not turning out as she'd planned, and spending her sleeping hours tending a sick child.

"Thank you, Mr. Haynes. Now what's this nonsense about guns and knives?"

"No nonsense at all. I'm asking if you know how to use them."

"Well, certainly not, Mr. Haynes. I make hats. I come from Gleesburg, a most civilized village outside Gettysburg."

"Yes, ma'am. I know all about your civilized nature." He glared back and felt his mouth slip into a triumphant little grin as he recalled her hot and willing lips for that split second last night. Wondered how he'd be feeling today if they had made their wedding night real. Would he feel regret? Satisfaction? Victory?

She blushed, and he felt a bit of a coup. Right now she was surely remembering her time on his bedroll just like he was. God in heaven, he enjoyed the look of her, blushing at the memory.

Then a powerful thought hit. The Perkins gang might well see fit to expand their ill-gotten rewards to include pretty women just like his wife.

"I ask a good question of you, Miz Haynes. There's been outlaws spotted not fifty miles from here."

"Outlaws?" Her voice was a whisper, a whisper that ought to come from those sweet lips breathing his name in the dark.

"Yep. Ahab Perkins and his gang."

Her eyes were bright and wide as full moons, her face just as white. "Why, I read about them. On my travels. They're outlaws, but gentlemen."

"Those dime novels are miserable trash, Miz Haynes. No gentleman steals what isn't his to take. And..." He slowed down and pinned her gaze to his. "Around here, horse thieving's a hanging offense."

"But these are farmers around here."

Disgust tightened his lips. "Farmers have good horses, Miz Haynes. Like my brother's. Now, I guess that means you don't know how to keep yourself and the kids from harm?"

"How dare you, Mr. Haynes? I think I've shown that the welfare of these children means a great deal to me. Despite your payback." Her pansy eyes turned hard and black, but her voice trembled. "Norman Dale thought I was perfectly qualified in that regard. He never mentioned that I had to be a gunslinger as well."

It bothered him to hear his brother's name, especially from those lovely lips. He hadn't thought of Norman Dale much at all today, and neither of them seemed to be grieving for him. Maybe if he recalled that she'd come here to be nothing but his sister-in-law, he could squash his desire like a bug.

Sure would make leaving easier.

"So I guess that means you're a gunslinger," she said, her tone accusing.

"I know how to use a piece, that's a fact. There's rustlers along the trail, Miz Haynes, and diamondbacks. And once in a while a prairie chicken to hunt. But I never kill for joy. Now come outside and I'll show you a trick or two."

"But I..."

"Now, Miz Haynes. That's an order whether you like it or not."

Her mouth opened, and he longed to kiss it closed. Couldn't help himself. It's just what she did to him. The bug squashing was harder to do than he thought. Just like yesterday at church, he took her hand to lead her off into something she'd never done before. He almost trembled. How the hell could he teach her how to aim, him prickling like a schoolgirl?

Out by the fence posts where he'd lined up a row of bottles and cans, he showed her his Peacemaker and how to cock it. Then he stepped back and sighted, drawing her against him. Her softness and that smell of roses with his fingers around a gun was a strange mix.

"Likely this will take some practice," he said softly. "But I don't think I could leave without you knowing a little something. Just never leave a gun where the kids can find it."

He expected angry eyes to take him like fingernails, but she spoke in that same whisper that now almost sent him to his knees. "I'm a fairly smart woman, Mr. Haynes. You can trust me."

Trust. He shot and missed, cursed. Felt like a fool. Like he'd trusted Esperanza? But wasn't his own dishonesty just as bad? He had led Minda to the altar under false pretenses. And even now, he knew his brother had wanted a wife because he was dying.

"I think you're right, Mr. Haynes." She smiled, leaning into him. "A lot of practice. There's so much around here I need to learn."

Her eyes were bright. He was no womanizer, but he took a gamble that he knew the look. Wasn't this invitation pure and simple?

He holstered the gun and bent down to her. The moment before a kiss was almost the best, imagining what was to come. Her scent and warmth surrounded him, and for a second, there was nobody but the two of them in the whole wide world.

So close he could taste her breath, he grabbed a length of her hair and brought it to his mouth first. Tasted like roses. She was so close…

"Uncle Brix. Come quick. I think I heard a gun."

Damn.

"No, no, Neddie. That was me." Reluctant but

relieved, he let go of his wife. Ned's timing was just right. Brixton Haynes had been about to do something he shouldn't.

****

Over her mending, Minda looked nervously out the window, but the darkness was complete. Through the windbreak of trees, she couldn't see lights from even the nearest farmhouse. Never before in her life had she been so far from other living folks.

Her husband had made no secret of the fact he was leaving. Leaving her and the children alone. The nightfall was hot and humid and who knew what lurked out in it? More contagion?

Horse thieves?

At least for now he sat across from her, singing Priscilla a lullaby. He promised he'd never leave without kissing her good-bye. So what should she make of the almost-kiss? Did it mean he'd changed his mind?

Of course not. He'd never made it a secret that he was going. Besides, he hadn't looked her in the eye the whole rest of the day. He regretted it. Of that she had no doubt.

Even though he'd seemed to want the kiss as much as she did, at first anyway.

At least the lovely bunch of wildflowers in the center of the table kept her spirits up while she'd busied herself with supper and the fidgeting baby. She'd noticed them earlier in the day, long before the almost-kiss. Brixton must have plunked them in a crock of water behind her back before going to town.

Strange man, her husband. Guns and wildflowers.

But even a gun didn't help. How could she be anything but afraid? The baby wasn't well. There wasn't any money, and now she had to worry about outlaws.

If outlaws peeked in those windows, they would see nothing but a normal family. Her breath caught, and she got up to close the curtains. No matter that the fresh air wouldn't flow as freely.

What matter that he promised to send money? Children needed a father, too. She'd learned that from raising her sisters all alone. A husband who steered the right course for his family was every bit a man's man as one who stormed the plains guiding horses and cows.

But when she got up to dig through Ida Lou's leftover mending supplies, she reminded herself that she didn't intend to stay, after her payback at least. How could she? This wasn't the life she'd come for. Brixton would simply have to cope without her.

Throughout the day, Katie's *ma'am* had started to sound more and more like *mom*. She couldn't encourage the child. Under no condition could she let the children steal her heart.

At the thought, Minda's heart started to pound too hard. Maybe she'd picked up Priscilla's contagion. But she knew better. She had to cope with all of this, too. And the only way she knew how to sort things out and to think things through was to create a hat.

She glanced at Priscilla and at Katie through the open sleeping curtain. The little brown braid hung almost to the floor. Somehow, Minda would find time tomorrow to make the girls new bonnets for church on Sunday. And outlaws or not, that would mean a trip into town.

Brix wiggled in the big overstuffed chair, probably signaling he was ready to go outside to his bedroll.

"I'll put her to bed," she whispered, then added, "That was a pretty song."

"Don't bother me at all to hold her. She seems peaceful enough." He shrugged, then caught Minda's eye. “You aren’t one of those Temperance ladies, are you, Miz Haynes, who keeps a man from his blackstrap?”

She wasn’t, but his almost-kiss still confused and disappointed her, and truth to tell, she resented both feelings. She had every right to obstinate. But as she dared a glance at his face, at the cheekbones carved high and eyes shadowed deep, her heart beat harder than it ever had.

“No, not at all, Mr. Haynes,” she said. “So long as that man doesn’t liquor himself up and take it out on a lady.”

Brixton’s face darkened. “No real man vents his spleen any place, any time, on a woman, a critter, or a kid.”

His words pleased her, and she felt a bit more friendly toward him.

“We sing that song to cattle, out on the trail,” he said, laying the baby in her bed and heading toward the cupboard. His voice was soft and conversational. He moved like magic and music at the same time, and her skin grew warm.

She looked away from him. Last night, their wedding night, his lips traveling across her flesh, his hands sliding over her body, caused riots in her special places.

Her breath came quick. He was not just a man’s man, but a woman’s as well. Swallowing hard, she tried to get back to normal.

“Why?”

“Why what?” He poured something thick and dark into a cup.

Was he so unaware of her turmoil? Or had it been just another toss on a bedroll for him? She sighed in disgust, but asked anyway. “Why do you sing to the cows?”

“Lulls them just like kids, keeps them calm. They don’t know what’s out there in the dark.

Anything can spook them into stampede. Striking a match. Kicking a stone. Thunder rolling somewhere far off. Anything."

Minda raised her eyebrows. There was a lot to cattle driving that she didn't know. Life around here was nothing like Gleesburg. Now she had something out there in the dark to spook her as well.

Outlaws.

"You should know that Katie's right proud of her braid. She said you didn't pull once."

Shrugging, his shoulders rippled as he raised the cup to his mouth. He moved to the funny X-shaped chair and leaned against the wall. "No different from braiding strips of rawhide into a lariat."

His indifference infuriated her. He was so blasted off-hand about these children. That reminded her of her latest quest.

"I'm going to need to go to town tomorrow to obtain some sewing supplies."

"Like hell." The chair scraped flat on all legs.

"Pardon me, Mr. Haynes?"

"I said *like hell*, ma'am. It's not that I don't adore your company, Miz Haynes, but I got no time to go to town. The more I help with the wheat harvest, the less I got to pay the field hands."

"I don't need you go to with me. I can ride as well as any man."

Brix smirked over the baby's head.

"It's true," Minda said, pulling an angry needle to reunite a button with Ned's shirt. Why should she have to defend herself against this mannerless lout? "I earned money as a girl mucking Mayor Davis's stables. His groom taught me to ride. The mayor was a kind man who let me ride whenever I found the time."

"There's outlaws about, Miz Haynes," her husband drawled. "Up to now, they're content with thieving horses. But one of these times they just might want a woman."

He glared.

"You are not going to town."

Chapter Six

"That bird's nest top your head's gonna blow off in this wind."

Minda turned at the sound of her husband's voice early the next afternoon. She hadn't seen him all day. He must have done his washing up early on, and she admitted to disappointment at not getting to peek again at his bare, manly chest.

At Katie's suggestion, she'd cut some ham at noon and sent it with biscuits out to the men in the fields. Katie explained that Uncle Brix and the other workers weren't expected to come to the table. The children had also carried a pail of water to wash in, and cold water to drink later on.

So why was he in the barn? Neddie had explained there were still acres to harvest. Even at five, the little boy knew more about farming than Minda ever would.

The friendly horse she'd saddled nickered and nibbled at her shoulder. Before she could think of a word to say, Brix came toward her and reached for a homely, wide-brimmed hat hanging on a hook nearby.

He plunked the ugly thing right over the smart little cap she'd made special of real bird feathers and brown lace to match her new suede split riding skirt. Since this was her first real outing in Paradise, she wanted to look her best in front of her new neighbors.

However, she couldn't help wondering if the garment was as scandalous here as it had been back home. Norman Dale's letters had assured her otherwise, explaining the practicality of the people who inhabited the Plains.

Brixton's lips twisted in a little smile that was just like Priscilla's when Neddie tickled her. "Much better. Keep the sun off your face, too."

Brixton Haynes, her husband, smelling of warm July and the windswept prairie, fastened the ties under her chin. His hot fingers grazed her cheek as he formed the bow, and her heart stopped for a full second.

"You looked just like Priscilla right then," she said. Lord in heaven, she liked his face and every move it made. Just remembering the heat of him in the winter to come would warm her as much as any Pennsylvania fireplace.

Recalling the movement of his lips upon hers for their first kiss at the altar, and those lips so tantalizingly close yesterday, her breath caught like air on a cold day.

His eyes rolled a bit at her remark, but his cheeks darkened. She knew he was pleased. But then her mood darkened as well. Too bad he was obstinate and ornery without a care for those left in his charge. All this talk of leaving.

"Looks like you're out and about," he said pleasantly.

Sighing, Minda took a deep breath. Obviously he'd forgotten her trip to town today, and his order against it. She hadn't managed to slip away in time. And now she fully expected an uproar.

She hadn't forgotten about the outlaws on the loose and how they'd unnerved her last night. But if she had to live in Paradise, even temporarily, she might as well conquer her fears. Folks, and especially her husband, need not think she was a fainthearted ninny.

"Yes. I mentioned last night I need to visit the

mercantile."

"And I told you no. Not alone leastways, and I don't have the time to go along. Besides, who's tending the kids?"

"Neddie wore himself out caring for the heifer they're entering in the fair. He's napping now, and Katie's minding Priscilla. I won't be gone all that long. Besides, you're here, too."

He grumbled deep down, but didn't utter any real words or any kind of protest. Was it possible she'd won him over?

"As I say, I'll be back in plenty of time to start supper. And I won't get lost." Not with the sun to guide her instead of the hills and valleys of Pennsylvania.

"Silly been eating today?" Brixton asked.

Minda shook her head with a twinge of worry. "Not much. She is a bit feverish, but Katie thinks she might be 'growing teeth inside her mouth' and that makes her puny. While I'm in town, I'll see if the doctor's in."

As she led the horse outside, Brixton followed. At least Norman Dale's wife had had the sense not to go sidesaddle, for she was sure the dainty saddle had belonged to Ida Lou.

Her husband's eyes narrowed. "So you didn't make Silly that willow bark tea?"

She turned from him. Of course she hadn't. She would never experiment on such a tiny soul with something so primitive. If the doctor wasn't in, she would surely obtain some civilized medicines at the mercantile.

"Please, Brixton. The children will be fine. I just need to feel the wind on my face and get some fresh air in my lungs." That was the most important reason of all. She hadn't been away from the homestead or around other grownups for days.

For some reason, her answer seemed to be the

right one. He nodded like he might understand. But then he cautioned, "We got no spare coin to buy fancy trinkets for anybody's head."

"I'll barter for the materials I need."

He tensed, his eyes narrowed, and she expected the explosion now. "No wife of mine gets anything except by real cash money."

"No, Brixton. Listen to me. It's an honest transaction." She pulled from her saddlebag the black velvet cap she'd created back home. The silk plume plumped in the breeze. "This is my version of what's called a Huntley bonnet. My design caused quite a stir back home and became very fashionable. I'll trade it for the things I need. And then, if the mercantile happens to sell this hat, we'll split the price."

His face was creased with doubt, but she mounted the horse. "That's how it worked with the milliner in Gleesburg." She looked at him with a dare. "And yes, I know this isn't Gleesburg, but I'm going to try anyway. Good-bye. I'll be back soon."

"All right by me, then." Brixton shrugged. "Strawberry's lady-broke. Gentle enough for a gal."

Throwing her husband one last glare, Minda kneed the horse into a firm gallop.

The strawberry gelding didn't have but a mile of prairie under his hooves when Minda heard a rider coming up behind her. Even with outlaws lurking nearby, ready and willing to bully and rob honest folks, she felt not a single qualm. She knew right off who her follower was.

Her husband.

When he drew abreast, she tossed her head and raced the wind. She beat him into Paradise with a glow of satisfaction, then frowned with the realization that he might have let her win.

She dismounted in front of the mercantile and tethered her horse, but he pulled up and doffed his hat.

"Nice riding, Miz Haynes. I'll see what sort of refreshment Skinny Hank has to offer at his establishment, then see if the doc's back. But don't be long. You and me, we'll be having another shooting lesson this afternoon."

And from the way he said it, she knew exactly what he meant. The almost-kiss needed to be completed. Her spine tingled just thinking about the deed.

****

As Minda opened the door to Hackett's Mercantile, cool air from inside brushed her face. Elsewhere, however, a heat simmered where the shimmying tingles had settled.

Her husband sauntered to the saloon, his backside swaying above his boot heels. The deliciousness of the movement warmed her through and through.

Made her giddy as wine punch.

To calm herself, she paused to use the window as a mirror, pulled off the big hat and re-arranged her chignon around the dainty feathered cap.

Behind the counter was a man she didn't recognize. To be sure, she had a long way to go before she could set straight in her brain all the faces and names she'd met at her wedding. But the mercantiler she had remembered; his pleasant fleshy face reminded her of Gleesburg's mayor. His wife had been just as jolly and plump.

This tall, well-constructed man was far younger, with brown hair perfectly styled with macassar oil, just as handsome in his way as Brixton was in his. His gray-striped wool trousers and vest seemed better suited for a Pennsylvania businessman than one here on the prairie. A trim mustache sat above his smile and a pair of wire-rimmed spectacles added a touch of mystery to his eyes.

"Good afternoon, Mrs. Haynes. Welcome."

She hesitated. Obviously he'd recognized her, probably even attended the wedding. Could he tell she was still untouched?

Could anybody? In Gleesburg, a bride would likely not be shopping in public this soon. She might entertain friends after a week or so, but only by sending out her at-home cards first.

But, Minda reminded herself for the one-hundredth time, she wasn't in Gleesburg any more.

Leaving the counter, the young man came toward her and offered a suave little bow. "I'm Caldwell Hackett. At your service."

The mercantiler's son?

"I'm happy to make your acquaintance," Minda said, delighted with his manners. "I need some aconite for fever, but I also have a transaction to discuss with Mrs. Hackett, if you please."

"Oh, I can help in any way you need. I've got full authority. My mother's in bed with a megrim and Papa can't leave his garden these days. He's growing some mighty squashes to enter in the county fair and treats them like kin."

Minda laughed, remembering Ned's diligence with the heifer. He had asked to sleep in the barn to sing lullabies to her, once he'd learned that his Uncle Brix sang to cattle. She just might let him. The nights were hot, and Brix slept outside ten feet away.

"Yes, my..." She started to tell Caldwell Hackett about Ned but for a second, didn't know quite how to describe him. Neddie wasn't her stepson, as if she'd married Norman Dale. But Brix was his uncle, so that must make her an aunt. "My nephew is totally enamored of his heifer."

"Norman Dale left behind some grand youngsters." Caldwell peered over his spectacles. "I help out here at the store in the summers, but my true calling is schoolmaster. I've been to university, but Paradise will always be home. The children will come to school in the fall, yes?"

Of course. So this was the schoolmaster who claimed Katie had a fine brain. "Absolutely, Mr. Hackett. In fact, I've got designs to get Katie into college later on. There's a fine institution in Gettysburg, and there are others, of course, that admit females." She peered back with apology. "I regret that she's had to miss schooldays in the past. That won't happen again."

What was she thinking? She wouldn't be around to herd Katie into a college somewhere. After her payback, she had no reason to stay in Paradise.

"You sound settled in then, after these two days."

Minda moved on to the real reason she was here, unwilling to chat about her life's events with a perfect stranger. "Mr. Hackett, I would like to discuss a little transaction." She showed him the black velvet cap and explained her plan. "That way, the little girls can have new bonnets to, well, cheer themselves up."

This time, she didn't say "my nieces." Somehow that made the girls sound like they belonged to her. And while it hurt in a strange way to say so, they really didn't. She wasn't anything to them at all, other than their uncle's reluctant wife. The more she told herself that, the easier it was to guard her heart.

"I think that's a fine idea." Caldwell Hackett nodded vigorously, reminding her of her present business. "My parents are ever eager to help our friends and neighbors. I know I speak for them."

He set the cap on a hat stand and placed it prominently on the countertop, the plume curling elegantly. "Come along with me. Let me show you where my mother keeps her remnants."

With some amazement, Minda looked around the well-stocked store. Why had she thought the shelves would be shorthanded, with a poor selection of wares? Norman Dale's letters had assured her she'd find everything she needed in Paradise.

Well, that was probably the reason. He'd lied about so many things.

She examined a dainty calico of pink posies, perfect for a tiny sunbonnet for baby Priscilla, particularly when trimmed with a leftover yard of white tatted lace. She touched the materials lovingly. But she would treat Katie to something more than a big bow pinned to the back of her head, something brimmed and special. After gathering up some pink velvet, she found a handful of silver netting, some black grosgrain ribbon, and three silk rosebuds. She could make do with cardboard to support a brim.

"This should do, Mr. Hackett," she said, happy with the choices. Although he had looked away while she examined the goods, he had stayed nearby her the whole time. The store bustled with customers doing their Saturday shopping, but Minda soon saw why. His mother had obviously recovered from her headache, and was behind the counter now.

"Geraldine Hackett," the shopkeeper called out with a wave.

As Mr. Hackett wrapped her supplies in brown paper, Minda waved back, planning a friendly chat with his mother and other townswomen before she left.

"Mrs. Haynes," Caldwell Hackett said suddenly, back at her side, "might I invite you to join me for tea at Miss Lila Jean's boardinghouse? She runs a fine dining room."

His invitation startled her. Was this the state of manners in Paradise? She was a married woman, after all. And himself a handsome bachelor. He definitely hadn't included his mother.

"Why, Mr. Hackett? I don't think..."

He bent down close to her ear and moved his head side to side to make sure no other customers were close enough. "Mrs. Haynes, you need to know that not everyone in Paradise supported the trick played upon you in your marriage. Should you need a friend..."

His face reddening, he stood up again, as if realizing the impropriety of his nearness. "What I mean is, should you find yourself needing a means of support..." He stumbled over the words. "Hackett Mercantile could make a permanent business arrangement with you regarding your hats."

She fought for words. "Why, Mr. Hackett, your generosity is most kind, but I... Well, this is just my way of gifting the girls with something special. I'm quite all right. Really."

"Well," Caldwell said. "Should the day come when you tire of the trickery..." He reached for her hand and raised it to his lips.

The gesture was merely gallant and gentlemanly, but at the same time she caught a scent she recognized, the scent of oceans or pine trees or downright manliness that her husband wore like a second skin. Caldwell Hackett didn't drop her hand, but Minda watched him stiffen from the toes of his brogans to the oiled strands of his hair.

"Keep your hands off my wife, Hackett."

****

Caldwell Hackett hung over Minda's hand for another split second. Then he looked straight at Brix, his mud-brown eyes turning black. It was a challenge any man would recognize.

"Afternoon, Brix. No cause for ruffled feathers. Just being gentlemanly." His smirk was big and real.

"Known you since we were kids, Hackett. You're no gentleman." Brix's fists tightened. Hackett needed his pretty face busted up, but hell, the buffoon wore spectacles.

"Why, the people of Paradise allow me to be in charge of their schoolchildren, Brix. I think they just might disagree with your assessment of my character. And this lovely lady might disagree as well, hmm, Mrs. Haynes?" Caldwell Hackett acknowledged Minda with a debonair little nod. "I think she and I are fast on the way to becoming business partners. And friends."

"No matter what the town thinks of you, you got no right to put your perfumed paws on my wife. Damn, if you weren't wearing those spectacles, I'd..."

"What, Brix? You'd bloody my nose? Seems you settled a matter that way once already, remember? When we were twelve?

"You weren't wearing spectacles back then, and you deserved it. Taking Norman Dale's slingshot. Something else that wasn't yours."

"Well, Norman Dale's *bride* seems to be yours now, and only through trickery. Shall we let her speak her opinions on that deal? Perhaps she doesn't accept that she's yours at all?"

Brix fumed. "Hackett, Minda's a married woman. My married woman. Now, get out of my way."

"Or what?"

"Or you can take off your spectacles and meet me in the back of Skinny Hank's. But not here, not in front of the ladies." He sure didn't need to harm his reputation, now that he had a wife and kids to his name. But likely he had anyway. From the corner of his eye, he caught a glimpse of the town biddies looking straight at them with wide, interested stares.

"How remarkable, your respect for womenfolk. Yet you trick one into being your wife," Hackett peered over his spectacles at Brix like he was a naughty dunce in a corner. It wasn't a feeling Brix liked at all.

"As I see it, our matrimony is none of your business." Brix's back teeth clenched just as he saw his wife's jaws clamp together, like she might want to say something but not sure she should. Well, whatever it was, it was between the two of them.

Then Minda took his hand. She wasn't gentle at all, he figured she was angry, but his heart still set up a racket that made his ribs crack. "Well, *gentlemen*," she said. "I've had enough of this, discussing me like I'm not even here. Good-day, Mr. Hackett. Thank you for your assistance. Come along, Mr. Haynes."

She hugged her package and led Brix to the door.

"My pleasure, Mrs. Haynes. Any time. Any time at all," Hackett called after them. "Especially if you change your mind about anything. Anything at all."

Outside by their horses, she dropped Brix's hand and stuffed her package in her saddlebag. Hell, she wasn't acting offended at all.

Or flustered. His heart was beating twice as hard as it should.

Minda said in a tight little voice, "Just so you know, Mr. Haynes, Mr. Hackett's behavior was not untoward."

"Save your big words, Miz Haynes. This is not Gleesburg." Brix mounted his horse. "He's got no right to put his lips anywhere on you."

"For your information..." She looked up at him in the saddle. "It was unexpected. I was very surprised."

"Didn't seem like you minded it."

She sighed long and hard. "Mr. Haynes, he was just being gallant. Polite. You needn't act insulted. He's right. You did trick me into marrying you. And you're leaving." She raised her arm, put her hand on his sleeve. His skin burned through the twill. "But I'll still be here, and I'll need friends. Mr. Hackett seems like a fine man, and he speaks well of Katie. I assured him she'll be back in school come autumn. It'll be time for Neddie, too, then."

"Don't think he'll be satisfied, just being your friend." Just saying it tied Brix's stomach into a sickly knot. He wanted to make yesterday's kiss the real thing. He was a healthy man, and she was a beautiful woman. It wasn't any more complicated than that. Especially since he was leaving first thing in the morning.

"Nonsense. Mr. Hackett's simply being kind." She put on her riding gloves.

"Now, get on your horse and hurry home, Miz Haynes. We got time for a short lesson with my Peacemaker. Then I got to help Monty and Clem. Finish up our day in the fields."

"Monty and Clem?"

"Field hands. Their pa, Donny Black, farms the next place over. You ought to come out and meet them sometime. Now, those fine hardworking boys are *my* opinion of a gentleman." He gave her quick nod, caught her in the corner of his eye tying Ida Lou's old sunhat on her head. That gave him a twinge of satisfaction.

Brix kneed Norman Dale's buckskin into a full gallop. Storm clouds clumped overhead like West Texas grew sagebrush, dark as his own spirit.

Hell, he might be a rough and tumble cowpoke, but he knew what was proper and what wasn't. Truth to tell, Minda hadn't done anything like Esperanza's vulgar embrace with Rawley Snate, but that sorry memory wrestled with his mind. And he was leaving tomorrow morning. Leaving with another man in hot pursuit of his wife.

He heard her hoof beats behind him. With each thud of his horse's hooves, his own confusion pounded. He didn't want a wife, but now that he had one, she was his and his alone.

But what if she didn't want the same?

Her payback would oblige her for a time, but what would happen after that? She might want a man like Hackett who didn't wear denim and buckskin and who spoke with fancy words.

At the homestead, he stabled his horse, gently in spite of his temper, saw her dust close behind him on the road from town, and went inside to check the kids.

Silly's face felt warm, but her eyes were bright. Still, he worried. Was it some strange new disease killing her slow? The loss of so much of his family already came back like a rash he couldn't stop scratching.

He looked around but didn't know where Minda had stashed the willow bark. Had she tossed it away? Damn better not.

Katie hustled over to him, freckles making her bright cheeks look like strawberries. "Uncle Brix, I got peas shelled and potatoes peeled for stew."

She was a wonder, that girl. Most kids were trouble, but he'd miss these when he left. "Sounds good to me. Cookie's chuck along the trail isn't anything like the table you set here."

The little girl preened.

"And me, Uncle Brix, I want a dog," Neddie said.

"You got your chickens to care for, and plenty of barn cats. And that heifer."

"But that's the reason. Dogs herd cows."

"We only got one cow," Katie told her brother. "And Mabel doesn't need a dog. She minds good. I want a pup just for fun."

"But the heifer? That's two." Neddie said, and Brix felt a stab. The young'un likely didn't know his prize pet might be bound for somebody's dinner table. Maybe even his own. But Brix's mood cheered a bit. Maybe he'd turn the lad into a cattleman like himself.

"No dog. I like dogs fine, but you got your hands full. Now there's Minda coming up." Her name settled sweet on his tongue. "Don't you get scared now, if you hear a bang. All right? I need some time alone with her to show her how to handle a gun."

And some time alone with her for other things.

"Papa had a gun. He taught Mama, too." Neddie nodded. For the first time, Brix realized Minda had somehow made time to trim the lad's hair. He reached out and ruffled it, and felt a twinge. Hell, that boy's smile could bring a statue to life.

"Now, you keep Silly's ears covered if you've the need. Minda and I, we won't be long."

Outside, he waited for her by the fence. She came out of the barn, her face cautious as she looked at him.

"Time for your lesson," he called.

Her cheeks turned pink like they had then and there at the altar. Just the thought of it, of their wedding kiss, made him know he was a man. Against his trousers, his arousal came to life.

"In a moment, please. Let me put my parcel away and check the children." She wasn't in the house long and didn't seem as peeved with him now.

"Over here, Miz Haynes."

When she came across the farmyard over to him, he thought he saw a glimmer of a smile. Like before, he held her next to him, her shoulder and arm under his, showed her how to hold the Colt, explained how to peer and aim, cock and fire.

He gave good directions, else he wouldn't have made it long as a point rider, but right now, the smell of roses in her hair was too distracting. And that tuft of feathers and cloth on her head, why it wasn't silly at all. It settled just right inside the rolls and coils of her hair.

He breathed deep, wishing he had the courage to let her hair fall down long and loose like yesterday. Holding her along side himself, heating up at the warmth of her, he recalled full well what glory lingered beneath her jacket front. He'd seen enough in the lantern light to know he wanted to see more, see it all. Have it all.

But then he reminded himself that what he wanted could well bring on a child. He had enough worries with these three. No need to bring on more responsibility.

But she was his. He'd heard her *I Do*, watched her sign her name. She had his ring on her finger, but did he need to put his brand on her to keep men like Caldwell Hackett off her trail?

He fired and missed. She fired. A green glass bottle shattered to bits.

"Oh, Brixton! I did it! I did it!" She stuck the gun in her pocket and clapped her hand like she was at an opera or some other fancy thing.

"You did all right, Minda." He whooped with her, but inside he knew her aim was just beginner's luck. She had a long way to go to hit a moving target, or even a second bottle.

"Brixton, I learned something new, and I did it! I think I'm a fast learner! Thanks for teaching me."

At that, he turned her inside his arms and tightened his hands at the back of her waist. Drawing her close, he wished he'd taken off her thick suede jacket first. But that would be later.

This was now. "You got a lot more to learn, Minda. And I'm real glad to be your teacher." He breathed the words just before his lips touched hers, reminding him he was a man who needed every kind of nourishment there was. Her arms came up around his neck, and he knew she stood on the tips of her toes. He bent to her mouth and tasted cherries warmed by Nebraska wind.

Chapter Seven

The twilight was hot and thick with dark gloomy clouds, and once in a while, thunder smacked the prairie miles away.

"I'll be sitting outside on the porch, Miz Haynes, lighting up this long-nine," Brixton said after supper, wiggling a cigar at her, "unless of course you need me to help you some."

Minda knew that little came between a man and his smoke, and he likely didn't mean the offer. But his assistance actually would be welcome. "Why, it'd be nice if you braided Katie's hair. We've just washed it, and she enjoys it so."

"Sure thing," he said, not without enthusiasm. But he didn't meet her eyes. Nor had he all through supper.

She sighed. He was back to using her formal name, too. His last kiss during their shooting lesson, the kiss that had taken all the power from her knees, had brought on her deepest fear. He truly was leaving. That was the farewell kiss he'd promised her.

Her heart paused for a second while her throat clenched.

Had he even told the children good-bye? He'd be gone by sunup.

Shaking her head with a strange sadness, Minda rinsed Priscilla in the washtub. Now all three had had their Saturday night baths. Maybe she could get her husband to sing the baby to sleep like he had last night. One last time. Neddie, too.

Neddie-boy drooped like a morning glory closing up until the next day, but still he fought sleep. In his arms, he held tight the foolish toy dog she'd tried to fashion out of Ida Lou's old brown shawl.

With his fingers gentle on Katie's hair, her husband sat in the rough X-shaped chair. He'd finally revealed to her that he'd made it himself years ago.

Well, he wouldn't be sitting in it much longer. Her heart hammered with a cruel disappointment. He hadn't been the husband she came for, so why was his departure so painful? Was it the humble lifestyle Norman Dale had left behind? The children she hadn't expected?

Or simply a woman's heart? Thinking of Brix's touch, his lips that seemed to give her life, the closeness where she felt the raging power between his legs... No. He'd taken her to be the children's mother, nothing more. He was just a healthy man with masculine urges.

She tried to close off her unhappy thoughts. Priscilla fussed under the drying towel. Even though she'd eaten a bit at supper, her skin felt warm despite the cooling bath. And, Minda remembered with horror, she'd left the mercantile without the fever remedy she'd come for.

As she dressed the baby, her thoughts of the mercantile reminded her of Caldwell Hackett. Had he been impolite and indecent? And had she been demure enough? Whether she'd been tricked or not, she was a married woman.

But for how long? Did Brixton intend to hold her to her vows once her payback was done? Couldn't she seek an annulment if the marriage were never consummated?

Her cheeks burned. Caldwell Hackett had made it clear he never supported the subterfuge. That she had a friend. And as Brixton had ranted, more than a friend… Did that mean Minda had a beau?

She certainly didn't have a husband.

"What's your brother got there?" Brix asked Katie, interrupting Minda's murky thoughts.

"Oh, it's a toy dog now, but it was a shawl before." Katie giggled. "Mo…Minda rolled it up and tied some ribbons here and there so he's got a head and ears. And some legs."

Minda hid her warming face by tucking Priscilla into her little bed. It was a homely, amateur toy, and she didn't want her husband's ridicule. But Ned had fallen in love with it right away. Then, she made up her mind. She'd heard her husband refuse the children's request a number of times, but he was leaving. What did he care if the children had a dog or not?

"My sisters had a grand playful dog growing up, and I'm thinking of getting the children one," she said.

Ned stirred long enough to cheer with his sister. Above Katie's lengthening braid, Brixton's eyes widened at Minda's defiance.

"She was a wonderful pal to them, and I loved Patches, too. Besides—" She stared unflinchingly back. "—she was a watchdog as well. Always set up a ruckus when strangers came to the door."

There. That should do it. He was leaving them, alone and unprotected. Although she'd managed to hit five of the dozen cans he'd displayed during their lesson, it was luck, pure and simple. He may not care about her—other than stolen kisses—but a decent man ought to have a worry or two about his brother's children. His own blood.

With outlaws like Ahab Perkins and his miserable cohorts roughing up the countryside. Her flesh goosed.

"Pups are a ton of work," Brixton said, his eyes deep black holes in the lantern light.

"We don't mind a grown-up dog," Neddie said, but then his face paled, Katie's too. The pulsing sound of hoof beats coming up the drive had Minda's skin crawling, her heart thumping.

Katie and Ned looked at her, then out toward their uncle, their little faces white with dread.

After glancing at his gun belt hung high out of the children's reach, Brix got up to peer out the window. The overall tension alarmed her. Obviously, around here night visitors never brought good news. Neddie came to Minda and wrapped himself around her legs.

Or was it somebody even worse, like outlaws?

Nervously, she combed her fingers through Ned's little thatch of pale brown hair that she'd trimmed just this morning.

"Looks like the Blacks," Brixton said, and Minda relaxed somewhat, recalling the neighbors. Boots clumped on the wooden porch steps, and Brixton let in their callers, making hasty introductions.

Monty Black tipped his hat to her. "Sorry to barge in, ma'am. We just come from Skinny Hank's. Sheriff Pelton got word the Perkins gang hit a place over in Platte Center last night. Lute Mohlman lost four pretty fillies. Took 'em right out of his corral during supper. Weren't even all the way dark yet."

"Damn shame." Brixton shook his head, and Minda didn't chide him for his language. She didn't know where Platte Center was, but from her husband's tense face, she figured it wasn't all that far away.

"Lute all right?" Brixton asked.

Monty shook his head. "Perkins shot him in the knee when he came after 'em. He'll live, but won't be walking until doomsday."

"Damn worse," Brixton muttered. "Gang's getting bolder and meaner."

Minda shivered, and wished she'd covered Ned's

ears, and not because of the curse.

Clem tipped his hat now. "We got a few places up ahead to warn, so we'll be on our way. Lock up tight, you hear?"

Closing the door after them, Brixton raised his eyebrows like he might be concluding something important. Maybe it meant he was going to stay.

"You'll be safe, children," Minda said. "Uncle Brix will see to it."

"Did you shut up the barn tight?" His eyes were almost accusing.

"Certainly," she said, somewhat annoyed. "After you went back to the fields, Katie and I fed the horses. Ned took care of the cows. And I locked the barn door tight when we were done."

Minda pointed to the key hanging by the back door. The lock was so rusted she'd been surprised the contraption worked at all. Next time she was in town, she'd barter for a new lock and key.

"So there's outlaws?" Katie's little voice shook. "That's why you locked the barn?" She looked at Minda first, then addressed her uncle. "We told her around here nobody locks up tight."

"Well, Firefly, sometimes we just need to," Brixton said, laying his left hand on Katie's shoulder. Minda was struck that he'd noticed the little endearment she'd come to using for the girl. "Besides, I'll be sleeping out there."

"Could I sleep in the barn?" Ned asked.

"You'll be all right in here, tucked safe in your bed."

"Uncle Brix, no. No. *No.* Don't leave us alone." Katie's eyes were wide, and Minda's heart ached. The young girl was old enough to understand the seriousness of the situation, and had already experienced so much trouble in her short life.

"I'm scared." Neddie switched from Minda's legs to his uncle's. Brixton didn't seem to mind, laid his big hands on the small brown head.

"Please, stay inside with us, Uncle Brix," Katie said. "Papa used to sleep with Mama."

"In the same bed, too." Neddie's hair bounced.

Katie nodded, a bit calmer. "And I think he liked it fine. Sometimes he'd keep the door shut and tell us he'd licorice-whip us if we bothered them."

Minda almost smiled. It hadn't occurred to her that the children would find their odd sleeping arrangement, well, odd. What would it be like, sharing a bed with her rough-hewn husband?

A delicious tremble danced up her spine.

"And Miss Gracey sleeps with the reverend," Ned said. "Seen 'em when we stayed over with Philip and Martin at Eastertime."

Katie nodded. "We spent the night to be in town already for sunrise service. And the egg hunt."

"I found three eggs," Neddie said.

It was certainly time to end the children's prattle about sleeping arrangements. Despite her wonder and the lingering amazement of their last kiss, Minda knew sharing a bed with her husband would be intensely unwise. And from his reddened cheeks, clearly Brixton thought so, too.

"Come on now, kids." He touched Katie's braid. "You all get in bed now and start your prayers. Be along in a sec to tuck you in."

"Then will you tell us another story, Uncle Brix? About that magic cow that talks on Christmas Eve?"

"Maybe."

They scampered off, Ned's toy dog firm in his arms.

Minda's surprise must have shown on her face, for Brixton met her eyes again.

"What? Who you think tucked 'em in before you got here?"

She heard prayers and Brix's soft mumbles before he came out from behind the children's sleeping curtain.

"I'm going out for that long-nine, now," he said, scooting his old chair behind him. Tossing her a grin, he remarked, "That storytelling wears me out."

While she cut up material for Katie's bonnet, Minda stole a glance at him from time to time through the open curtains. In the dark, the tip of his cigar danced like a firefly. But she didn't see any real fireflies skipping around the pasture. She knew a storm was likely, figured the creatures had taken shelter. She wondered if outlaws did the same, or if they preyed and prowled no matter the weather?

Her heart skipped unhappily in her chest. She felt safe tonight, but what about tomorrow after he was gone? She said a quick, fervent prayer for poor Lute Mohlman and his crippled knee. Taking to the upholstered wing chair, she calmed herself by designing Katie's hat. Priscilla's little snuffles and snores comforted her. Hopefully the little one was finally well.

It was almost like they were a regular family, but Minda knew better.

Brixton came inside about an hour later. "Starting to rain," he said. He had his bedroll in one arm and a wooden contrivance in the other. Tossing the bedroll in a corner, he looked at her straight on. "I'll be hunkering down here unless you agree with the kids. About you and me sharing a bed, that is. During our lesson today, I figured you might be interested." His eyebrow rose in such a rakish way her stomach tumbled.

But she ignored him with an eye roll. "What's that in your hand?"

Her husband shrugged. "Neddie got a toy. Seemed right to make one for Katie." Seeming shy, he held out his hand. It was a beautiful wood insect with whirligig wings and a carved opening in its abdomen. "And when she's grown too old for toys, this hole's a place where she can set a candle."

"It's a firefly," Minda said. "Oh, Brixton, it's lovely. She'll be delighted."

"Back to using my first name again?" His mouth twitched in what was certainly a tease.

She ignored that, too. "And you made it just now?"

Brixton nodded. "I whittle fast. Night watch on the trail bores me silly. Got to keep my hands busy." He reached in his pocket for his knife and made one last quick smoothing motion with his left hand.

"Why, I didn't realize you're left-handed. I'm all but certain Priscilla is, too."

Once again, he shrugged away her words. She continued, "I made Ned the dog because I'm making Katie a new bonnet."

"Then I'll whittle him a whistle soon's I can. Each will have something from both of us that way."

Somehow his voice had taken a sad tone. She figured that meant he'd carve it his next lonely night on the trail. "You're leaving then, like you planned," she said dully. "Our lesson. That was your good-bye kiss."

He looked down at her long and leisurely, making her body tingle and shimmy again. Remembering the last kiss, she put down her needle and placed her fingers on her lips, wishing he'd do the same with his mouth. But all he did was breathe out loudly.

"Ah, Minda. You claim to be a fast learner, but I haven't taught you near what you need to know. 'Night now."

He nodded politely and hunkered down to pull off his boots. Then the bedroll rustled beneath him. Hearing the sound had Minda's mind roil with the memories of his kisses and caresses on that very same bedroll on their wedding night. Sighing, she dimmed the lantern and headed for the bedroom, her mind awhirl, her womanhood alive.

Braids and lullabies. Bedtime prayers and stories. Whirligigs and whistles. And Brixton Haynes didn't consider himself a family man?

****

After Minda shut Norman Dale's bedroom door, she left behind a scent of roses floating on the night air. Brix imagined her, fragrant and drowsy, tumbled in the covers of a bed big enough for both of them.

He sighed, deep. His wife's kisses told him she just might be willing to share it with him. And for the first time he could remember, he found himself liking rain falling on a roof better than dripping down his brim.

And he didn't like that a bit.

Beneath his bedroll, the plank floor wasn't any harder than the packed dirt of West Texas, but tonight he longed for a real bed and a real wife in it. Likely she might even welcome him, especially if he told her what decision he'd come to.

He wasn't leaving, even though he couldn't stay.

The children's appealing little snores forced a smile from him. Silly fretted in her sleep, so he pulled her trundle closer so he could move it in a rocking motion. What kind of plaything should he make for her?

He couldn't leave Paradise until Silly was all the way well. Until the Perkins gang was behind bars. The decision had come long and hard, with anger and plenty of cussing, but he'd no choice in the matter. His brother wasn't even cold yet, and Brix didn't need to add another sin to his list.

Sure, he'd be missing the drive now, but he'd head for Texas soon enough. Ranchers in Butter Creek would pay him good cash money for riding supplies to their line shacks, fixing fence and digging post holes, breaking mustangs and readying things for fall round-up. He'd earn enough to tide the family over. But when another drive commenced, he'd be on it, no question and no doubt.

Until then, he had wheat to harvest, toys to carve, and a wife who seemed intrigued by his kisses. An erection started with a pleasure that was almost pain.

But that wife hadn't seemed to mind another man drooling over her hand. His temper burned all on its own. Caldwell Hackett wanting something else that belonged to a Haynes.

Suddenly, lightning slashed the darkness and three seconds later, thunder pounded Paradise, louder than a flash flood.

As Silly howled, Katie and Ned poked pale little faces from behind their curtain. The horses screamed, and the crash of splintering wood broke through the sound of rain.

Brix sprang to his feet, lit a lantern, and peered out.

Minda, hair tussled from sleep, dashed from Norman Dale's old room, wrapped in a quilt. "What was that dreadful noise above the storm?"

She took his breath away, but now wasn't the time. Disappointment in himself all but choked him. He might need a woman, but he didn't need a wife.

"Storm spooked the horses," he said. "Broke out of their stalls and kicked the barn door open. Thought you said you locked up good and tight?"

He'd believed her, yet he knew his voice had turned cold. Right now just might have been their moment, but he had to leave her and it was her fault. There was no money to replace livestock that got itself lost or hurt.

"I did! Don't put this off on me. That lock is as ancient as Methuselah."

"Held just fine last time I used it." After pulling on his boots, he found his brother's old slicker in a cupboard.

"You're going out in this weather?"

"Damn straight, Miz Haynes. Hell, I should have checked the barn myself. That's what I get for trusting you. And don't you dare come down on me for cussing. I got to find them fast. Remember those horse thieves? They work best in the dark."

Minda came close, smelling like roses again, and speaking too soft to hear. He leaned close, liking it but steeling his heart.

"But Brixton, they shot a man because he came after them."

"I'm not after them. Just after what's ours."

"Exactly." Her tongue was sharp.

He paused to reassure her. After all, she was his wife. "You did all right with that gun today. You know where Norman Dale kept his hog-leg. You'll be safe enough. Stay tight and comfort the kids. Likely Strawberry won't have gone far." He headed for the backdoor. "Buttermilk's got adventure in his blood, but I'm bound to find him quick. Be back soon's I can."

For a flash, he wanted to kiss his wife's wide eyes closed and hold her like a man held his woman. Tell her to wait for him underneath the covers.

But he had things to do, and women were nothing but trouble.

"And don't you worry," he said, looking back at her before he closed the back door, feeling some regret for his pique. His heart pumped in a way it never had before. "Norman Dale put up lightning rods."

Outside, the rain splashing down his brim welcomed him, like it had a hundred times on the trail. Welcomed him back to the life he loved. A night like this in search of a wayward animal pumped him full of satisfaction. The fires inside him cooled down. This was what he'd been born for, not farming. Not family.

Like he'd thought, Strawberry stood drenched and unhappy, pawing the ground near Minda's rose garden. He saddled the horse, then set out to find the buckskin.

Breathing deep, he almost said a prayer. He was outside where he belonged. What had he been thinking a while ago? He didn't need four walls closing in on him or a woman he couldn't trust. Must have been loco to think anything different. True, he had to help his brother for just a little while longer, but then he'd be gone.

He started to enjoy himself, wind at his heels and mud in his eyes.

****

Minda watched him leave like her eyes were in someone else's head. Fear slammed hard against her mind and heart. For a black moment, she figured she'd lost him. And he left, believing she'd let him down. Oh, she had felt dread before. She'd been afraid to leave Pennsylvania, but sure she'd arrive to Norman Dale's waiting arms.

And afraid at Mama's tragic death, but comforted by friends and neighbors. Right now there was no one around, other than three frightened children who depended on her. And on a man who now had to face lightning strikes, flash floods, crazed animals, and gun-slinging outlaws.

What would happen if he didn't make it home? What would happen to the children? Her throat choking with tears, she remembered Gracey Satterburg's hands on Priscilla, and some selfish farmer, Tom Holden, wanting baby Ned as a slave.

She had no money, likely no legal standing to the farm or the children's guardianship. Not even Caldwell Hackett transacting to sell her hats could bring on sufficient support.

Although he had implied that she could come to

him for anything, anything at all. He might truly have appealed to her back in Gleesburg, with his fine manners and intellectual occupation, but unruly Brixton Haynes had conquered her heart.

If she didn't love him, she was close. It had come on quick but slow at the same time. He'd never know, and wouldn't care anyway, but she held the secret close inside for herself alone.

Neddie came to her then, embracing her legs, in a flood of tears of his own. "But Minda, our heifer. We raised her since a calf. I got to check on her. I reckon she's scared to death."

"No, no, sweetheart." She bent to hug him tight. "You know Uncle Brix made sure she's safe."

"Will he come back?" Katie asked. And like a stab in the heart, Minda realized the child hadn't asked "when." Poor thing had already suffered such unimaginable losses. Thinking she'd lost her uncle was just a natural course of events.

"Of course he will, Firefly." That reminded her of Brixton's wonderful carved toy, but she held on to the hope that he'd be back to gift it himself. "Remember, Uncle Brix is used to being outside, helping animals. That's his job and he's good at it."

Maybe her own words could convince herself.

Katie's lip turned out in a pout. "But the thunder scares me." She held her weeping baby sister, and Minda wrapped her arms around them both. Heavens, Priscilla was feverish again. What next?

"Now, you and Ned need to try to sleep. You're safe and warm in here. I'll tend to Priscilla. Why don't you two cuddle up in my big bed?" She led the jittery little pair toward the bedroom. "You know, my little sisters used to like crowding together during a noisy storm, and hiding under the covers." That was true. The girls had liked nothing better.

In the doorway, Katie's face turned paler yet,

although it might have been the flickering candle. “But our mama and Paulie died in that bed.”

Minda didn’t now how much more her heart could bear before it broke completely. “That was a tragedy, Katie, but the Lord does promise not to send us more than we can bear.” And Minda had believed it, once. “But your papa bought a brand new bed for me. I promise. I’ve been the only one asleep on that ticking.”

At least Norman Dale had told the truth about that.

She had imagined her husband beside her. But she’d let him down. She’d missed her chance. After all, he hadn’t even kissed her before he ran off into the storm.

To erase the image of herself and Brixton sharing a transcending love, she tucked the children tight and kissed them soundly.

The storm seemed to hold the little house in angry hands and shake it. Minda’d be lucky to get the children to sleep. Why hadn’t she listened closer to Brixton’s lullabies and stories? She sang them a hymn she thought she remembered, but the words fizzled on her lips.

Priscilla slept, but her fever rose. Worry inhabited every inch of Minda. A nightmare word Brixton had said once came to life before her eyes.

A conniption, as Brixton would call it, brought on by the fever. Priscilla stiffened, eyes rolling back, and trembled for a terrible moment. Minda prayed and prayed some more.

Was it too late? Was she losing Priscilla and Brixton both?

Minda did the only thing she could think to do, and brewed the baby some willow bark tea. And afterward, the baby settled, like a tea kettle’s steam that had been released.

Chapter Eight

He was soaked through and through but didn't mind a single bit. The clean night air filled his lungs with life itself.

And brought him to his senses. The outdoors was where he belonged.

Buttermilk had been a dickens to catch, but Brix hadn't minded all that much. The tall cornfields had barricaded some of the horse's maneuvers, and the expedition had taken them across miles of sludged roads and fallow fields. Likely a vegetable garden or two.

Right now, he saw the lantern light glowing in Norman Dale's window up ahead. He had sight like a night owl, and a comfortable thought came upon him. It felt nice, just this once, to have a home and woman waiting for him.

Unless that light was a beacon of some sort of trouble.

Blood thumped in his veins like a crooked wagon wheel, and he hurried Buttermilk through the muddy road. Strawberry was tied behind, but he'd chosen to ride the high-spirited buckskin so as not to give Buttermilk any further chance to misbehave. His successful retrieval of the animals now gave way to a sense of dread.

By the time he'd stabled the horses, Minda waited on the porch, wearing Norman Dale's old dressing gown. The downpour had stopped, but the lively wind blew her hair across her face like a veil. For a moment his breath caught, thinking of the veil on their wedding day. Hell, he'd be gone soon, out of temptation's way.

"Brixton!" She stayed put, likely unwilling to muck through the farmyard. "Brixton, you're safe. You're back. Hurry inside. Get dry."

He didn't like the worry in her voice. Had she thought he'd left for good, like he'd been promising?

She pulled the wet slicker from his body while he managed his muddy boots. "My goodness, you're completely drenched. Come on. Here's some toweling."

As he stopped at the doorway, she shrugged the dressing gown from her body. "Now, you get those wet things off and slip into this. I'll put some Arbuckle's on to warm you up."

"Summer rain, Minda. Never hurt nobody. Wet doesn't mean cold." But he liked her fussing. She ought to be mad at him for the mean things he'd said as he left, and for not kissing her good-bye. "How're the kids?"

Then she finally looked him in the eye, face bleak. "I fear Priscilla suffered a bit of a convulsion. A conniption, Brixton. She's sleeping sound now, but I was terrified for a time."

He opened his mouth to ask, but she didn't let him. "Yes, I finally used the willow bark. You know I was hesitant at first, but now I am convinced in my heart that you'd never take a chance on any of the children."

His fists clenched around the towel. "You sure she's all right?"

Minda sighed. "Far as I can tell, yes. It didn't last long and seemed to tire her out more than anything. Then the fever spiked and broke. I'm thinking she's on the mend."

"Yep. The remedy's tried and true," he said, feeling a funny pleasure that she'd trusted him after all. Still, the worry over Silly's ailment had gone on long enough. "But the doc needs to be telegraphed."

"Yes. In the morning. For now, get out of those sodden clothes," she said again. "Just leave them in a pile in the corner. If the sun's out tomorrow, I'll set to washing them."

Maybe she wasn't remembering that tomorrow, today now, was the day he'd set to leave. Seemed like a good time to tell her he wasn't. "Minda…"

"No arguing with me. Get undressed. You're worse than Neddie. Land sakes, I'm not going to peek."

She turned her back, and he obeyed her, wishing she would peek, truth to tell. He wondered how it might be to have a wife for real. His clothes on the trail turned rank mighty fast. Without the dressing gown, she wore only the dainty nightdress she'd worn that first night. Their wedding night on his bedroll. He could see near through it.

"Minda…"

"Mr. Haynes, if you don't need hot water, there's plenty of cold to clean yourself up."

She sounded too wifely of a sudden, and he grew miffed, figuring he didn't want one for real at all. He knew perfectly well how to look after himself. He'd been doing it for years. Truth was, he took more ice cold baths in creeks than warm ones in a tub.

There wasn't a tie for the robe, unless he'd dropped it somehow. Just as it flapped open, she started to speak in a shaking voice. "I can heat some if you'd rather."

"No need." Looking at her made him hot enough. He set to scrubbing in the little washtub by the stove, wondering at her tremble.

Then she turned to him, and he found her crying. "Oh, Brixton, I'm so relieved now, but I was so scared, those long hours you were gone. I thought Priscilla might die, and you'd get drowned in a flood or shot by the outlaws and I'd lose you, too. Even though I never had you, not at all. Not really."

Tears bathed her beautiful face and her eyes opened wide when she noticed his open garment. His erection rose in invitation, and she didn't look away. For a second, an interested smile tugged at her berry lips, and he knew then and there he wanted that mouth pressed around his flesh. He could teach her that, in a gentle and kind way, letting her know what came between a man and his wife was their business alone.

But the suggestion might frighten her, this first time at least. For now, he was almost giddy, thinking how snug he'd fit inside her tight maidenhood, swelling until he released deep within her. Hell, he swelled almost to bursting now.

He couldn't stop to dry himself. Waiting even one more second was out of the question. Pulling her to him with his right hand, he unbuttoned her night dress with the other.

"You could have had me any time at all." He breathed into her hair. "And there's so much I want you to learn."

"Well, I think this is the right time," she said, "and I want to learn as much as I can in whatever time we have."

"I should check Silly."

"I just did. She's sleeping peaceful. You'd just make a commotion and wake her up."

"The kids?"

"The thunder scared them. They're sleeping behind the bedroom's closed door." Minda said the last two words with a slow meaningful smile.

"Then where? Us, I mean?"

"That bedroll over there. Like the first time." Her finger pointed eagerly, but her eyes looked away, shy.

"But I wanted the first time outside, under the stars." He touched her cheek, soft as silk.

"Well, sometimes you make do with what you have. For as long as you're lucky to have it." Her voice was barely a whisper.

Like a starving man, he suckled her breasts for a moment, then picked her up like a groom carrying a bride over a threshold. He laid her on the bedroll in the corner, snug at his side, letting his fingers glide up her leg. His free hand rested under head, her hair a counterpane of bliss, and turned her face to his. Nibbling her lips, he started a tender exploration there, then traveled to the miracle of her bosom. He licked and tugged with starvation, tensing at her groans.

"Now don't you get frightened, Minda. This helps ease the first time." He slid a finger in her core, shuddering as her body trembled. He could wait long enough to drive her to pleasure, so he quickly settled himself on his knees between her thighs. While his fingers resumed their teasing, he lowered his tongue to her.

It didn't take as long as he thought, lucky for him, and he had the joy of watching her face the whole time. And finally, when her legs tensed around his neck, he knew it was time.

Time to go home.

****

Minda's mind swirled with a thousand colors and her body felt blessed by a higher power she'd never imagined. The intimate touch of his fingers deep inside her, and his tongue mastering her so deliciously, forced her eyes to close in shyness.

"No, darlin'. Look at me." He raised his face to her own, resting on his elbows, close enough for her to see the magic and passion in his gaze. "Hold on. Hold me."

Needing air, she grasped his head. The manly scent of his hair claimed her senses as the colors faded and her knees relaxed. Then the warm weight of him pressed over her body. He lowered his face to kiss her hungrily, and she tasted herself on his lips. Her chest heaved at the intimacy of his actions as her husband, her first lover, began his journey to claim her body and her soul.

He slid back to her breasts, and they suddenly tightened, aching with a fullness she didn't recognize. Pleasure so delicious it almost hurt washed over from top to toe.

"Ah, Minda, what you do to me," he mumbled, his breath heating the skin of her belly. Fumbling for her hand, he wrapped her fingers about his throbbing shaft. In the lantern light, she stole a peek.

"Oh my goodness," she whispered, awestruck at the sight. Even as she ached for him, her wonder grew. "I don't know..."

Brixton gasped out his words. "Ah, it'll be fine."

His fingers reached for her core again, igniting fire and need. Suddenly she had no doubts at all. She wanted him. She needed to be complete with him, to have him fill her emptiness. It wouldn't be forever, but it would have to be enough. If all they had was tonight, she wanted every single second he could give her.

"Brixton, I..." She turned shy again. "Yes, everything will be fine."

He moved between her legs, a hand gentle but firm on each breast. "Spread wider, darlin.'"

As she did, he pressed his manhood into her, patient at first, then with increasing pressure. She was untouched, but desperate to please him in spite of the twinge of pain. She relaxed, and they were joined, true man and wife. His rhythmic thrusts matched the pounding of her heart.

Then he shuddered and tensed, eyes shut tight, as he lay across her. His endless moans let her know she'd pleased him. His harsh breath landed hot on her shoulder, and he kissed her without a word. Turning, he held her backside against his front, and his gentle snores started almost at once.

She could hardly bear the rough bedroll against her sensitive skin, but his warmth and embrace comforted her. Goodness, she was a married woman in every sense of the word.

It might not be exactly what she came to Paradise for, but tonight it would be enough.

Finally, Minda drifted into sleep. But not for long. The length of him that nestled against her back grew hard and woke her, and her husband drew her to him again.

****

Sunlight blessed her face, but Minda kept her eyes shut tight. The bedroll soft under her bare skin, she remembered her husband's warmth, his callused hands that felt like velvet as they learned the secrets of her body and taught her the mysteries of his.

She relived his trembles when her own hand had closed around his manhood, the wonderful weight of him atop her again and again.

She sighed dreamily. He had filled her every way a woman can be filled, and she had enjoyed every minute of it, even the brisk discomfort of the first joining.

Shyly, she turned to hold him close as she'd done before they finally slept in the summer darkness. But she opened her eyes to find herself on the bedroll alone, covered with the old dressing gown.

She knew why, and the distress slammed into her heart like the storm just passed.

He'd left.

Of course. She understood now. Last night's lovemaking had been the farewell kiss he'd promised, with something more.

She swallowed hard, but couldn't let her heart break. Not when she reminded herself that he'd never offered to stay. She was the one who had foolishly contented herself, thinking his blossoming rapport with the children would expand to something permanent. All he'd vowed was to care for them in a monetary sense, and the cattle trail was the only livelihood he had.

It was her own fault for losing her heart. She'd tried to guard against this very thing, but at her first sight of him, it hadn't been possible. She knew that now.

The little locket watch her mama had left her was in the bedroom, but she'd gotten good these past few days about telling time from the sun's station in the sky. When it was out, that is. This morning, the rain clouds were gone, other than the ones dampening her disposition.

Between eight and nine o'clock, she figured. They'd missed church, and she tightened her eyelids with more hopelessness. Missing services in Gleesburg had always incurred gossip, but out here, folks might believe her responsible for preventing the innocent Haynes children from righteous worship. Those wanting to take the children might feel justified in resuming their pursuits.

Scrambling into the dressing gown, she gathered the bedroll in her arms, up to her nose, breathing in the scent their lovemaking had left behind. She'd find time to cry later. Right now she had children to feed.

The bedroom door opened as she wound up the bedroll. Of course he'd left it behind. He likely had another one back in Texas. Maybe this one was Norman Dale's anyway. Borrowing off his brother had been Brixton's way in Paradise, after his long travels with a light load. The wedding suit, the horse he planned to ride to the train depot in Columbus.

Strawberry would wait there at the livery until a stablehand could bring him home.

"So did you and Uncle Brix sleep out here on his bedroll?" Neddie asked, arms clamped around his homemade dog.

"Of course, you ninny," Katie said, in the same big-sister way the oldest of her three had always used. "We were in their bed, remember?"

Their bed. The words hurt.

Priscilla sat in her little bed, clapping her hands and mouthing an unintelligible word.

"That's her word for hungry." Katie placed her hands firmly on her hips.

Despite her heavy heart, Minda rejoiced at Priscilla's health. At least she had something good this day. Maybe Brixton had hugged the children good-bye while they slept. Katie wasn't extolling about the whirligig firefly though. Had he stashed it somewhere like a treasure hunt, reckoning she'd find it somehow?

Or did that mean he hadn't gone?

A girlish hope trilled in her heart, the same one as when she'd purchased her wedding dress, as when she'd first caught sight of Paradise from the stagecoach.

But that had merely led to her strange marriage to a man who had no desire to remain at her side.

"Well, now, you two dress yourselves, and I'll do the same." She held back the trembles from her voice. After all, she had things to do.

"Mom…Minda," Katie shouted from the sleeping area, "look what I found on my bed!"

"And me, too. A whistle!"

Even at the children's joy, her spirits fell. He had presented his gifts after all before taking off. When had he made the whistle? He'd claimed to be a fast whittler, and obviously that had taken precedence over one last hour in her bed.

Her sadness was almost complete. But it didn't include regret. Whether he was close by or a thousand miles away, Brixton Haynes was still her husband. And he would come for visits now and again, wouldn't he? To see the children, at least?

She set to her toilette and Priscilla's, then sliced stale bread, leftover from the wedding feast. Lord's day or not, there'd be no rest for her today, not with baking to do.

And Brixton's pile of sopping clothes. However, a quick peek in the corner and she noticed it was gone. Her mood gladdened as she recalled the morning he'd laundered up after Priscilla.

But she could see the clothesline outside, and nothing hung on it now.

Fully dressed, Katie came to the kitchen workspace, her shining eyes belying the fear and sleeplessness of the night. The firefly's wooden wings spun in flight. Minda had given her a piece of the grosgrain ribbon meant for the pink velvet hat, and it was tied in a jaunty bow at the end of Katie's beloved braid.

Ned followed, needing sleep dust washed from his eyes, but his short trousers hung straight. In his hands, he held his toy dog and whistle.

"Now we got something from you and Uncle Brix," he announced cheerfully. "My doggie from you and my whistle from him. And Katie's bug and the hat you're making her."

"Can I see it?" Katie asked. "Did you work on it last night?"

Nodding, Minda walked to the sewing basket by the upholstered wing chair. "Yes, indeed I did. I waited up for Uncle Brix, and it gave me something pleasant to do. Come, have a look."

She took the bonnet and set it on Katie's head. It wasn't finished yet, but Katie beamed, although the twinge of worry Minda often saw in her eyes was once again apparent.

"He got back fine, right? And the horses, too?"

"Yes, thank God."

"He sure was riled up."

Minda sighed with a head shake. "Yes, and I am positive I locked the barn. But everything turned out well." Unbidden, images of their lovemaking flooded her. She managed to hold back the pain of his leaving. "But never mind that. Let me get some breakfast down you children."

"What does Silly get?" Neddie asked, holding his toys just out of his baby sister's reach.

"Well, see those strips of velvet? I don't need them, so I'll stitch them up and stuff it full of cotton wool and make her a ball."

"And Uncle Brix?"

Fortunately, Katie interrupted that chain of discussion. "Will my hat be done by next Sunday? I will be the prettiest girl in Sunday School."

Minda laughed. "Now, Katie, it's far better to be kind and smart."

"Mr. Hackett says that very thing. But I still want my pretty hat."

"Mr. Hackett?" Minda's sadness stirred a bit. Her husband had wanted to stake a claim on her then.

"Oh, he and Miss Gracey teach us a Bible story on Sundays after the reverend finishes up with church."

"Do you attend, too, Ned?"

But the little boy seemed fretful for a second, and she did not persist. Then she saw that of the ribbons forming the dog's legs was loose, so she tied it with a smile.

Without being asked, the ever-efficient Katie began to set the table. "Here, you'll sit right next to Uncle Brix," she said happily, situating two plates and chairs close together.

"I think…I don't think he'll be around for breakfast," Minda said gently, wondering how she could explain the circumstance that lay so heavy in her heart and mind. It didn't seem fair at all, youngsters like this losing both men in their lives so close together.

"'Course he will." Katie nodded, her cheeks bright. "A man needs a hearty meal, Papa used to say. I saw Uncle Brix heading toward the field on my way to the privy at sunup. He'll be hungry by this time."

He was here? He'd stayed on? What had changed his mind?

Minda could barely breathe. It could either be a dream of love come true, or a nightmare of resentment.

"I'll go get him and blow my whistle," Neddie said, his little face covered with smiles now.

Minda made up her mind then and there. Brix had changed her life's plans. She deserved to know his. But her stomach both churned with dread and fluttered with butterflies.

"No, I'll get him this morning. Here's a nice scrambled egg for Priscilla. Would you mind feeding her, Katie? Then you two enjoy your breakfast. I won't be gone long."

"What's these?" Ned's eyes widened with interest at the full plate Minda set before him. She'd carved a circle in the bread slices and fried an egg inside.

"My mama called them God's eyes. Fitting for the Lord's day, don't you think?"

Nodding as he chewed, he wiped his face on his sleeve.

Oh well. She had washing to do later anyway.

But right now, she had a husband to find.

****

Brix watered the draft horse and rubbed the

hard-working animal's nose. Cornstalks taller than a man whispered around him in the wind. At least last night's rain meant he wouldn't have to be hauling water from the river for a while.

He felt the satisfaction Norman Dale must have felt, the wheat harvest near done. But his stomach grumbled, and his head started to ache just above his eyebrows. Not wanting to face Minda, he'd left the house before sunup without a bite or even a cup of coffee.

No true man could regret that night in her arms, lost in her body. It had been perfection. But he had doubts now in the morning sun. He'd made her his wife and a woman all the way, but he didn't want to be a husband.

And now, hell, any true woman would think that's just what last night meant.

He sensed her before he heard or saw her, took a deep breath and faced her. She had her hair down, long and wispy in the wind, and she wore a pretty purple dress, holding up the skirts although the mud had caked somewhat in the hot sun. He couldn't help a smile. Underneath the yards of purple and petticoat she wore Norman Dale's oldest boots.

A bashful smile turned up the corners of the mouth where he'd found a sense of heaven. He forced his brain not to recall how she looked, eyes wide with wonder, when he'd entered her.

It was time. He couldn't let her think he was what she'd come to Paradise to find.

"'Morning, Miz Haynes," he said as she neared, hating the disappointment that crumpled her face. They'd used their first names all night long. But it was for the best. He was here now but he wouldn't be staying long. And he should have told her his decision last night, before. For likely she thought he was here this morning because of her.

Her eyes didn't meet his now, and he was glad

for two reasons. He didn't want to read the hurt there, or lose himself in them.

"It's time for breakfast," she said with a quick glance, "and you should know the children adored their toys."

"I'll wash up first. Been wondering what kind of plaything to invent for Silly. Seems too old for a rattle."

"I'm sure she'd love anything you had to give," Minda said softly, and his heart pounded with real pain. She turned back toward the house, her backside ruffling her dress as she started out.

He swallowed hard against a dozen kinds of emptiness he felt inside. No denying he cared for her, in his way, and the kids, too. But this wasn't the life he'd been called to live. He'd never made it a secret to anybody, not even his dying brother.

Not at all. Now was the time to remind her again and let her know for sure. "Miz Haynes? Minda?"

She turned back, and her wonderful bosom rose in a deep breath. "Yes?"

"Last night? It was a powerful mistake. I'm not saying I didn't enjoy it, but I had no right." Enjoy it? He'd gone to heaven and back a dozen times, taking her with him if he did say so himself.

"You had every right, Brixton. You're my husband."

He shuffled his boots, disappointed in himself and not liking it. But worse, he hated hurting her and never thought that feeling would ever cross his bones. Not long ago, he'd held her to blame for his brother's death.

"Thing is, I should have told you before. Before it happened..." Once again he looked away from her face. It had grown quite pale. "What I mean to say is, I'm not staying around because of, because of last night."

“Why then?” She faced him, sounding strong and determined. The wind caught that scent of roses and drew it straight into his nostrils, and worse, his heart.

“I figured it best, me sticking around, but just for a while. Just ’til the doc’s around and says Silly’s well. And then, ’til the Perkins gang’s locked up.”

“But…”

He interrupted her. “Now, you got no need to worry about money. Today’s the last day I’m hiring Monty and Clem. There isn’t much wheat to bring in. I recall how to do it. Folks in town say wheat prices are high. And corn won’t need taking down ’til September. By then…” He paused, comforted a little by her eyes. They weren’t dripping tears or fired up with anger. “By then, I’ll be long back in Texas, earning good cash to pay field hands.”

She shrugged, and the cloth of her dress tightened over her breasts. His manhood moved.

“And ’til then,” he said, quick before he could change his mind, “I’ll be sleeping outside, like before.”

“All right then,” she said. “Come eat now. With breakfast so late this morning, Sunday dinner will be later, too. Oh and Brixton? Think about something else while you wash up. Just how long do you figure my payback should last?”

She turned and hurried back to the house. Brix tensed with another kind of emptiness.

He hadn’t given one single thought about *her* leaving *him*.

Chapter Nine

The next noon, Reverend Jake Satterburg drove up to the Haynes homestead in a smart buggy and helped down his three stair-step little boys and pretty yellow-haired wife. Minda swallowed down a tense and tightened throat.

The reverend might be here to chide her for keeping the children from yesterday's service. Worse, Gracey might have resumed her quest to take Priscilla.

Gracey knocked on the back door. Minda held the baby close as she opened it. For an unpleasant moment, Minda remembered Jake's enormous part in the trick played on her and resented him anew.

Jake remained outside with the children, giving Ned an affectionate hug and tugging Katie's braid. At least Brixton hadn't shirked that duty. Minda hadn't seen her husband since supper last night when she'd moved apart the plates Katie had set together. He'd never met her eyes, and true to his word, he'd resumed sleeping outside.

"Afternoon, Minda." At least the preacher's wife smiled as a friend, not as a scheming harpy intent on nabbing a child not her own. In the crook of her arm, she held a large basket covered in yellow gingham.

"Welcome, Gracey. Be pleased to have you join us for dinner." Minda could easily set up a bacon and potato pie.

"Nonsense." Gracey's smile grew bigger yet, and she wiggled the yellow cloth. "We're here to invite you and the kids on a picnic at the riverbank. After that dreadful storm, it's such a beautiful day. Sun's dried the mud."

"Why, I don't know. It does sound pleasant, but I've got much to do." The invitation both pleased and stunned her. Were the Satterburgs merely checking whether Brixton had left? A picnic would be a welcome diversion from her troubled life. The payback issue weighed heavy on her soul. Perhaps she had no legal obligations to the children as Brixton's wife, but she certainly had moral ones.

And, of course, Brixton's lovemaking had instilled new worries. She had welcomed him into her bed, and into her body, and still trembled about their glorious night. But what if he'd given her a child? Then they'd be bound together forever. She longed for children of her own, but he'd made it perfectly clear that a wife was the last thing he wanted.

Gracey glowed with summer sun and enthusiasm. Minda noticed the homely floppy bonnet, thinking how well one of her designs would frame the minister's wife's lovely face.

"Now everybody needs to eat," Gracey said. "Just a short dinner break to get some fresh air. The kids will love it."

Minda couldn't help thinking of her husband and the noon meal she ought to make for him. He'd been out harvesting since sunup and would be powerfully hungry. Despite Katie's proclamation that a man needed breakfast, Brixton had fended for himself.

And that had been good for Minda. It had been painful enough last night at suppertime, forcing her eyes away from the delightful movement of his muscles beneath his shirt even in the simple action of lifting his fork to his mouth.

Of course, the children would love an outing.

Right now, each held one of Jake's hands, dragging him off toward the barn, no doubt to play with the kittens and examine the heifer. His three boys followed like a dotted line.

"Why, thanks, Gracey. Let me see what I can rustle up to share."

"Minda, I..."

Minda paused. Gracey was starting to sound like she had at the wedding when she brought her cause of adopting Priscilla out in the open. "Yes, Gracey?"

"Minda, I had no right to think Priscilla could be mine. Jake had nothing to do with that, and I repent my selfishness. But in turn, I believed him and Brix terribly wrong to keep such secrets from you." Gracey closed her troubled eyes for a second, "If you'd like, that is, if you wouldn't mind, maybe we could be friends?"

Gracey's voice was earnest, but she looked away, cheeks flushed.

"Of course. I would like nothing better." Minda meant it, and reached out to touch Gracey's arm. They were of similar age, and land sakes, she could certainly use a friend, especially one who understood her misery at being duped.

Although Gracey's smile was friendly and bright, her voice remained serious. "But Brix is a good man, Minda. Truly. He, Jake, and I have been pals since we were all kids ourselves. He, well, he heard the call to ride the trail, same as Jake took the call to preach. It isn't all that easy, doing what you're meant to do." She looked away.

Unsure what to say, Minda moved to the workspace in the kitchen area, slicing the fresh bread she'd baked, and gathering up a pot of jam.

In her heart, she knew Brixton was a good man. He just didn't have inside him what it took to be a good husband.

And, she reminded herself sadly, he'd never made that a secret.

It was better to discuss harmless topics right now with someone who'd been her friend for just five minutes. "So you grew up in Paradise?"

"My pa's the blacksmith. My brother, Nathan, mostly runs the smith and livery now. But Pa likes to keep his hands in. Jake's ma was widowed early on. She runs the boardinghouse. You likely met them all at the wedding." Gracey's face flamed at mentioning the controversial event, and she awkwardly moved toward Minda's sewing basket.

Minda couldn't help a friendly smile to ease her new friend's embarrassment. "I'm certain I did. But it'll take me a while to rethink everybody's faces and names."

"We figured the storm kept you all from church yesterday. Caldwell and I always teach a Bible story after, and your kids don't like to miss."

Caldwell. Caldwell Hackett. Minda froze the memory to a standstill, saying instead, "Yes. Brixton was out all night rescuing Buttermilk. I was terrified. He'd kicked himself out of the barn during a lightning strike. I'm certain I locked the door, but he sure was riled."

"He does have something of a temper," Gracey said. "There's a bit of gossip in town about him and Caldwell."

Minda's face muscles screwed together in consternation. She had to face the townsfolk tomorrow to buy supplies.

"But everybody's used to it," Gracey said. "They're good fellows, but they enjoy wrangling over anything and everything. Everybody knows how Caldwell spoke out against Brix marrying you. You know, without your knowledge or consent."

Gracey's words sounded like those Caldwell Hackett might use. According to Brixton, the schoolmaster wanted to be Minda's beau. Could she fend off Caldwell after her husband left?

Or would Caldwell be the kind of husband she'd come for, one who stayed home and honored his vows? It didn't matter. Minda had a husband already, for better or worse.

Just then, Priscilla reached for Gracey, who hugged her eagerly. As usual, the baby stuffed her fist into her mouth and gnawed.

"She's eating healthy now, but she's been a bit puny," Minda said, no longer fearful that Gracey would deem her a bad mother. She explained the symptoms of the mysterious ailment. The short convulsion still terrified her.

"Growing teeth sets every bit of a baby into disarray," Gracey said. "And a raging fever can be a big part. You did the right thing with the willow bark to get the fever down. We prairie folks understand nature's remedies more than city medicines."

Well, only thanks to Brixton. But at least Minda knew now. Relief filled her like air.

"Come on, let's call the children and get them washed up," Minda said, bright, eager for companionship and a change of scenery.

"Oh, they can wash up at the river. Minda, what's this?" Gracey had found Katie's new hat in the basket.

Minda's cheeks warmed, though she'd heard compliments on her hats for years. "I…I worked for the millinery back home. But now I find it relaxes me, as well. Fact is, that one helped calm me the night the horses got loose." She wanted to let Gracey know she intended to make her a new hat, but Gracey burst in quickly.

"Well, now Minda. Do you know about the Bonnet Race? You simply must construct a new hat for yourself."

"Bonnet Race?"

"For the Platte County Fair."

"The fair. Of course." Minda remembered seeing playbills announcing the event pasted on the mercantile's windows. She'd been searching for wanted posters about the Perkins gang.

Oh, the gang. Her heart thumped anew.

"You see, ladies and girls decorate special hats for the day." Gracey giggled, taking Katie's new hat and positioning it atop her own bonnet, and went on to demonstrate. "There's a row of fence posts outside of town. We hang 'em on the posts. The men race their horses three miles from the Lewis place at Shell Creek to the finish line past the cemetery."

Gracey's hands pointed to different directions. "But even the fastest man can't win the race unless he's retrieved his sweetheart's bonnet." Her pale green eyes gleamed and she gave a hearty laugh.

"I tell you, Minda. It gets a real mess there at the gauntlet of fence posts. All those men and horses finding the right bonnet. Some men can't even get close enough to reach the one they want."

Minda's mind was busy with the image. Just like Katie, she wanted her hat to be the prettiest. But even if he was around, Brix would never declare her his sweetheart. "Brixton wouldn't...

"And there's a forty dollar prize." Gracey nodded emphatically.

Forty dollars? Even Brixton might go for that.

"But best of all." Gracey smacked her lips. "The traditional celebration is a good, long kiss for the winner and his sweetheart. In front of everybody."

No, Brixton definitely wouldn't.

"But what if a man doesn't have a sweetheart? Or a lady, either?"

"There's always a secret admirer who wants that kiss, even if the lady's married," Gracey said. "No one takes offense. It's all in good fun."

"Well, Gracey. Let's go get that picnic over and done. Sounds like we've got some new hats to plan."

Gracey pinked again. "Oh, I'll just plunk some goldenrod and meadow flowers on this old thing."

"Nonsense. I've got just the idea."

"Don't matter. Jake tries but he'll never win. Even as a kid, he wasn't that nimble on a horse. Not like Brix. Now being the preacher, Jake stays dignified. It would never do for him to take a tumble."

"Whether he wins or not, I want to make you a new hat, as a thank-you for caring for the children so many times."

"Why, thank you kindly, Minda," her new friend said bashfully. "I'd like that."

Jake came inside to join them. "Afternoon, Minda." He nodded politely, then offered her his arm. His smile was genuine, and her resentment eased. What had Gracey said? It wasn't easy doing what you had to do.

"Minda, let's go out to the field and get your husband to join us. The children just told me he didn't go back to Texas after all."

"Yet," she said softly, but she knew Jake had heard.

****

Brix leaned his scythe against the wagon and watered the draft horse. Sweat ran down his aching back, and he groaned as Jake approached the wheat field. He was hungry, hot, and hurting, and definitely in no mood to get preached at.

Hell, then he saw Minda at Jake's side. The drab brown dress she wore was the ugliest thing outside of a convent, but it didn't stop his manhood from throbbing. She could wear a feed sack trimmed with buffalo chips and he'd still hanker after her. He knew exactly what she looked like without any clothes at all.

Damn Norman Dale, despite the fact he'd likely already crossed the Pearly Gates. Marrying Minda had seemed like a good idea at the time. But Brix also damned himself. Making love to Minda had seemed like a good idea, too. Since then, he could hardly meet her eyes.

"The kids told me you're hanging around," Jake said pleasantly, his feet stumbling a bit on the stubbled field. Truth to tell, Jake might have lived much of his life in Paradise, but he'd spent it stripping beds and keeping his ma's accounts.

"It's not what you're thinking," Brix said, avoiding his wife. "Silly's been sick. And Perkins is still on the loose. Unless you heard different?"

"Sadly, no." Jake's jaw clenched. "Sheriff Pelton heard that the gang hit up the livery in Genoa yesterday morning while the townsfolk were in church. They don't even rest on the Lord's Day anymore.

"Well, they don't strike me as a god-fearing bunch. Don't like it that they're striking in broad daylight. Sneaking up under cover of darkness seemed their way up to now." He couldn't help a glimpse of Minda then. Her face turned white as that wedding veil. All he could think about was holding her close for comfort. Forever.

Jake's talk chased that thought away. "Bob hopes they leave us alone now and head for the Sand Hills. That's far enough away for them to dupe those ranchers into buying their ill-gotten steeds."

Brix felt a smidge of confusion. He'd been wanting Silly's health to return and the gang to leave, so he could be on his way. But the scent of Minda's rose perfume right now trounced over the smell of fresh-threshed wheat, making him think he just might miss her.

She spoke, and out of politeness, he turned to her. Her eyes were shadowed with worry, but bright as rainbows anyway. "Surely along the way the horses would be recognized."

At those eyes, his heart thumped, and to cover his feelings, Brix scoffed. "Ahab and his boys are mighty good at disguise. They paint over a blaze or socks on the fetlock."

Jake looked confused, and Minda gave a little shrug that moved her bosom. Damn, Brix had only tasted her breasts a hundred times that night, not the million he wanted.

Needed.

"That means covering up a horse's white legs and spots on its forehead," Minda said.

A dance of pride rippled Brix's spine. "Yep. They also dye manes and tails. Dapple a chestnut to look piebald. And they can counterbrand. Burn in a bar over a regular brand, add something bogus top or below."

"And I do know they can expertly forge bills of sale," Jake said.

"My heavens." Minda gave off that scent of roses again. "I had no idea."

"Not so much like your dime novel." Brix couldn't help but grin.

Minda gave him a shy smile. "Not much at all. That plot had them rescue abused horses from evil landowners. They didn't shoot innocent men in the knee or rob decent folks during church. It was the bounty hunters after them who were the mean old villains."

Heat, not from the high noon sun, warmed Brix's face. She was so damn beautiful. Could Jake tell Brix had made his unwanted bride a true wife? Had he defiled her for some other man who might care for her with honest love?

The image of Caldwell Hackett kissing her hand raged in his mind, and Brix puffed out angry breath. Whether he—or she—wanted it, Minda was his wife fair and square.

Minda's little smile disappeared. She moved on her heels, impatient. "We're taking the children on a picnic. You're invited to attend."

"I just might do that, Miz Haynes." He smirked at Jake's big wide eyes. He didn't care a whit that Jake and Gracey had been on first-name terms for twenty years.

****

The bread melted on his tongue like snow on sunshine, the jam reminding him of his wife's sweet lips. And the river tumbling along its timber-studded banks might as well flow with whiskey, so relaxed and peaceable Brix felt.

"Good fixins here, Miz Haynes," he drawled, leaning lazily against the trunk of a cottonwood tree. She sat close, but not close enough. So he slid next to her until they touched. She twitched away, and he couldn't help grinning. "Won't be long before Cookie's sourdough'll be breaking my teeth."

Yep, this picnic had been a good idea. The wheat would wait. No reason not to enjoy the green of God's rolling prairie hilltops and the wind rippling the tallgrass. Not to mention sensible food and a fine-looking woman, too.

"Well, thank you for joining our picnic, but you might at least use my given name in public." She stuck her pretty nose in the air.

"That's only for private, Miz Haynes," he said, hating the sudden reminder, "and it won't happen again. Promised you that."

"Yes. So you did," Minda murmured after a long stare. She turned to Silly napping on the blanket next to her.

Her hat was as ugly as her dress, but that didn't stop his desire. He'd noticed the pretty pink thing she was making for Katie, but instead of some sweet confection of her own, it was Ida Lou's grubby brimmed hat that kept the sun from her face today. And her hair was stuffed tight under it.

But he recalled with no effort at all her long flowing hair and the pretty purple dress she'd worn yesterday when he'd told her he'd be leaving soon, when all along he wanted to kiss her senseless and renew their night of love. Right now, a ways off, Jake and Gracey bickered with affection, and envy stabbed him.

Minda got to her knees and looked over at the kids playing at the water's edge. "I can't see them all from here."

"Don't worry. Taught the kids to swim myself. Jake's too."

That seemed to surprise her. "Why, when?"

"Now, Miz Haynes, you don't surely think this is the only visit hereabouts I ever made?"

She gave him another stare deep from behind those pansy eyes. Damn, she was beautiful, even in those revolting duds.

"Well, Mr. Haynes, I don't rightly know anything about you at all," she said, nose high once again.

Like it had wings of its own, his hand flew up to touch her face. And she let him.

"Hey, Brix?" Jake interrupted, busy loading the baskets.

Brix left his fingers on Minda's cheek for an extra second, and he felt not a smidge of guilt for not helping. He'd started hacking wheat in the dawn's rosy light and hated every second. No high minded moral person would deprive him of some relaxation right about now.

And, he grinned, Minda hadn't nagged once.

"Yep?"

"You and Minda are entering the bonnet race next week, aren't you?"

His wife's eyes tossed him a dare. A wicked little

smile flickered at those delicious lips. "Silliest notion I ever heard," Brix said.

"The winner gets a purse of forty dollars," Jake said, loading the wagon.

"Won't be around then, most likely." Brix said, hearing Minda's harrumph. She got up quick, and he lolled, liking the look of her helping Jake with the cleanup.

Still, Brix had to admit forty dollars was a fine goal.

"I heard after church yesterday that Caldwell Hackett's got a new medicine hat mustang." Jake nodded casually, bending down to fold up a blanket.

A stew started in Brix's head and heart right then that would likely simmer for days. Damn Hackett. Those black-speckled ponies were considered powerful luck by the Indians.

Brix himself had a high regard for the people of the Plains.

He got to his feet and headed for the riverbank. "Gonna check the kids." He needed something to do to cool his face and fury, and the long ridge of flesh inside his denims. It had started to heat up at the swish of his wife's backside. A cold swim might do the trick.

Damn. Hackett with a new horse was a powerful threat. Jake couldn't sit upright on a pincushion but Caldwell now, he downright wasted his horsemanship plunked behind a teacher's desk. He might be a town boy, but he'd ridden like the wind before he could walk.

And the fool had already humiliated Brixton once.

Just then Katie burst through the thicket, followed by Jake's ladder of boys. "Uncle Brix, Neddie-boy's gone!"

"What do you mean, gone? Thought you kept an eye out?" Fear replaced his lust and anger.

"I did! We've been playing fine...but then he was gone!" She burst into tears.

"Show me."

The kids led him downstream ten yards or so, but all he found caught in the dead branches reaching out of the water was a soaking length of brown wool.

Katie sobbed. "That used to be his toy dog. Oh, Uncle Brix, does that mean he fell in after it? Did he, he didn't drown did he?"

"'Course not." His own gut tightened with unspeakable dread. Sure the kids had learned to swim last summer, but likely they hadn't practiced much. The river was still full from that storm, the current stronger than a kid even during drought.

Besides, Brix knew from bungled river crossings on the trail just how strong panic could be.

He scurried to the water's edge, ready to jump in. But as he kicked off his boots, he tossed a quick prayer up toward heaven, too. Although he was by no means a worshipful man, he couldn't bear losing something else he never thought he wanted.

Chapter Ten

Heart pounding with each footstep, Minda rushed through a thicket of willow and larkspur to gather the sobbing Katie in her arms. She held off her own tears even though the pain of losing Ned cut into her flesh as cruelly as a whip.

The terror she'd felt during Priscilla's mysterious illness had returned ten-fold. Katie held on to Minda like she herself was drowning.

Next to them, Jake tended his knot of boys tied together by tears.

Waist high in the river, Brixton grabbed the water this way and that as if defying the current. Minda shivered with a new and tortured fear. She might lose him, too.

Back in Pennsylvania, she'd seen the Allegheny once, and compared to it, this was a rivulet, but she knew the power of water. Brixton was sure to return, but it wouldn't take much to claim such a little child.

"I'll search downriver on foot," Jake said to Brixton, then told Minda, "Hopefully he just wandered away and didn't fall in at all. But if he did..." He touched her shoulder in gentle reassurance. "Brix has years of know-how rescuing bogged cattle. Neddie won't be any trouble at all."

Brixton turned his head to acknowledge Jake, and Minda saw his bleak, hard eyes. They hadn't been married but days, yet she knew what the look meant. He didn't like losing control, and he'd heaped this tragedy on her. After all, she had charge of tending the children.

That was the only reason he'd wed her, and she had failed the night of the storm, after all. Neddie had confessed to sneaking to the barn to lullaby the cows, leaving it unlocked when he came back to bed.

But the situation between her and Brixton didn't matter one whit now. She prayed silently as the river sent her husband on.

Katie left Minda to wave her uncle along the bank for a few feet.

"Be careful," Minda called, fearing she'd screeched.

Jake's eyes turned black with worry. "Damn fool," he said under his breath, but Minda heard anyway.

"Reverend!"

"You can call me Jake, Minda. But right now, I don't have any other appropriate word. I pray you and the Lord forgive me for my lack of sanctity."

"But Brixton can swim. He taught the children," she said anxiously.

"Sure he can. But sandbars can grab a leg and break it. And there's quicksand in the shallows and in many places along the riverbank."

"Oh, merciful heavens. Quicksand?" Minda's world teetered on its end and sink into an abyss of dread. "Doesn't Brixton know all that?"

Before Jake turned on his heel to start his search, he nodded and gave Minda's hand a squeeze. "Sure he does. Quicksand won't snare a man, but a child can easily get mired up in it. But right now, Brix's thinking with his heart, not his head."

"But he knows the outdoors," she said, squeezing back in a definite panic.

"Minda, can't you see?" Jake kept his voice gentle, but Minda heard what he was really saying. "I'm not just thinking of Brix out there."

Of course, he meant Neddie. Most likely it hurt

him to say the name as much as it did Minda to think it. But think about Ned she must. She must be prepared, a luxury she hadn't been given about anything in Paradise.

Neddie might be able to thrash his little limbs in swimming motions against the water for a time, but he would soon grow weary. Roots and sandbars might trap him and hold him under, and quicksand might take him from them forever.

The hot, moist wind swirled around her body like the tragic images twisting inside her brain, and Minda willed herself not to faint dead away. She had work to do.

She had a child to save.

Gracey came through the woods with Priscilla in her arms. "I'll go to town for help. Some of the men are awful good swimmers."

"Yes, and hurry!" That's how it would have been in Gleesburg. Even though she was in Paradise now, folks everywhere gathered together to help in times of need.

"Yes, indeed. Go alert Sheriff Pelton." Jake said. "And have everyone bring nets and poles. And Gracey, take all the children back to the parsonage. One less thing for us to worry about here."

"I'll stay here and start looking upriver," Minda said, drawing fresh air into her lungs to stabilize herself. Staying busy might help keep her calm. "I'd like to lend whatever hand I can."

And, she realized glumly, she'd be close on hand to hear whatever news emerged, good or bad. Icy prickles pierced the back of her neck. She had two people to worry about.

Katie came back after waving Brix on. "I'm looking, too," she said in a firm voice. "He's my brother."

Minda nodded. "I do need you now, Katie. You've been a wonderful helper to me at home." Indeed, the girl was a most efficient youngster and might be of help. Her tears had stopped although the dusty trails of them marked her cheeks.

"Sure thing." Jake stomped off through the cattails at the water's edge as Gracey took Priscilla and her boys back to their buggy.

"Katie, tell me..." Minda knelt and drew the little girl close. "Did you hear Ned call out? Did you hear a splash?"

"No, Mama, I didn't hear a thing. Uncle Brix taught us to swim one time, but Neddie will be mighty scared. I know it. And I'm scared, too."

"Of course you are, Firefly. But Ned is a smart boy, and Uncle Brix knows about the outdoors. He'll find your brother." She tamped down the panic in her trembling voice.

"Are you sure?" Katie pulled away to look at Minda straight on. Her voice had lost some of its energy.

"I am sure." Minda believed it so it so firmly that her confidence began to steady her shaking knees. She hadn't known Brixton all that long, but she knew full well he liked getting his way.

His sleeping outside was sure proof of that.

"Come on, Firefly. Let's start the opposite direction from the reverend. Ned might have slipped by and I didn't notice. Neddie? Ned?"

"The sheriff's coming soon, isn't he?" Katie said, tiny lines crinkling her forehead.

"Yes. And he's going to bring help. I'm sure they'll all be here in no time at all." Minda tried to brush away the little girl's worry with a gentle hand. "I think we should look behind any tree branches and poke at all the clumps of weeds and clover."

Katie nodded, plunging ahead, but called out anxiously, "Watch out! That's poison ivy there."

"All right. At least we're wearing long sleeves."

"Well, your hands touched it just then," Katie

said. "See? It has three leaves."

Minda couldn't worry about that now. Rinsing her hands off in the river was her only choice. Back at home, she could scrub with the fine French soaps her sisters had given her for her wedding. But now, she had more important things to think about.

"Neddie, Neddie!"

"There's burrs, too. And thorns," Katie said, too late.

Minda pulled her scratched hand from a bush. "I need to be more careful. But don't you worry. We'll have plenty of searchers." She struggled to catch her breath, but most of the shortness was fear and nerves. "A missing child is a dreadful circumstance. All hands are needed. And I suspect everybody in Paradise is fond of your brother."

"Papa always said he was a mischief maker. Maybe a turtle bit him. Some of them snap, you know."

"Then I think we'll find him sooner than ever. He would want a bandage to show for his wound, don't you think?" Minda tried to smile. Katie's description of her little brother was most apt.

Katie carefully waved a branch from Minda's face. But turtles reminded her of something else.

"How about, well, snakes?" Minda asked. Reaching into grottos and searching behind rocks would certainly disturb plenty of wild creatures.

"Just water ones. They don't hurt."

But unseen bugs of dread climbed up and down Minda's bones and underneath her skin anyway, and tears spilled down her face as she thought of never again seeing little Ned's glorious smile.

Or Brixton.

"Ned? Ned, where are you?" Katie yelled, and Minda was grateful because she found she had no voice just then. Her feet carried her up and down the hummocks of riverbank without any real thought.

Fighting for self-control, she surged through the undergrowth. Mud grabbed at her feet, for the cottonwood trees kept the sun from drying it out. "There's a big tuft of weeds, Katie. Let's go check. If he tripped, why..."

Minda closed her eyes to the unimaginable. His lifeless body might have been brought to shore by the current. She misstepped. Her shoe caught between two roots and she bobbled slightly, twisting her ankle.

"Mama. Are you all right? You can lean on me if you must."

She shook off the twinge. "No, I'm fine. I think I need to head lower to the water's edge. There are tangled roots. He could be stuck."

"I'll come too."

"No, Firefly. You look in the brambles here." She didn't dare mention the quicksand.

"That's chokecherry. Makes good jam. Neddie likes it."

"Ned? It's Minda. Can you hear me?"

****

He'd paddled, waded and swum for likely a mile, maybe more, longing to find the boy clinging to roots or grabbing onto cattails. His shoulders ached with a hopelessness he'd never felt ever before.

Not even, he thought bitterly, when he'd taken on a family he didn't want. Scrambling up the bank, Brix gasped for air and grunted in pain. His bare foot met a thistle he'd known about since childhood and should have watched out for.

The fish-hook shaped barb had already found its way inside his arch.

Hell, it wasn't anything he couldn't dig out later. He had better things to tend to now. But even with the heat of the day, he shivered inside his wet clothes and struggled to find a last bit of hope.

Likely Ned had washed all the way to the Platte

by now. It wouldn't take anything at all to move a little lad so quick and far.

And hell, quicksand might have swallowed him whole.

Well, not exactly. But the fearsome bog could trap a kid as tiny as Ned, hold him under until the river did its final damage.

Damn, why hadn't Minda watched him better? Why hadn't he taught Ned to swim stronger?

Brix's veins pumped hard but without power. He figured he might have died himself and gone to hell. He hadn't wanted to take on the kids, but he might have tried to be more of a pa. Most times, Brixton Haynes took on any job the best he could even if he didn't like the task. Else he'd never have reached inside a troubled cow to relieve her of a tangled calf.

Or sucked snake poison from a cowpoke's filthy leg. Or bartered his last half-eagles for safe passage for the pitiful remnants of a Kiowa tribe.

"I should have played with you, boy." Thorn or not, he got to his feet, regret taking over his grief. "What kind of man don't play tag with a kid when he asks? Come on, little fella. Talk to me."

Brix forced his knees to stand him up. Damn, his brother hardly dead a week, and Brix had another grave to dig.

If they found Ned at all, that is. The little boy's body might become a feast for the fishes. Hell, the coyotes and bobcats along the river were hungry, too.

These nightmares darkened the daylight around him, but Brix shook closed his aching imagination. Like it or not, he was head of a family now and might as well act like it. Might as well head back to the wagon and tend to Katie.

Even Minda. Whether he wanted it so or not, she was his wife, despite her carelessness and uppity ways.

How had they all enjoyed a picnic barely an

hour ago?

Nothing but the river made sounds now, not the meadowlarks or bobolinks or the frogs. Not even the chatter of prairie dogs or the whisper of a grasshopper. Maybe the heat of the day had baked them into submission.

But sometimes that meant a human had come by, startling Mother Nature into silence. It could mean himself.

But it could also mean the boy.

He dared to let hope seep into his bones. He made his feet land light along the undergrowth of switchgrass and prairie clover. A blooming jack-in-the-pulpit had the gall to cheer him.

Gracey'd taken to calling them jake-in-the-pulpits, after her husband.

Well, Brix didn't go easily into defeat and would himself die fighting the light.

"Ned? Neddie-boy, can you hear me? It's Uncle Brix. Let me know, boy." The lad might be wounded, stuffed under a root cave, maybe unable to call out.

He moved along sand bar willows, poking under chokecherry brush, poison oak and ivy too, but damn, he didn't care. His arms reached into any type of hidey-hole he could find.

"Come on, Neddie. I got more stories to tell about that magic cow. Yep, I know Katie likes her, too, but she's busy with that new pink hat. You and me, we got things to do."

Finally he gave in to the only choice he had left, besides praying, which he was none too good at. The lullaby Neddie liked came from Brix's throat in a harsh way that meant he might have swallowed a tear or two.

For not even when he was alone did Brixton Haynes give in to weeping.

He rounded the bend and saw Jake up ahead. His friend's stern face indicated there was no good news to report.

Jake shook his head. Brix's insides tangled up right. "Gracey went to get help right away. Upriver is probably already crawling with folks."

But Brix wasn't giving up, not yet, at least.

"I got some hope left, Jake," Brix said. "Might be foolish, but Norman Dale's already got one of his boys with him in heaven. Just don't think it's Neddie's time."

"I like to think so. But Brix, I've lost a child. It can be difficult to accept. If you need a friend..."

"Last I heard, you are my friend, Jake. And I haven't lost a child. Better believe it." Brix grunted. "Why the hell aren't you yammering about how miracles happen? Now get moving."

Even under Jake's prying eye, he started up his lullaby, then stopped after every refrain and listened, cautious.

Jake opened his mouth, but Brix hushed him. "Get your silent prayers going and listen up."

For a second, the river seemed to hold its breath, like the wind blew against it and stopped it up.

In the brief space of silence, Brix sure as hell heard sniffles and sobs coming from a stand of tallgrass higher than any small boy. Mule deer and jack bunnies didn't make any sound like that.

"Ned? Ned? Here I am. It's Uncle Brix. Are you hurt? Let me know. Reverend's with me, too."

Time lasted forever. And at the end of it, he heard the tiny voice, and a little hand reached through the stalks.

Like Brix had wings on his feet, he was there, kneeling down and pulling the boy gently from the thick grass. Ned hiccupped with sobs that had gone on far too long.

"You all right?" Brix didn't see any blood or awkward limbs. And Ned wasn't soaked. At least he hadn't tumbled into the river to fear water forever after. Sending up his own silent prayer of thanks, Brix crushed the boy close. "Neddie, we been powerful worried. Now, let me know what this is about."

"You scared us silly, little man." Jake tussled Ned's hair. "Brix, I'll run along ahead and tell everyone you're both safe and sound."

Brix held Ned, drinking in the sight of him.

"Uncle Brix, I tripped and drowned my doggie." Ned gulped. His face was lined with muddy tears. "I didn't mean to. It was on accident."

"Sure, boy. You loved that thing pure and simple. Minda won't mind, I can promise you."

And she wouldn't mind, not at all. Brix knew that. Even forced to it, she'd been a real good ma to kids she barely even knew. At least that part of Norman Dale's plan had come true. Now that Ned was safe, Minda would likely smother him to death to make up for not watching over him today.

Neddie nodded, dripping sniffles down his cheeks. "I know that. I knew she could dry it on the clothesline. And fold it up again with those ribbons. Katie showed me some pretty ones she has. But I dropped my whistle, too. It floated off."

Ned's tiny shoulders shook with new sobs. "I tried to follow it, but it went far away."

Whatever beat inside Brix's chest melted. He rubbed the boy's back. "Well, making you another whistle won't take any time at all, Neddie. Won't bother me a bit. But why are you hiding? You hurt?"

Ned shook his head and jammed his thumb in his mouth. It was a babyish habit Brix had never noticed before.

Then Brix understood. He read it in the boy's eyes, read it clear as the first time he'd ciphered alphabet words in front of a schoolmarm. Ned was hiding in fear, not in shame for spoiling his toys.

Had he seen a wolf?

"Ned, tell me. What did you see? What scared you?"

The boy shivered against him. Even with his own wet clothes, Brix figured his arms warmed Ned somewhat. For a second, he hummed the lullaby again to comfort Ned. "Bobcats and coyotes? A wolf maybe?"

Ned removed his thumb and tightened his grubby hand around Brix's index finger. He liked the feeling.

"No. It wasn't that, Uncle Brix. It wasn't a wild critter at all."

"What then? You can tell me. I'm here now. Keep you safe." For the first time ever, his lips touched the boy's hair.

"The outlaws," Ned whispered, closing his eyes against the memory. "More than my fingers. They wore masks. I hid."

All Brix's aches vanished. Blood pumped fast and furious in his veins, and words came tight off his tongue. "Come on, Ned. Sit on my shoulders. Let's go find my boots."

He tried not to let Ned know, but his skin crawled so fast it almost left his bones. The devil himself, in the form of Ahab Perkins, had arrived in Paradise.

****

"Sheriff Pelton, ma'am." The lawman's horse had stopped on a dime when he came upon her and Katie investigating the riverbank. They were almost back to where they'd started, but Minda wasn't about to give up or slow down.

However, she did want a short break for Katie. The girl's skin was pink and clammy, and Minda feared a state of shock coming on.

Did Brixton have a riverside cure for that?

"Minda Haynes," she said, surprised at the

firmness of her voice. She'd grown nearly hoarse calling for Ned.

He tipped his hat. "My deputy's sending wires downriver so those towns keep watch for Ned."

"Thank you, sir." The arrival of searchers from town was a good thing, but at the sheriff's words, hopelessness all but crushed her bones. Ned was too little to hike miles and miles to other towns. Of course, the sheriff meant it was his *body* they'd keep watch for.

Or maybe they'd be keeping an eye for Brixton's, too? She choked on a tear.

"Call me Bob. We brought equipment in case we need to drag the river. But don't you worry, Miz Haynes. We got no reason to suspect he's not just wandering the river bed. Kids like to explore. Turtles, frogs. Maybe made a fishing pole out of a branch."

Minda considered the possibility. Ned might still have the cords she'd used to make his toy dog. But no. He would have stayed close by. And he'd have wanted the Satterburg boys and his sister along.

He would have heard folks calling out his name.

Besides, he would never have left her. Of that she was sure.

"Maybe he had a tiff with his sister and ran away in a bit of temper?" Bob said.

"We did no such thing, Sheriff," Katie said, indignant, breaking into fresh tears.

Minda kept her voice as light as she could, without censure. Without losing control.

"Sheriff, thank you for coming so quickly. Hopefully we'll have some good news soon." Minda hated the reality that the news might be bad. She had a great deal to lose right now.

But Minda wasn't the only one suffering. Katie's stricken face and shaking hands were hard to endure. How much more suffering would the little girl have to bear?

The peaceful picnic area had come to life with an awful tension. Men had crossed the bridge a half-mile away and both sides of the river teemed with searchers bound for the missing little boy who had captured her heart.

She held Katie close. “Firefly, I think you need to rest. But I’d like to look a little more. Let’s settle you in the back of the wagon for a while.”

“I want to still look, too.”

“You’ve done your best.” Minda kissed her cheek as the little girl sagged against her.

Suddenly, Minda heard Jake’s voice resonating through the trees and calling out news as good as a gospel. “He’s all right. He’s all right.”

The sheriff let out a whoop.

“Thank you, God.” Minda’s heart pumped with new vigor along with her prayer, and Katie came to new life. “Now you wait for me in the wagon, all right?”

Minda ran toward the reverend as he rounded a copse of trees.

“Jake? He’s all right? You’re sure?”

The reverend gave her a friendly embrace, eyes twinkling, and caught his breath. “Which one are you asking about?”

“Both, of course.” Minda hugged her arms around herself, longing for Brixton there. Not just the little boy, but the man had stolen her heart, too.

“Brix found Neddie, and he’s fine.” Jake breathed. “Really fine. They both are. I came ahead to let you know, but they can’t be far behind me. Brix might have needed a space of time to sort things out with Ned, but he can walk through fire, you know.”

“Then I’m off to meet him. Tend Katie, please.” She had to see them with her own eyes.

Hold them in her own arms.

It wouldn't matter if her husband slept outside tonight. She needed this moment with him now.

Some of the searchers followed behind her through the trees, and with joy, she first saw Neddie's head bobbing over a rolling knoll ahead, then Brixton's under it. The boy was perched on his shoulders. Brixton had grabbed the little legs that hung down his chest and ran quickly as he could.

The crowd cheered.

"Oh Neddie, sweetheart. Brixton, I've been so worried. So scared." She let the prairie wind carry her words to his ears. Her arms were spread wide.

They met at the smooth bottom of the knoll. After Brix stopped and balanced himself and Ned, she held her arms wider yet.

"Been worried myself, Miz Haynes," Brixton mumbled, thrusting Neddie into her waiting embrace.

She grabbed Neddie so hard he groaned. When the boy finally struggled for the ground, she reached for Brixton and held him just as hard against her, and he let her, his chest hot against her cheeks.

"I am so glad to see you both." She placed one hand on either side of Brixton's face and rose on her toes to kiss him.

He clasped her hard against him, his mouth closing over hers. She parted her lips, taking inside his tongue like she had his manhood. The memories throbbed in her heart and lower, deep down, reminding her she was a woman.

Then he pushed her away, like she'd touched something she shouldn't. Her cheeks burned. But before he nodded to the cheering onlookers, she caught a brief look of regret in his eyes. And she understood completely. He wasn't hers to have.

Then Neddie called out one single word that silenced the good people of Paradise.

"Outlaws."

Chapter Eleven

"Aha. Perkins at last." Sheriff Pelton nodded, resolute. "Now all of you skeedaddle back home. The boy's found now. Go get your stock under lock and key."

Like the Baptizer, Bob Pelton waved his arms over those gathered at the river. Faces of folks celebrating Ned's safe return now crumpled with worry.

"Gang's likely to split up in two's or three's to save time. Hit more places. Now, get," the sheriff yelled.

"Sure enough, Bob. Hurry up, Miz Haynes." Brix shook away his worry and desire. After all, he had a gun and had taught Minda well. He looked down at her blushing face, and those eyes that didn't meet his. He didn't dare let folks around here think that kiss meant anything at all, that he was some kind of happily married man.

Still, he couldn't deny liking her touch when he took her hand and pulled her toward the wagon.

"Hurry yourself up."

"I am hurrying," she said, prim, pulling her hand away. Stubborn, he grabbed it back.

He reckoned he'd shamed her, breaking off that kiss. Hell, he'd like nothing better than to clamp himself against those bosoms. But despite those eager lips and the secrets below that only he had uncovered, he reminded himself that he couldn't have her. Just a few more days and he'd be gone.

And he had a heap of things to do in the

meantime.

"Well, hurry up some more. I got wheat to thresh yet."

"We should thank everyone for helping," she said, pulling her hand away again. Her swishing sent that aroma of roses to ease the stench of his soggy clothes. He admitted he enjoyed it. It would be a good thing to recall on the trail when his nose was weary of manure and sweat

"They know already." He grabbed her hand. "They're in a rush, too."

"Why are you limping? Are you hurt?"

Brix declined to explain the thorn he'd stepped on. Right now, all he wanted was to enjoy her fingers wrapped in his so he could recall that night when they'd closed hot and firm around his cock.

At the wagon, Katie turned spunky as hell at seeing her brother, and Brix tugged her braid. Forever after, he'd think of her each time he twisted new rawhide strips into a lariat. He settled Ned and tucked the picnic blanket around him. The boy's fear had caught up, and he was shivering.

Moisture started up behind Brix's eyelids, and his heart did a funny pitter, hurt a bit. He'd downright miss the kids.

Jake came over with a big smile and troubled eyes. "We'll have special petitions come Sunday for Ned's safe return. Delmar and Geraldine Hackett are giving me a ride back to town. I think it best that we keep Silly overnight with us. No need for anyone to be out and about extra right now, with hooligans on the loose."

Along Brix's shoulders, fear kicked him like little Ned's legs had done just moments ago. Perkins was getting closer and meaner. Brix had to do anything he could to keep the kids safe.

"All right by me, if my wife doesn't mind," Brix said, giving Minda a cautious look. Sure as hell she'd set to complaining about such a transaction. Once upon a time, Gracey had wanted to pilfer the baby.

Instead, he caught a smile that surprised him and made a manly thing happen inside his trousers. Strange how sweet the word *wife* had sounded on his tongue.

"No, I don't mind at all, Jake," Minda said. "As a matter of fact, I think Gracey would like it a great deal. Please tell her I'll be by to get Priscilla tomorrow when I run errands. If it's safe, of course. We can discuss our hats."

"I will do that. Good-bye now."

As he helped her into the wagon, Brix reckoned a lecture on the Bonnet Race was about to start, so he decided to hedge it off. And damn, if there was any righteousness in the world, Caldwell Hackett's mustang would be the first pony Ahab Perkins thieved.

"See you lost that big hat," he said, as he climbed up.

"I did." Just for an instant she gave off a breathy little chuckle that reminded him of that night in her arms. The manly thing happened again. "It blew off in a bramble patch somewhere. I didn't even care. I was so worried about Ned. And I'm so worried now." Her voice and lips tightened.

"Well, Miz Haynes, you can shoot as good as any female around here. Let's see now how fast this churn-head can get us home." He urged the draft horse along, and a cuss slipped out.

"Churn-head? What's wrong?" Minda asked, face pink as dawn.

"Churn-head means he's stubborn. This horse works strong, but he's slow. And I'd like to get home quick."

"Well, I think we all want that."

"Worse than that. Anybody with ears in any saloon in Platte County knows Norman Dale's horses are the best in these parts. He spent more cash than he should have on that pair. Even Dobby is a valuable piece of horseflesh."

"Dobby?"

"This churn-head." A grin slipped out even with his bones weary from the river and outlaws skulking up ahead and that unfulfilled kiss. "None of my doing, I'll have you know. My brother allowed his kids to name everything from pullets to, hell, barn mice."

She frowned. Without that hat, sunshine turned her hair to spun silver and gold, tied here and there with copper wire.

"Must you speak so? Around the children? And I *am* a lady."

He sighed deep. Another reason to leave. The trail was a place where a man could cuss in peace, smoke long-nine cigars at will, and engage in blackstrap whiskey without beseeching permission.

A man on the trail had no chance to get nagged by a wife, no matter how pretty she was.

No matter how much he liked the hot, sweet mysteries of her body.

"Sorry," he muttered in such a way she'd know for sure he didn't mean it at all, and looked straight ahead. The miles of corn and prairie grass around him contented men who liked muddying their fingers, but his only peace came from riding from place to place. That was a fact, and everybody in Paradise knew it, including his wife.

And it couldn't happen soon enough.

"What's yours?" she asked, and confusion filled his head at her words.

"My what?" He looked sideways at her.

Even with the worry tweaking the edges of her eyes, she smiled a little, and he couldn't help but enjoy the glimpse of her lips. He recalled their taste, regretted that he'd halted that kiss. Turning a little more, he watched her mouth full on and thought of the few kisses they'd shared.

He almost wanted to die in her arms.

"The name of the horse that waits for you in Kansas," she said, bringing him to his senses.

It sounded a harmless enough question.

"Fara. Farajido." He wondered for a flash how his pinto was doing. It wouldn't be too long before the two of them were on their way back to Butter Creek.

"Hmm. I must guess that's Spanish?" A bump in the road made the word tumble on her tongue.

"Yep." Her inkling surprised him. What did a Pennsylvania girl know about south of the border?

"So, what is the translation?"

"Outlaw." He couldn't help a grin.

She didn't giggle or make any other sort of humorous sound. The word must have reminded her of their true quest, now that Ned was found.

"Oh, mercy, Mr. Haynes, we truly must hurry," she said, her voice fluttering a little.

"Been saying that very thing. Dob's doing his best." Brix scowled, suddenly spent of grins. He hadn't even had time to improve his mood over nearly losing Ned. Now he had to consider outlaws practically lined up at the homestead, waiting to strike.

She whispered close to his ear, his hands all but trembling on the reins just at her hair flowing so close to his nose. "Do you have your gun along?"

He nodded and tightened his lips together, thinking he had best speak his mind. Soon, she'd be the only one looking after the kids.

"You ought to have kept your eye on Ned." He forced the words out, wondering if he should. She'd been a splendid ma up to now.

Those flower petal eyes turned dark with anger. "Why, Mr. Haynes, don't you dare cast any such blame on me. You have a pair of eyes, too. Besides, you yourself told me not to be concerned."

He ignored her. "Well, it worked out good. Found him right as rain."

"Well, I tried, too."

"That you did," he said, with some surprise. She truly hadn't carried on in any fainthearted way. "Truth is, it could have been you, except you went the other direction."

The bouncing of the wheels had lulled Ned fast asleep in Katie's arms. Tilting the brim of his hat, Brix checked out the sun overhead. That meant only one thing. He could get in four more hours threshing that damn wheat. It didn't matter about his burning foot.

In July, night came late to Nebraska.

"It sure was a fine thing, all those people coming to help find Ned," Minda said, interrupting his unhappy thoughts. "I actually felt a bit like I belong in Paradise now."

What did that mean? She was staying on after her payback? That might answer some prayers. But he couldn't help grumbling about the wasted day and his aching foot.

"Shouldn't have gone on that picnic, any of us," he groused. "Ned getting lost took a heap of folks away from their business. Myself included."

"Why, Mr. Haynes, you just hush and reconsider. In a roundabout way, Neddie alerted Paradise to the presence of the outlaws."

"Nothing but trouble."

"Ned scared us all to death, but we might not have known about Ahab Perkins any other way."

He grunted. They had reached the homestead, and with some unease, he turned the wagon toward the barn. Minda tensed beside him, but things looked undisturbed. His sigh sounded just like hers.

"Listen, Miz Haynes, I got hours left in the field.

Taking this day off was not wise." He raised his eyebrows.

"Well, again as I recall, you had the chance to say no to the invitation." Her pretty nose went high in the air again in that way he had to admit he liked. "I remember perfectly well how much you hate farming. How much you hate Paradise. But at least after today, I'm assured that you don't hate the children!" She stomped down from the wagon seat all by herself.

Her words knocked into him like a hungry calf finally finding its ma. He had taken on the kids without a moment's hesitation, tossed his whole life upside down. How had such an uncharitable thought ever crossed her brain?

He jumped down beside her.

At that precise second, the sleeping kids stirred and calmed him down.

"Let's keep our voices down, Miz Haynes. Now you got kids to tend. And I got wheat to thresh."

"I'll keep supper warm for you." Her voice was stiff.

"Something else you need to keep, Miz Haynes." He leaned close to whisper in her ear. "Keep my brother's hog-leg pistol at your side."

****

Neddie continued his nap inside, and when Katie wasn't looking, Minda tied Norman Dale's gun to her leg with his old suspender.

Her husband had scared her into obedience, but she didn't want to frighten the children. When she tried out her new contrivance, the homemade gun belt held fine.

They'd have to feed the chickens somehow, but she hesitated to leave Ned alone in the house. And while she missed Priscilla, she felt comforted with the baby safe in town.

As Jake had said, one less thing to worry about.

Brixton's blaming her for Ned's accident troubled her. And breaking off that kiss had been downright humiliation. They'd seemed to find a bit of accord during the picnic.

But now, outlaws crept around the prairie, threatening them all. Nervously, she peeked out the window.

"Let's start supper, Firefly," she said. Keeping busy would chase away her runaway thoughts and feelings. "Then we can work on your new hat while the meat pie bakes."

"Can I go to the pasture and pick some wildflowers first? They always look so pretty on the table," Katie asked. "Uncle Brix might like it."

"Not today." Minda reached for her rolling pin and felt a twinge. He wouldn't be around long enough to see flowers wilt. "I'd like you to stay inside with me."

"It's the outlaws fretting you, isn't it?"

She nodded. "Well, Katie, I don't like to think of them so close by. And I keep imagining just how terrified your brother must have been when he saw them ride practically right next to him."

Katie peeked out the window. "But I don't see them now. And the pasture isn't all that far from the house. Besides, they don't want to steal Mabel. They're horse thieves, not cow thieves."

Minda had to laugh, even with her nerves. "I believe your Uncle Brix calls them cattle rustlers. But no. Not today. Hopefully, things will be back to normal soon."

The thought saddened her, even though she wanted the brigands locked tight behind bars. Brixton had said, allowing no argument at all, that he'd be going back to Texas the moment things settled down.

"Well, did you like the flowers I brought you before? You never said."

In mortification, Minda paused her flattening of the pie dough. She prided herself on her good manners. Had she missed something?

"Firefly, I am sorry if I overlooked anything."

"Oh, the other morning. Your first morning here. I put 'em in a jar on the table before you got up."

"Oh." Minda couldn't find any other words, and her spirits sank to China and farther yet. All this time, she'd thought her bridegroom had brightened her day. But her disappointment didn't mean the child's offering shouldn't be appreciated. "Yes, I did. They were lovely, and I thank you for your thoughtfulness. I, well, I've had quite a lot on my mind."

Katie chewed on her brown braid for a second, making her plump red cheeks look like apples in a basket. "Yes, I believe you have. And worrying about Neddie today just made it worse. But I hope you found out you should stay. We need a mother around here, and you're doing just fine."

At least someone welcomed her. Of all people, she understood the heavy weight Katie had borne on her small shoulders since her mother's death. The girl's lost childhood touched Minda deeply. After all, she'd experienced something of the same.

"Thank you, Katie." She hugged the little girl in spite of the flour. "I have had plenty of experience raising children, don't you think?" They'd already had discussions about Minda's three sisters.

"I say you did. And Papa knew that, too. Why, he was most excited when you accepted his proposal!"

Minda smacked the rolling pin down hard. That couldn't be the only reason Norman Dale had wanted her here, could it? He'd sent letter after letter, claiming that he cared. That his feelings for her had grown real.

"I know Uncle Brix's got to leave us, but you

won't, will you, Mama? Please say you won't."

Hearing the impossible words, and the even more impossible "mama" that she'd heard before along the river, Minda dropped the rolling pin with a huge clatter. Neddie whimpered from behind the curtain of the children's sleeping alcove. She tried to calm herself. What on earth should she say? She didn't even know the answer herself.

"Well, Katie," she began carefully. "Pennsylvania is a long way from here. And today, with all those folks eager to help us, Paradise did start to feel more like home."

There. She hadn't said anything untrue, but Katie had more to say. "No. Now that I think of it, Uncle Brix needs to stay with us, too. Be your husband like other men do."

Once again, Minda had no real reply, so she gave Katie a direction, fighting down the hurt. "You snap some beans, and I'll cut up the potatoes."

"Will you put dried chokecherries in the bacon pie, too? There's some in the cupboard. Uncle Brix likes them."

She wanted to say she didn't care what he liked, but truth was, she did care, deeply. She wanted a wife's opportunity to please him.

"Yes, of course. Please go get them. Then we'll crimp the crust and get this pie in the oven. Finally, Firefly, we'll have time to work on your hat."

Katie handed Minda a small brown paper package. "And then you can tell me about your bonnet race hat."

Minda laughed lightly, but heard it ring false. There would be no bonnet race for her. She had no sweetheart here. Brixton would never stay.

As the scents of the meal cooking filled the little house, twilight fell and crickets chirped outside. Maybe she ought to feed the children early. It had been quite a day.

Brixton would no doubt be angrier with her than ever, for she and the children had left the evening chores for him, unwilling as she was for them to leave the house. She sighed long and deep, peering out the window. The wind chasing itself across the prairie, the sunset danced in the farmyard with the shadows it made.

She stitched for a while, and instinct trickled up and down her spine like a poisonous spider. Pulling the curtain taut, she glanced out the window. Ground-tethered at the edge of the windbreak that lined the farm's north ride were two horses she'd never seen before. Her throat drained dry.

She hadn't heard riders on the road. Dear Lord in heaven, what kind of mother was she? Her heart thumped so hard she held her hand to her chest.

Two shadowed men sawed against the barn-door lock, stealthy but arrogant at the same time as if they dared someone to see. One tossed a glance at the house and set right back to his task. Still, she knew he'd seen her.

The Perkins gang, coming in two's or three's, unconcerned by a woman cooking supper.

That meant they knew her husband wasn't inside. Her veins froze. Brixton had worn his gun belt to the fields, but she'd heard no gunshots. Had the gang come upon him by stealth and harmed him in some other way, eliminating the threat of a husband? Her heart pounded.

No. It wasn't possible. On the trail, Brixton lived with the threat of rustlers and guns and knives.

The horses inside the barn whinnied, and Katie looked up from her tasks at the unusual commotion.

"Katie," Minda whispered, "you get Ned and hide under my… under the big bed."

"But…"

"Now, Firefly," she ordered "And you two stay there, no matter what you hear. You stay put until

Uncle Brix or I, or the Reverend or the sheriff, or some grown up person you know by name, tells you otherwise."

The girl trembled but obeyed. With the children safely hidden and the quilt pulled low, Minda returned to the parted curtains and watched in continued disbelief.

How long would the old lock hold?

Hot blood raced from her feet to her head. Her husband had taught her shooting but no strategy. And he was still out in the field.

Unless… She chased that tragic thought from her mind. Ahab Perkins had not widowed her. Neither Brixton nor God would have allowed that. Her fright gave way to ire. The nerve. Taking what wasn't theirs. Taking what a man had worked hard for and what innocent children had tended like kin.

After the fear of losing Neddie, nothing frightened her any longer. She reached underneath her skirts and stepped onto the back porch. "Halt, thieves!" she shouted in a firm voice.

The outlaws ignored her, so she aimed low, and fired, holding herself tight against the recoil. The bullet shrieked in her ears. "I said halt, thieves."

Two hats tipped insolently, so she yelled again. "I said halt, and get off this property." She sighted and fired again. The animals inside screamed.

"Minda!"

At her husband's shout, relief laved her like warm spring rainwater. From the far side of the barn, he came up on the thieves, his gun drawn. She'd never been so glad to see him, not even when she thought him to be Norman Dale.

"Get in the house," he ordered.

"No." She and Brix fired at the same time.

One outlaw crumpled, but the other shot back.

Minda fired the gun again, just as her husband slumped to the ground.

"Brixton!" She fired again, but the second man was too far away. Her bullet danced in the dust. As she ran toward her husband, the outlaw dashed across the yard to the waiting horses, jumped atop one effortlessly, grabbed the reins of the other, and disappeared into the trees.

Falling to her knees, she placed her ear on Brix's chest. His heart beat firm, and his hand came to rest on her hair.

****

"Brixton, Brixton, are you all right?" She knelt before him in the dust, and he pulled her close, her loose hair soft as sunshine on his face.

But pain sliced through his outer thigh, and blood flowed free. He'd been gored worse by a feisty longhorn, and more than once, but the motion now put a gasp in his throat that stopped any possibility of a kiss.

She raised her head right away, likely not wanting to cause him more injury. Damn, he'd like to die wrapped up in her hair at the tail end of his life.

"Are you all right?" She breathed, close by.

"Yep, think so, Miz Haynes. Leastways I'm not dead." He wanted to let her know he'd be all right and confess he'd wanted a stolen kiss, but he started fuming deep down. "What the hell are you doing outside? I was sneaking up just fine. Your job's to tend the kids."

"They're safe. Let me help you up." She started to rise, keeping her arms under him to bring him along with her. "Just what did you expect me to do? You yourself taught me to shoot and ordered me to keep my gun handy."

Brix groaned and sat up. Across the yard, the outlaw wiggled and whimpered, grabbing at a shot-up knee.

"You didn't kill a man, but looks like my lesson

worked," he said, low, almost amused, then breathed sharp again at the pain.

She frowned, her face pale as moonlight. Hurting folks never sat well with a woman. "It could just as well have been your bullet."

"What makes you think it isn't?"

She ignored him. "Now let me get you inside. Then I can tie up our intruder."

"He isn't going anywhere, and nobody's coming to get him. The other thug's long gone. That's Perkins's way. His gang doesn't rescue anybody who gets shot or caught."

His leg warred with itself, and he ground his teeth tight as they got to the porch.

"We've got to get you some help. You're losing blood." Her touch was gentle but her voice sharp.

"Lost more than this other times. Chester isn't back yet, anyway. Any doctoring's got to come from you, Miz Haynes."

She pulled a sash from her ugly dress and tied it tight around the shredded, bloody denim on his thigh. "I, you need to know, Mr. Haynes. I have never dug out a bullet before."

"Won't have to. Flesh wound. A graze," he muttered.

A powerful groan rattled the night air, but it didn't come from Brix. He knew well how to hold in the hollers and was doing so right now. The outlaw had gotten to his feet, balancing on one of them and not getting far at all.

Minda looked down the road. "Land sakes, he's running away."

"He's not running anywhere. Saw Monty and Clem along their north forty. They heard the shots. They'll be here any second and get him to the sheriff."

Brix leaned hard against her. His stomach churned like butter, but something tasty on the stove did tempt it a bit, and that rose perfume of hers dulled every sense except the one between his legs. Outside the bedroom, he heard Katie and Ned, full of tears and hope both. Minda comforted them with the right words.

"Let's get you to bed," she said.

"Might mess up that fine new tick."

"Here's an old blanket and plenty of towels. Now, unless you want me to undress you, Mr. Haynes, get those clothes off. I'll be right back."

Shucking off his duds, he fought off waves of pain, feeling something like pride at her strength. He lay down.

A deep sleep would feel mighty good after this day. Those roses came into the room before his wife did, bearing her sewing basket in one hand and a bottle in the other.

"Here's some rotgut against the pain." She settled a flock of pillows under his head and shoulders and handed him the blackstrap whiskey. He took a healthy swig. "I've got some willow bark tea brewing."

She leaned down to check his wound, and those pansy eyes closed for half a second, like they'd done the first time he'd entered her. Brix had seen worse gunshot, but figured she'd never seen anything like it at all. She pursed her lips with a resolute little nod. His pride gushed at her strength and lack of squeamish frowns.

He drank deeper.

"Let me see just what kind of doctoring I need to do, Mr. Haynes." Her eyes traveled up and down the length of his leg, stopping just shy of the place he was warmest. "Hmm. It appears I have a thorn to cut out, too."

But first she pulled out a needle and thread.

"Put that down for a minute, Miz Haynes," he said, draining the bottle.

“Whatever for?”

“For this,” Brix pulled her face to his. “Your sweet lips intoxicate me better than anything a man can brew.”

“Oh, balderdash, Mr. Haynes,” she muttered, but she relented, her hands reaching inside his shirt and smoothing themselves across his shoulders.

Her lips opened beneath his, then moved below his ear, soft as petals. Sweet breath warmed his sudden shiver.

Then she pulled away, with a whisper. “Really, Mr. Haynes, enough for now. I must get to my task.”

She reached for the needle.

Deep inside, feeling cold and alone at the loss of her warmth, Brixton Haynes knew it wasn’t enough then, and never would be.

Chapter Twelve

Well past dawn the next morning, Minda woke up next to her husband, her head resting on his bare chest and his fingers combed through her hair. Soft with sleep, his eyes opened, and a little smile played on his lips when he recognized her.

She'd dared to kiss those lips goodnight while he slept, and now she blinked shyly at the memory of his taste. His other hand traveled down to her backside, drawing her up closer.

"Miz Haynes?" he drawled, slower than ever. She couldn't determine whether it was the wound or leftover whiskey. "You stay here all night by my side?"

"Yes, all night," she murmured, daring to lay her own arm across him. "You told me the doctoring was up to me."

"Damn, wish I'd woke up more often."

"Well, you seemed more peaceful the longer you slept. How are you feeling?" She decided to indulge in one last cuddle, although it would surely be wiser to get up. Even through her purple dress, his body simmered against her. She'd concluded that sleeping beside him in her nightgown might not be wise.

"A morning kiss would make things better," he said, low.

"Now, Mr. Haynes, you're in no condition to leave."

He tussled against the pillow and tossed her a puzzled look. "Don't get your meaning."

"Meaning, Mr. Haynes, you keep saying you'll

kiss me when you go."

Lying back, he breathed deep, his hair black against the linens, and he shifted against her again. "Now there's truth in that statement, Miz Haynes. But good-bye isn't the only kiss I'm going to ever need. Or..." The hand cupping her head moved to her cheek and brought her mouth against his. "...or you either."

His lips parted over hers, and she remembered what he'd taught her that stormy night on his bedroll. Opening slightly herself, she drew the tip of his tongue inside her mouth, reminding them both of their acts of love. As her body quivered, he reached gently for the buttons of her bodice.

"God almighty," he murmured, "this sure is a good way to wake up."

His manhood quickened against her skirts, and despite the layers of fabric, she knew its heat, length, and breadth. Against her inexpressibles, a wetness flowed.

But as quickly as a lightning strike, she sat up, remembering the hopeless feeling of him pushing her away at the river. "You're the one who sleeps outside, Mr. Haynes."

Against her movements, he winced and masked it with a yawn.

"Notice you're back to using my formal name again." Then he pulled her down once more.

Before their lips met again, she moved back, and his hand dropped to her knee, giving it a squeeze that was gentle and firm. She almost called out in joy, but only said, "As I recall, it was a custom you began."

"So I did." He sighed and moved his hand up her thigh with the same enticing pressure. "You did real good yesterday, Miz Haynes."

Her skin tingled under layers of crinoline, and her breath puffed in short gasps. "But I wasn't sure what to do at all," she said, emotion pouring from her like warm honey. "I was so relieved to hear your voice."

"But you didn't listen," he mumbled, hand still strong and busy. She placed her fingers atop his, cheeks warming at her boldness.

"And you shot him…"

"Fact is, Miz Haynes—" Brixton interrupted the mist of desire. "That bullet was yours."

"What?" Shock exploded against her yearning. "How can you know?"

"I aim to kill," he said in a flat voice. "Better a bullet through the heart than a slow, strangling noose."

"Merciful heaven." Distressed, she moved her hand to his forehead, fever mild under her touch. But she let her fingers linger along the heated flesh, treating herself to the feel of him.

"Yep, Miz Haynes. Horse thieving's a hanging offense in these parts. But I'm right proud of you." His voice slowed. "The kids'll be in good hands once I leave."

At the reminder, she pulled her hand away. He'd never spoken anything differently, but the hurt continued to pound every time he mentioned it. She didn't care about the pride he had for her. She wanted his love.

She strode to the doorway, needing to leave the room before she felt even more bereft or confessed something stupid. "I think I'll go heat up some of that willow bark tea and prepare you a soft-cooked egg."

"Good idea."

"Oh, Mr. Haynes, I'll be heading into town today to retrieve Priscilla and get some things I need." She'd decided to wangle some goods for a new bonnet for herself after all, and to consult with Gracey about possible designs.

"No you don't. Perkins's gang might still be out and about.

Minda looked at him, perplexed. "But you said they never rescue a man who gets left behind."

"They're changing their tactics all over the place. Won't let you take a chance. You keep a gun underneath the bed last night like I told you?"

"Yes, I did." Even though she'd watched Monty and Clem truss up the criminal and cart him to the jailhouse in town, her fear would not be gone for a long time. It prickled now. Maybe Brixton was right. Even though the thief's partner had ridden off, she didn't know how far. The weapon close by made her feel a little better.

"Fact is, it wouldn't be a bad idea to keep a gun on you all the time," he said.

"Every single day?" Minda's brow furrowed.

Brixton tried to sit upright, his breath full of tiny groans and gasps. "Yep. Every day. Later on it could be something simple. Like scaring off a 'coon in the henhouse. Or something complicated like an outlaw. Me, I always keep my Bowie knife in my boot. Now, I'm going with you."

He bit out the words, and she wondered, not for the first time, how a sick man could still look so handsome.

"You most certainly are not. Have some sense, Mr. Haynes. You need your rest. And I need some chicken stock to make you a nourishing broth. Bandages, of course, and an unguent to relieve your wounds." She swallowed against her nerves. "I simply must visit the mercantile."

"No, you do not," he said, snorting. "Get some white oak leaves or skunk cabbage and make a poultice, that's what. Rip up a pillow case. And Ned's got a henhouse full of chickens. Fry us up one for supper. You got no needs at that mercantile."

"Oh, I understand. You and Caldwell are still

behaving like schoolboys. Well, I…" She looked away. She couldn't confess she'd never butchered or dressed a chicken. Her hard-nosed husband would think her a ninny. Gleesburg had a fine meat shop. Many times she'd traded a hat for a rib roast and capons and home-smoked bacon.

As he nodded, a knowing smile wrestled with his moustache. "Reckon I got you figured out, Miz Haynes. You haven't ever wrung a neck or plucked a feather, now, have you?"

"No."

He laughed deep at first, but shuddered in sudden pain. "Well, get Neddie to show you."

If he weren't hurt, a cup of spilled water over his head would have cooled her aggravation. "Nothing you can say will keep me from town."

"Hackett isn't the reason I want to go with you. Well, not the entire one anyways." His eyes flashed some honesty just then, and she wished again to touch him, to reassure him Caldwell meant nothing to her. "Need to consult with Bob Pelton. Likely some kind of reward out for that fella you nicked."

Hmm. A reward sounded like a fine piece of unexpected fortune for her nerves and his pain, particularly with supplies to buy. "Well, if that's the case, it's certainly something I can do all by myself."

"But more important, if you're collecting Silly, I'd like to be there, too. Don't seem right around here without her."

His tender declaration lightened her heart, and she almost relented, but it throbbed heavy the next second. Why didn't his lonely cattle trails seem wrong without her?

Her husband's face split with a saucy smile. "How many stitches did you notch me up with, Miz Haynes?"

"Twenty-two," Minda said firmly, then smiled. "I figured if I didn't count diligently, I'd empty my stomach all over you."

Under the covers, he grimaced and moved, grunting like he shouldn't have changed position. "You doctor up your sisters like that back home?"

"No need, thank the Lord. But once I helped the surgeon in our town stitch shut the haunch of our poor dog. She'd been struck by a cartwheel. That long slash sideways along your thigh seemed somewhat similar. By the way," she said with confidence, "our pup lived a long, happy life without a limp."

Brix's eyes shone bright with something that wasn't fever. It was something she easily recognized and would force herself to resist. "I will never go limp on you, Minda."

It was her first name, an invitation. They were alone and they had the time. His loving her body would be a dream come true.

If he weren't leaving her.

"I'll get some warm water for your bath, Mr. Haynes. Then it will be time for breakfast."

****

Brix exhaled with regret. He understood her looks and her touch. She might be inexperienced, but she wanted him as much as he wanted her. Sometimes a man's wounds brought a nurturing woman to her knees

It would be wrong to take advantage. Likely it was a good thing he hadn't known she spent last night next to him.

Minutes later, she returned with the washtub, towels folded over her arm, a prodigious apron hiding her bosom. "Kids still asleep?" he asked.

She nodded, looking at the hill his toes made under the covers. If she'd glance higher, she'd notice his manhood tall with life just from the swaying of her backside when she walked.

Damn, at least the kids would be a diversion.

He'd felt their hugs last night through his haze of pain. Recalling their sweet tears started his heart pumping in a way that was entirely new.

Recalling Minda's morning kiss started a throbbing all over.

She looked away from his eyes, but her face was still that pretty pink from moments ago. He remembered her shyness in the lantern light, that night on his bedroll when he'd made her his own.

Damn. That night had started a hunger he wouldn't be around to satisfy.

"Mr. Haynes," she said, with a deeper blush than before, "last night I had to cut away the right leg of your drawers. So I've brought you a pair that is fresh and intact."

Damn, how he wanted her help getting naked, and how he couldn't allow it.

"Don't need a bath." He grumbled to hide his need.

"Of course you do. Cleanliness is part of godliness."

"Don't have any godliness in me. You know that most of all, Miz Haynes."

She sighed nice and loud. The apron tugged here and there, and while he couldn't see the shape of her breasts, it didn't matter. He knew. He'd seen. He'd tasted.

"Please, Mr. Haynes, don't be an infant. Get out of those garments, and let's get a start." She gave him a good long glare, dark as gloom like she just might be reading his thoughts. "I do have other things to do today."

"No woman's going to get to wash me. Been tussying myself for years." He pulled at the bedsheet in protection.

"Well, not today. And I'm not just a woman. I'm your wife. Now get on with it. I tended your wounds last night, but miasma from the river has likely already corrupted the rest of you. You need to be clean."

"Well, you got it right there, Miz Haynes. You aren't just a woman. You're my woman." His erection squirmed just at the words, and he scorned his poor self control.

Damn, she'd slept next to him all night. How could he not have known?

Her tongue clucked, and she shook her head, both signs of disgust, he knew, and that helped tamp his desire. Then he returned to using his brain, not his body, and considered her words. He reckoned mud had seeped up into his foot due to that thorn, and that likely wasn't a good thing. Then he shuddered at a blurry nightmare. His wife had dug that barb out with a knitting needle!

But nothing mattered now, other than her hands. She moved over him fragrant as flowers and soft as a song he'd once heard, and he near burst with need.

"Then I'll have to cut away some more." She clattered some scissors in his ear. But there was something maidenly about her. She didn't strip him bare.

Damn.

His manly member that she'd once touched stayed hidden beneath a scrap of wool with four buttons and a tie-string. Yet his mind pounded with recollection of her hand closing around it, bringing it to urgent life. He recalled his resolve to teach her how to pleasure him with her mouth without fear and suspicion.

Now that goal could never be achieved.

"This doesn't change anything." He redirected his thoughts and pointed to the bandage on his thigh. As she bent down with a washcloth, she looked at him full-on, making a sound without words that made him want her all the more.

For it reminded him of her moans in the dark. His manhood flamed, and only a blind woman wouldn't see it rising up higher yet. Her latest blush told him she noticed.

He couldn't help a smidge of triumph.

"About me leaving, I mean," he said, meaning it. "This pain isn't much. I could ride a hundred miles without stopping."

The soapy swirls she made with the rag halted on his chest and her hand glided across one nipple. He held his breath, doubting she knew what she did to him, and figuring he'd better complete his wash-up himself like he'd threatened.

That was the safest course of action.

"That might be, Mr. Haynes." Her voice trembled a bit. Maybe she did know, after all. "But you don't need to ride a hundred miles today." Her tone was soft as dawn.

Her soapy hand slid just to the point his drawers lined up with his gut. If she slipped down inside he'd die and go to heaven.

But she didn't.

"Minda, I can finish scrubbing myself." He scowled in frustration.

She stopped at once. "Brixton, I suppose you're right. I'll start breakfast and see to the children."

Damn. Her voice took on that sad sound Katie's had, when he told her that her pa had just passed. Minda refreshed the rag, squeezed out the drips, and laid it on his chest. She left before he could take her soft, warm hand. It was best that she had, of course. He'd be hale soon and then he could leave.

At least she'd used his Christian name.

****

"Uncle Brix," little Ned asked after supper two evenings later, "those outlaws aren't out there anymore, are they?"

Avoiding Brixton's eyes, Minda looked up from

her stitching at the anxious little boy.

Despite Minda's insistence that dreadful evening, both children had initially thought their uncle would die. Katie had sprung back to her usual enthusiasm, but Ned hadn't yet returned to the cheerful child he'd been before the picnic at the river

"Course not," Brixton said from his X-shaped chair, his wounded leg slung straight out. He didn't look at Minda, either. "One rode off, and the other's already in a prison in Missouri by now. Far away."

"But how can you know for sure?"

Brixton's eyebrows rose, and anxiety crawled down Minda's back on scratchy little feet. Brixton got up carefully and moved over to Ned to rub his head in one of those touching gestures Minda would remember forever.

Even with his injury, Brixton moved with grace and song, another memory Minda would treasure, but she knew he was restless to be out and about. Clem and Monty and other nearby farmers had generously offered to finish the wheat and tend the livestock so he could recover without worry. Her heart swelled at the loving generosity of her new neighbors.

Minda had never had to go to town. Each day, kindly folks from far and wide brought provisions and desserts when they stopped by with greetings and congratulations. Doc Viessman had come home, his house call full of approval at her technique and satisfaction with Brixton's progress.

With much noise and celebration, saloonkeeper Hank Clark had sent along several bottles of celebratory whiskey, and Geraldine Hackett had arrived in style, wearing Minda's Huntley bonnet. Unable to resist purchasing it for herself, she'd promptly paid Minda her share of the transaction, and eagerly invited more business.

Needing materials for her own new hat, as well

as a remnant of brown wool, Minda traded the pert little cap of brown lace and feathers she'd worn only once. A delivery boy had gotten the supplies to her before day's end. With her good-bye, Geraldine had assured Minda, with bright knowing eyes, her son Caldwell would be back in time for the Bonnet Race.

Stitching a real toy dog with button eyes had kept Minda up late each night and her mind too busy to consider complications. And had allowed Brixton go to bed alone. Even the doctor had insisted her husband needed a proper place to sleep.

She had read apology and reluctance in his eyes, and he never turned toward her during the night. Never exchanging her day dress for her nightdress, she couldn't continue to give her heart to a man who didn't want to remain at her side.

Ned clutched his new toy dog tightly. Her heart wrenched looking at the troubled child. She wasn't the only person Brixton was abandoning.

"Look here, Ned. Got a new whistle done for you," Brixton said in a soft voice that made her eyes moist. "Now let's go check that heifer of yours. Might be time for a song. Almost time for bed, anyway."

"Don't like the barn," Ned said, pouting. "Too dark."

That didn't sound encouraging at all. Until lately, Ned had used any excuse he could invent to spend time with the heifer. The fair was four days away. Brixton's leg was healing mighty fast. Heart sinking, Minda realized he might not even be around then.

"Now, Neddie." She tried to keep her voice light. "You know she needs plenty of tender care to ready her for the fair. I'm making a nice red bow for her to wear."

Suddenly, he was all smiles. "I know that. I'll brush her tomorrow. But Uncle Brix, our heifer will get dirty and tired on the way to the fair."

"Well, that's the way of it, Ned." Brixton tousled the boy's hair with what Minda knew was real affection. She shook her head slightly at the sight. It still stunned her that he'd leave the children.

After all, men left wives all the time.

"We'll walk her to town real slow," Brixton said. "You and Katie can brush her clean and add that bow when you all get there."

Well, that sounded like he'd still be here.

"Uncle Brix," Ned said, eyes wide, "she'll be tired."

"Now, Neddie, Nathan at the livery's got good stalls and pens set up. She'll be plenty rested before you lead her to the judging. You pick a name yet?"

Katie and Ned shook their heads. "Not yet," Katie said, "but we'll come up with something in time. Something real special. Uncle Brix?"

"Yep?"

"You're riding in the Bonnet Race on Monday, aren't you? Strawberry's good and fast"

Heart pounding, Minda listened, expecting a firm no. It wasn't a question she had felt confident enough to ask her husband. Her bonnet would be ready in plenty of time. If he explained to the children he'd be gone already, she'd simply wear her new hat to church on Sunday. Unless...

Well, Caldwell intended to race. His mother had made that perfectly clear.

"No, Firefly, I just can't. Nothing but foolishness."

Katie cried out, "But Uncle Brix, that's not so. It's a grand race. You're the best rider there is. And Mama is building a beautiful new hat just for the race."

Brixton's brows rose over his dark eyes, but she wasn't sure if it was a response to the proclamation of her new hat or to Katie's name for her.

His eyes narrowed at her. "Thought you were

making that new hat for Geraldine to sell at the mercantile."

Minda shrugged, feeling ornery. He might want to leave her. She hadn't been in his life much over a week. But the children were his own blood and bone. "Perhaps you thought wrong. I believe I may display my hat whether you race or not. After all—" She lowered her eyelids demurely. "I just might have a secret admirer."

When he tensed in quick displeasure, Minda realized he still considered Caldwell Hackett a threat.

"And Uncle Brix, I entered your name." Katie's eyes, troubled, anxiously beseeched both Minda and her uncle.

"How? You haven't been to town."

Katie raised her little nose. "When the reverend was here yesterday, I put your name on a paper and told him to put it in the box."

Brixton groaned, and Minda glared at him with unspoken questions. What could it hurt to grant a little pleasure into the child's life, which had been fraught for months with grief and worry?

Brixton wasn't heartless. Minda knew that.

"And your leg's better. You said yourself," Ned said with his normal bright smile.

"And today you climbed all those stairs up to the loft," Katie persisted.

Minda hid a smile.

He wasn't weak, either. How better to prove to the townsfolk that not even an outlaw could keep him down?

Breath puffed hard from his nostrils, as Brixton apparently pondered his decision. "Well, I guess I can't disappoint you, Firefly."

The children whooped and cheered.

Then Brixton's voice turned somber and mournful. "But you kids know, don't you, that I'll be leaving soon after?"

"G.T.T.?" Katie asked sadly. Minda hadn't the faintest idea what the initials meant, but she hated his words anyway.

Brix squatted in front of the children, his face tightening, and put separate hands on their shoulders as if to draw them close. "Yep. Going To Texas. But you know that's where I live and what I do, don't you? Told you time and time again."

"No. No," Neddie said. "I told you I needed a brother."

"And we got a mama, but we need another papa." Katie said, awash in sudden tears.

Brixton raised bleak eyes to Minda, but she shook her head, feeling both anger and pain.

Neddie had told Brixton he needed a brother? Now Brixton had more reasons than ever to leave. He'd never chance putting an unwanted wife in the family way.

"Let's get you readied up for bed," Brix said.

Minda's heart cracked a little more. After tucking in the children, he grabbed a bottle of whiskey and his bedroll.

"'Night, Miz Haynes." With a polite nod, he went outside.

She hardly had the strength to swallow, but she wouldn't cry. Not one single tear.

Chapter Thirteen

Minda smiled ruefully at her hand. Poison ivy. The blisters were healing nicely and the itching had stopped. Brixton's remedy, buttermilk rubbed on the rash, had worked wonders these past few days since Ned's escapade along the river. But she wouldn't be able to wear her Sunday gloves.

No matter. The little girls' new bonnets were finished, and if she did say so herself, the hats would do her proud. Showing them off at church might mean she was greedy and irreverent, but after all, she did have a new venture to promote.

She might even expand the possibilities. Even her hard-nosed husband had exclaimed over the new toy dog she'd stitched and stuffed for Ned.

Every evening, Brixton had teased her about the quality of her stitchery, his eyes sending messages she couldn't quite read. Then he went outside to sleep. Friday night's rain had sent him inside the barn.

At least he hadn't fallen back to calling her *Miz Haynes* every chance he had. Still, her hopelessness was complete, and the sleeping arrangement insulting. After all, they'd spent nights together during the worst of his infirmity and managed restraint.

Hearing Katie's giggle, she looked toward the barn. Brixton, wreathed in laughter, helped the children hitch the horses to the wagon. They might get their clothes dusty, but that sweet tableau would stay framed in her mind for a long time.

Minda's heart started another crack.

Brixton's reasons for staying on no longer existed. With her outlaw extradited to Missouri and the rest of the gang seen in Wyoming, he'd be leaving soon. The children were safe and healthy now, the wheat harvest in, his leg sore but healing well.

"Come along now," Brixton said, so striking in Norman Dale's second-best, ill-fitting suit he took her breath away. His eyes brightened when he saw her, and her heart tumbled down her chest like it had the day he met her stagecoach. "The girls sure look pretty enough in those new bonnets. And you, why..."

His thorough glance from her toes to her eyes filled Minda with a new kind of ache. His chest rose and fell.

Her go-to-meeting green velvet jacket-bodice had long been out of fashion, but she'd restored an old beehive-shaped straw bonnet of her mama's with silk ivy and brown veiling.

"You look lovely, Miz Haynes," he said, finally. She was certain he meant every word, but her emptiness grew even at the compliment. Miz Haynes again.

She grumbled and climbed into the wagon by herself while the children scrambled happily in the back, Katie in awe of her hat and the *two* braids Brixton had made time for today. But Minda's mood improved. Although the morning was steaming hot, she started to feel alive and well. Along the road, they passed other wagons and buggies full of folks who had helped so much these past days, bringing food and cheer. She waved and called out to her friends and neighbors.

It would have been a fine day in Paradise, but for Brixton's constant threats to leave.

At least they had tomorrow. He'd promised to

get the heifer to town, and to win the race.

Her heart thrummed, and she wondered if he'd give her a public kiss for all the town to witness if he won. Plain and simple, she wanted to touch the man she loved. Bathing him that day had tantalized her into desiring more. Her face warmed as she recalled his hot flesh nearly igniting under her fingertips.

Land sakes, what thoughts to have on the Lord's Day.

Paradise was already decked out in bunting and streamers for tomorrow's fair. Channeling her runaway emotions, Minda caught a touch of the gala spirit. As Brixton braked at the pretty white church, women gushed over the bonnets, and Geraldine Hackett, resplendent in her own new hat, led the excitement.

"Why, Minda, those girls of yours look glorious. Are those your own stunning creations?"

"Yes, Geraldine, and thank you." Minda laid her cheek against Priscilla's, feeling Brixton's eyes on her. "It was a joy to make them."

Marylaura Gerstenschlag from two places over ordered a Huntley on the spot. But Minda trusted her instincts when the doctor's wife requested the same. "Elizabeth, I envision something soft-crowned, gray velvet to match your eyes perhaps, sashed under your chin with wine-dark satin."

"Well then, so it is," Elizabeth Viessman said. "I'll wear it to our new granddaughter's christening."

Gracey's hat, with its bright blue satin tie and wide brim trimmed with silk cornflowers, stole every female heart in the congregation.

Brixton guffawed. "You'll have plenty of time to gab tomorrow at the race. The reverend's inside there chomping at the bit to start his oration." He took Priscilla in his right arm and gave Minda his left.

She felt his pulse even through the thick wool.

With her husband next to her, Minda had a hard time relaxing. The elation she'd felt outside had vanished. This was the sanctuary in which they had been wed. She knew that he cared about the children, but did he still regret that day?

Next to her, sitting close as proper, Brixton started a hymn in his beautiful, low, soothing voice.

Why did the comfort of dumb beasts on a lonely trail mean more to him than the children?

Her heart burned with sadness. Why did it mean more to him than she did?

There was no sense going back to Gleesburg with a failed marriage at her feet. At least here in Paradise, she had a means to earn money and a town full of people who appreciated and accepted her. Her payback wouldn't last forever. In fact, she could likely reimburse Brixton with hat-making cash soon.

But what about the children?

She hardly paid any attention at all to Jake's sermon. While she knew in her heart she loved Brixton and cared for the children, she had doubts of her stamina to raise another family all by herself.

With some money of her own, she could start over.

"What bee's in that bonnet of yours?" Brixton said after the benediction, leading her outside. "Church's supposed to ease your spirits. You're pouting like Silly."

Even if she recited him the epics in her heart, he wouldn't change his mind or the way he felt. But when he reached for her hand to rush her through the other worshippers, his touch shocked her like a lightning bolt.

She was saved from answering.

"How's that leg?" Gracey's brother, Nathan, who ran the livery, asked.

"Not bad at all." Brixton grinned, nodding at her

with a pride that almost eased those spirits he'd mentioned. "I had some mighty fine doctoring."

Chester Viessman laughed loud and agreed. "Those stitches his missus laid on him could hold up a bridge."

"Gonna race tomorrow?" Nathan asked.

"Wouldn't miss it for the world," Caldwell Hackett said, pushing through the crowd. His arms were full of materials for the children's lesson he taught after church, but he wore riding clothes. "I made another practice run from Shell Creek at sunup this morning."

Caldwell didn't say another word, but his face and mannerisms bespoke bragging rights.

"Go on, kids," Brixton said, like he hadn't heard, "you get to your Bible story. We'll wait on you over coffee at Miss Lila Jean's." He straightened taller than ever, even with Priscilla in his arms. "Oh, Hackett? Just so you know. *I* intend to win."

He grabbed Minda's hand hard and started down the street. His soft grunts indicated he was straining his wound. In truth, his injury had prevented him from any heavy exertion all week. Certainly, he must believe Caldwell had the advantage.

Her heart and feet stumbled at the same time. Caldwell wouldn't win. He couldn't.

Before they reached the boardinghouse dining room, Sheriff Pelton and his young wife stopped them. Minda's trained eye instantly framed Lisa Pelton's face in a small flared brim of copper gossamer satin swept with an orange plume to match her red hair. The vision lightened her mood for a moment.

"'Morning, Brixton. And Miz Haynes, my apologies for transacting business on the Lord's day. This here—" He handed her one envelope. "—came by messenger from Columbus last night. Your reward money for the capture of Brentwood Peavy."

Minda peeked inside. Fifty dollars. All her own.

****

Later that afternoon, Brix put the horses out to pasture and mucked the stalls, bemoaning the waste of good manure. He considered hanging on for a few days to start up Ida Lou's old kitchen garden. His brother sure hadn't had the time.

Likely a Gleesburg hat-maker didn't know she could have fresh kale and cabbage through the winter. Now that she had that reward money to tide them over, he might not have to hurry.

He all but smacked his mouth at such an inkling. That money was hers and hers alone. He'd get out of here Tuesday, if his leg allowed, and head for the livelihood he knew how to make, the life he knew.

The life he missed.

She caught his eye at the rose garden, trimming dead heads as well as she could with Silly toddling about. Damn, she was good with the kids. Truth was, if he'd ever wanted a wife on his own, she might be the one. She'd spoiled him for other women from here on.

Silly—*Priscilla*—prated something and Minda bent down, picking her up and resting her on a hip just like Brix had seen Gracey do with Jake's babies. Ned came over to yank at her skirts, and Katie, hands tugging her braids, gave Minda some kind of childish request. Damn, Minda wasn't just patient and beautiful, she was a natural. He remembered Katie calling her Mama, and how right it sounded.

As his little family walked back to the house, he wished he had a daguerreotype machine to capture the moment. Then he could look at it all he wanted on the trail.

A new inkling struck him, and it was powerful and true. Minda had that money now. She could pay back what she owed in a heartbeat and leave them all. His heart stopped. Back inside the barn, he struck the hay bale with a vengeance as he strewed it about Strawberry's stall. Hell and damnation both.

Even with the healthy barn odors, he caught the smell of roses. She was smiling behind him, still in the green thing she'd worn to church.

"Brixton, I can help you do that. Remember, I used to work in the mayor's stables."

"Yep, the one who taught you to ride as well as a man."

"I just don't want you to burst your stitches. You should take truly a day of rest." Her smile was shy.

"That sure was nice of Jake's ma to treat us all to Sunday fixins," he said, ignoring her. A day of rest was no such thing. Minda smiled bigger yet. He knew she'd enjoyed a meal she hadn't had to cook. It was Miz Lila Jean's way of saying thank you for getting the outlaws out of town.

"I enjoyed it so. I'm planning something light for supper. But Brixton, I'm worried about Ned. He is still frightened, and he's been having nightmares."

"I expect that's natural, for a time. He saw those outlaws close up, then heard the gunfire in his own yard. And me taking a bullet..."

"Well, last night was better." Her eyes accused now because he hadn't been inside. "But the Bible story today was the Good Samaritan. And all he talks about is someone nearly dead lying by the road."

Brix sighed. "Guess we could talk to Doc Viessman, but I'm thinking Ned'll outgrow it soon enough."

"Just how soon is soon enough, Brixton?"

The smile was gone. She looked serious.

"What do you mean, Minda?"

"I think you already know."

He did. He knew what was coming. She was paying him back with her reward money and leaving them all. "That reward money…"

"Exactly. It makes no sense for you to leave now. That money will get us through for quite a while."

"That reward money is yours, Miz Haynes. Money I earn is ours."

"Nonsense. I earned it protecting this family." There was pain in her eyes. He'd seen it often lately, when he unrolled his bed outside, whenever he talked about going. "Brixton, I have things to sort out myself. I'm not running out on the children just because I have a windfall. But you have an obligation to them, too. Much more than I do. They're your kin."

He turned away roughly. "I'm supporting them the only way I know."

For a long, painful moment, they turned away from each other. Finally, she spoke. "Brixton, I actually came out here for another reason."

He looked at her.

"Could you teach me how to milk Mabel? Katie said it's almost that time of day."

"She's doing good at it."

"I know, but I'd rather her have a good night's sleep than wake up early to do it. School's starting soon. She can do the second round with her other afternoon chores."

"I milked cows myself before I went to school," Brix said. "Besides, you're all dressed up."

"I can change quickly. Just let me know if you can find the time."

"Go change then, and we'll get it done now."

"All right. I'll be back in five minutes."

Muttering curses nobody could hear, he got grain for Mabel and a T-shaped stool. But at least he'd have a good reason to touch Minda and sit close behind her, his thighs wrapped around her backside.

The thought stirred him.

She came back in the purple dress he liked, not that ugly old brown thing. Come to think of it, he'd bled all over that one. Hopefully she'd burnt it up.

"Mercy, Mabel's so big, close up." Minda looked downright skittish, something he hadn't seen even when she'd sewn him up.

Without thinking it through first, he laid his hands on her shoulders to relax her, kneading her flesh and liking it more than he should. "You'll do fine." The words stuck funny, back of his tongue. "She's gentle as a lamb. You like cows?"

"What? I like animals fine."

"Well, Mabel's going to know if you don't like her. You can't get nervous, neither. She'll know. Now, start brushing her. Rub her back. Get her to feel comfortable with you."

With a nod, Minda followed his directions, fast and sure, like she had with the Peacemaker. He couldn't help thinking of those hands in his hair on that magic night, or hell, that morning she'd bathed him.

Changing his thoughts was a must. An erection started to come to life.

"Now, you sit here and rest your head on the flank," he said, wanting her head to lie no place else but his side.

He balanced her on the stool at a right angle to Mabel, and squatted on his haunch right behind Minda to catch her if she stumbled. The stool had only one leg. "Now, rub your right knee there, too." He propped her knee against Mabel's stomach and brought the wash pail close. Touching her brought a whole new battle between his legs, making the painful strain upon his stitches nothing at all.

"Wash with this soap and rag. Get your fingers rubbing in a circle, way at the top." He took her hand to guide the massaging of the teat, and folding her soft hand around waiting flesh made him swallow a groan. He pictured that morning bath with her fingers on his nipples.

By now, his arousal raged, and he figured she could feel it against her back. Hoped she did, truth to tell.

“Dry her now.” His voice was harsher than he intended. “And you ought to sing to her, something gentle. Or talk in a low tone.”

“You’re the one who knows cow songs.” Minda chuckled, soft and low, like that night on his bedroll, the night he dreamed about every time he stretched out on the filthy thing.

“All right.” Anything to keep his mind off her closeness. “I’ll sing, and you learn along. Now, I like to treat her like she’s the most important lady I know. Take it in your palm…”

He gently showed her how to squeeze the top of the teat. “Thumb. Pointer finger here. Then squeeze each finger one at a time until all your fingers are wrapped around.”

Her hand closing around long, pink flesh caused an image to burst into his mind that he’d die to repeat, and his cock flamed. Never before had the everyday motions of milking a cow reminded him he was a man.

And she was a woman.

The milk streamed into the bucket.

“Now release. And do it again ’til it’s empty and soft.”

Barely breathing, he started to sing the lullaby that Neddie-boy liked so much. The sweet melody reminded him of stars going blue on the night she’d spent in his arms, with him deep inside her.

Just then, she lost her balance and teetered back into his arms. Irked, Mabel kicked over her bucket.

“Oh, land sakes, Brixton,” she said, but his arms

closed about her to keep her from the white puddle.

With a quick maneuver, he turned her to face him, and brought her soft body down upon him in the clean straw.

He held his lids open as long as he dared while his lips claimed hers, for he wanted to see her own eyes widen before those butterfly-wing lashes closed on her cheek.

For a perfect, sweet moment, she drank from him, and he reached gently for the beautiful buds inside her bodice, but she climbed to her feet quick as a cat.

"Oh, Brixton, I...I've made a righteous mess here. And the children need fresh milk for supper. Will Mabel let down some more?" The flower petal eyes didn't look at him at all now.

"Yep, but she'll wait a while. She's got grain to keep her happy."

Then her eyes met his, wide and bold.

****

Still trembling from his touch, Minda rejoiced. She didn't see regret in his eyes and refused to show him any in return. True, it wasn't the life she had come for. But maybe it was the life she was called to live.

Her heart thundered as hard as it ever had. She'd made bold decisions before. She'd left family and friends for an unknown man and undiscovered territory. She'd stood up to outlaws, and stitched up a gruesome wound with only a vague notion of what to do.

And she'd watched her husband take a bullet. She could have lost him at that moment. She'd been given another chance, and it was a chance she had to take.

Smiling shyly, she unbuttoned her dress and started on the ribbons of her chemise. The barn was dark, but it was still daylight, and a blush warmed her cheeks.

"What are you doing?" Brixton asked, eyes half-lidded, but letting her know he was aware of her intent. He'd raised himself up on his elbows, his shirt half-open, calling attention to his sun-bronzed chest and black hair.

"Getting ready."

"Ready for what?" His hot dark eyes told her he knew. The words came through his mouth, tip of his tongue peeking between his lips, and she kept from kissing him for another coy second.

"For you."

"The next time should be in a bed."

"You had plenty of chances."

"Minda…the kids…"

"Priscilla's asleep. Katie and Ned are playing with the ball I made for the baby. I just checked."

"Still. At least let's get to Strawberry's stall. Plenty of fresh hay." He got up to bar the door.

But when he came back with a saddle blanket, she read hesitation in his eyes despite the physical proof of his need burgeoning beneath his denims.

"Minda, this isn't a good idea."

"It's a wonderful idea, Brixton." She resolutely spread the blanket. "I'm your wife. You've said it yourself."

"Won't change a thing," he said, although his hands further untied her ribbons. "I'm still leaving."

"Then we can make the best of the time we've got left."

Dropping his fingers, he shook his head. "No. I'm not up to it."

"Oh, I think you are." She smiled, laying her hand on the lump beneath his trousers. Her boldness shocked her, but the woman who had shot a man to protect a husband and home she hadn't had a week wasn't a fainthearted ninny after all.

A low, guttural moan rumbled from her

husband's perfectly-sculpted chest. She helped him slide out of his shirt, and they lay down. Minda leaned toward him, placing her fingertips lightly across his copper-coin nipples. She'd noticed during his bath that he liked her touching him there. It had surprised her somewhat. But remembering her newfound bravery, and how much his lips on her breasts tantalized her, she placed her mouth and tongue on his nipple.

"Oh God." Brixton's whole body tensed. "Oh, Minda." Sounds seethed between his teeth. "I think I died and am now in heaven."

She moved to his mouth, silencing him with her lips and tongue in ways he had taught her. He tasted only of manly health in spite of his pain and injury, and she wanted more, all of him.

She sat up and slipped off the rest of her clothes, feeling the power of her nakedness.

"Ah, heaven indeed." Brixton breathed, taking one breast gently but firmly into his hand, his warm fingers sculpting her flesh to new pleasures. She raised her face, her hair streaming down her back. "Now, you know..." He looked away, almost blushing. "You know, don't you, you'll need to get on top of me? My leg's sore down to my knee."

Heat covered her. She had never considered such a position.

"I'll get you started. You'll figure it out." His laugh came with gentle amusement. "Now, lie here beside me for a time. Then when you're ready..."

She knew what that meant. He touched that special place of hers she'd never heard mentioned in real words, just blushing mumbles after her sisters' honeymoons. That special place that had a life all its own, and music only she could hear, colors only she could see. It wouldn't feel like this with any other man. She knew it in her soul.

For moments that lasted forever, his hands

blessed her, his lips feasting on her breasts as if they gave him life. She moaned, her mouth searching the hard, muscled span of his neck, and she nibbled him.

His strong firm hands guided her to her knees, and she straddled him. A smile of ecstasy lurked under his moustache, and she leaned down to cover his mouth with hers.

As her hand searched for the manhood raging and reaching for her through his open trousers, she lowered to him. His tip nudged her core and as she settled, he slipped inside, deeper than before. Her knees went weak as her thighs tightened around him, and placing her hands firmly over his nipples, she rose and fell upon him. His eyes praised her, his hands fervently cupped the mounds of her breasts. Then he gasped, and her world turned bold colors.

Triumphant music sang in her ears. They shuddered at the same moment, and she collapsed on his chest.

When she could manage words, she spoke.

"Brixton, will you at least miss me a little when you're gone?"

"Minda, I'd miss you even if we'd never met at all."

Chapter Fourteen

Brixton slept in the barn again that night, but with Minda's full permission.

She'd tingled in her bed alone, arms wrapped around her body as she recalled every delicious detail of their magical lovemaking in that most unlikely place.

Determined to keep his heifer comfortable before the fair, Ned had insisted that he and his uncle spend the night in the barn, singing lullabies to her. Minda had given her prompt consent, thinking it a chance for the boy to conquer his demons.

Her husband had behaved tenderly at supper, sitting close like Katie always arranged their settings, and giving her a real good-night kiss in front of the children.

It appeared Minda had taken her chance and won.

Although the mottled looking glass in the bedroom was all she had to go by on Monday morning, Minda considered her new bonnet a masterpiece. It thrilled her even more than her wedding veil.

She'd envisioned a variation on the high-crowned Regency hats of years gone by. Her scissors had seemed to know where to cut the purple wool brilliantine without measurement. She hadn't had to rip out one single stitch.

The spray of velvet violets drooped perfectly over her left ear instead of the old-style feather, and for drama, a ruche of lavender taffeta tickled the back of her neck.

As the final inspiration, the right amount of silver netting left over from Katie's new Sunday hat draped with perfection into a whimsical veil.

She smiled to herself. Yesterday at church had been nothing but triumph with a half-dozen down payments.

Not to mention her reward.

Katie grabbed Minda's hand. "Oh, you look beautiful, Mama. You would win a prize for the best hat."

Minda glanced coquettishly at her reflection through the veil. "Well, that's not the purpose of the Bonnet Race."

"I sure hope Uncle Brix wins the money. Then maybe he'll stay.

Maybe he would. He'd certainly been attentive enough since, well, that moment in the barn.

She touched Katie's cheek. "Firefly, let's think only happy thoughts today." She forced the nightmare of Caldwell Hackett winning the race from her mind. Ned's babbling and Brixton's brisk voice, though normally delightful, prickled her skin. Why were they back? They should be long gone, getting the heifer to town.

Around here, she didn't expect a change of plan to mean anything good.

Brixton smiled sheepish from the doorway, looking at her in a way that made her heart thunder. More than ever she was glad for the gorgeous hat and the purple dress she sensed he liked. For a change of pace, she'd design a different gown in a similar color soon as she could. But right now her everyday gown smelled of sunshine, starched thick as a plank.

"Now, Clem didn't want me to wear myself out before the race," Brixton said. "So Ned's heifer's already on the road to town with him. I hitched

Buttermilk to the wagon. You get the kids to town. I'll be taking Strawberry directly to Shell Creek."

"But..." She wanted to ask if he'd have time to get a practice run in, but he rushed, looking at her square on.

"I'm going to win that race, Minda."

Ned burst into the house, leading something black and white and furry close behind him on a twine. "Clem and Monty gave us a puppy! Uncle Brix told them to. But Mama..." His guileless eyes turned a brighter blue as he looked at Minda. "I will always love my toy dog best of all."

With a hangdog grin, her husband shrugged. In his denim riveted trousers and gray shirt laced at the neck with a leather strand, he looked every inch the cowboy he was. He held his Stetson in his hand, but tipped it at her anyway.

"Farm bitch whelped three months ago," he said. "Last one left. She'll be a herder." The grin left for a second, flashing instead a bleak stare.

Was this a good-bye gift for the children?

Had yesterday had been nothing but his good-bye kiss, and something more? She had started it, to be sure, but he hadn't complained.

A glimpse in the glass revealed a sickly pallor under her lovely hat. She pinched her cheeks. She'd already told Katie not to think unhappy thoughts today. Right now, Neddie's joyful face meant his nightmares might be chased away.

So she smiled. Katie shrieked with excitement and knelt to grapple the dog close.

"Now, the pup's housebroke, Minda. The kids've been yammering for one, and I..."

Minda was strangely touched. "It's a lovely thought, Brixton." At least they'd started to use their christened names. "You have every right to give your niece and nephew a dog."

She wanted to hug him in assurance, but he

turned away. "I should have asked you first. I don't want to cause you more bother, with Mabel now twice a day. But you sure learned that milking quick." His schoolboy smile was back, but the glaze in his eyes was a man's. "I bet you start a dairy of your own outside of a week."

Her face must have colored to match her hat. Her lips parted in remembrance.

His hot, dark eyes lowered to the children. "Now kids, your little girl cow needs a name before the judging."

Ned's good nature returned. "We named her Dicey, Uncle Brix, for Paradise. You always say G.T.T., but we reckon Paradise is better."

Minda almost couldn't bear it, so she checked Priscilla, who was prattling on the big bed with her cloth ball to her mouth. From the corner of her eye, she saw Brixton swallow hard behind his leather tie.

"It's a grand name," was all Brixton said. Ned and Katie tore out of the house with the puppy, and Brixton leaned down to Priscilla who hung on to his neck with a steady steam of *da-da* and *ma-ma.*

Minda's heart twisted when he kissed the baby's hair.

"I'm almost ready," she said.

He stood up and looked at her. "Like I say, I'm going to win that race. No man's going to kiss you but me, Minda." For a long time, his gaze never left her, as though he were memorizing her face. "It might not be the marriage you came for, but I'm the husband you got."

She knew. She'd accepted her call already. He was the one leaving.

"Wish me luck, Minda."

"Why, Brixton, you know I do..." He silenced her with a kiss, quick as a butterfly in flight.

Before she could make a sound, he was gone. Dashing to the window, she watched him ride off, one with the wind and the earth, atop a horse where he belonged.

****

He still tasted the kiss, and that purple hat would live on forever behind his eyelids. But even with Strawberry's high confident gait, Brix couldn't help but feel glum as he headed to Shell Creek for the start of the race.

He shouldn't have made love to her yesterday, for that certainly was what it had been. He'd taken advantage, pure and simple. As for the race, this horse wasn't his. While he could master any piece of horseflesh on earth, it took time. He didn't know Strawberry well, and his wound hadn't allowed for much training. He'd needed to save his strength for today.

Sighing, he looked around him at the cornfields and knolls and stands of trees that separated homesteads. As a kid, he could have got to Shell Creek blindfolded in the dark of midnight in a blizzard, but truth was, he hadn't scoped this land since those long ago days.

Along the road, other riders passed him on horses of varying age and competence, all with a howdy or a hat tip. Jake rode ahead on a mule-hipped broomtail, as foolish in the saddle as Brix would be sermonizing on a Sunday. But his pal's reasons were pure. He was doing it for his Gracey, no matter how humiliating it might be.

Brix's soul darkened. He was doing this only for himself. But he wasn't about to bring shame in the doing. His confidence surged. Do it he would, and win. Minda would have enough triumph of her own. Spying that hat, ladies from miles around would order dozens more. She'd have confidence enough to forget yesterday.

"How do." He cantered up to Jake with a smirk. "You do Gracey proud."

Jake flushed. "I don't know why it means so much to her, but it makes her happy. Her pa always outfits me with the slowest pudding-foot he can find so I can't fall off." He paused, and Brix guessed what was coming next. Jake had not kept it a secret that he admired Minda, and found her a suitable mate for Brix. No doubt he considered this a true sweetheart event.

"Don't you start preaching to me, Jake." Brix held up a warning hand. "I'm running this race for me. Could use the money. And Hackett isn't putting his brand on my wife. Minda won't be fair game after I go."

"What does it matter, if you aren't here?" Jake bobbled atop his horse despite the animal's big, sure feet.

"She's my wife."

"But you don't want her."

Brix gulped, tipped his hat lower. Of course he didn't, at first. And now, well, he admitted he did. He was a man, and a man could get lost in her body and never find his way out. That night in the storm, he'd liked having someone to come home to. But his way was coming home every once in a while. Everybody knew it. Jake, most of all, knew why Brix was leaving.

"A good woman's hard to find," Jake said

"You got lucky, Jake. You always knew Gracey was the one, ever since we were kids." Brix relaxed. Strawberry began to feel comfortable beneath him.

"Yes, I was lucky. Yours didn't happen to be here then. But she's here now." Jake cast him a sideways look, eyebrows raised high.

Brix grunted.

"And you can't possibly find someone as good as she is, traveling the trails the rest of your life. Who are you going to grow old with, a longhorn?" Jake's horse hit a pebble, and he grabbed the horn with both hands.

Brix decided not to mock Jake's lack of skill, but he downright disliked his friend's scolding. He'd planned on growing old with Esperanza, and look how that had turned out. It was better not getting anybody's hopes up, just sending money when he could. Dropping by to see the kids now and then.

"Well then, why not stay close at least? Don't cattle ranches in the Sand Hills need your skills?"

"I need the trail. Besides, folks in Texas know me, know they're getting a square deal. You might as well stop your meddling, Jake." Brix got ready to knee the horse into a gallop. "Been all right up to now. Never wanted family knots. You, best of all, know that."

"But you got them, just the same, no matter how far away you go. Your home's here." Jake leaned forward to grab Brix's arm.

"Norman Dale's home, you mean."

"No, *Minda*. She's your home, just like Gracey's mine. Unless, of course..." Jake paused for effect, just like he did during his orations. "Unless Minda takes that reward money and leaves Paradise."

Brix stiffened and Strawberry's gait quickened. He slowed the horse, waited for Jake to catch up, and shrugged. "Well, it's her money. But she said she won't leave the kids."

Jake shrugged back with that wise look he got when instructing the Commandments. "For now. But later on, you already know folks around here will take them in."

Brix bit his tongue. "Listen, preacherman, I got no time for this. I got a race to win."

Kneeing his horse onward to the starting line, he tried to pay Jake's sermon no heed. The idea had come to him, maybe working in the Sand Hills, but it didn't seem right.

That forty dollar prize. Jake might not know

that fine sum could get a farmer four improved acres.

Or buy a cattleman five healthy beeves, a fair start to a herd.

But Brix knew it. Right now, though, he had to keep his mind on one important thing—getting back to town first.

There was no set course for the race, so long as a man left the starting line at the pistol shot, retrieved the bonnet he'd declared at the start, and ended up at the finish line past the cemetery.

A man could take his horse up through the creek or through a fallow field, in between cornstalks or thickets, or overland on the main road. Brix hadn't had a chance to map his course. But Caldwell Hackett had, and made no secret of his many practice runs.

In case Brix didn't have enough on his mind, his foot and thigh throbbed, reminding him only of weakness.

A weakness he could not cave in to.

At least thirty men, either on horseback or leading their mounts, had gathered at the fence line of the Lewis farm. And damn, Hackett had already lined up, looking spiffy in denims from his ma's stockpile that likely had never been washed.

"Morning, Brix," he called out cheerily, "I've just declared Mrs. Haynes's hat, which is totally within the rules."

Hooves shuffled and men smirked, enjoying the taunt.

Brix shrugged, trying to appear indifferent. "You haven't even seen it."

Caldwell Hackett made a point of checking his spurs and stretching his broad shoulders. "It won't matter. It'll be the most beautiful hat there. Besides," he said, meeting Brix's angry gaze with a downright dare, "my mother described the materials

Mrs. Haynes purchased."

"Men, mount your horses and get to the starting line," Sheriff Pelton yelled. "Drew it myself right over here."

Dust clouded the creekside as the contenders obeyed.

"On your mark. Set." The sheriff's gunshot smacked the prairie wind.

Brix took off, realizing Strawberry knew the terrain better than he did. He'd trust him. Hooves clattered around him and dust blew through the air like little tornadoes, but he had one goal. Get Minda's hat.

Something from his boyhood niggled, and he recalled a footpath he'd snuck down many times to get to the homestead when he was running late after fishing. Might still be there. It was, somewhat overgrown, but Strawberry's nimble feet gave it no nevermind at all. Nobody followed behind or hindered him up ahead.

He stormed a thicket. Brambles caught, but couldn't pierce, his denims, and the gelding's nostrils flared. Fording the creek at its narrowest, outside Ben Pickler's place, saved them half a mile. He forgot his throbbing thigh.

Minda. Minda. Minda. Her name echoed in every hoof beat.

Sweat from the hot morning sun trickled down his face, reminding him of the liveliness he felt cutting cattle, but the wind cooled him down. By the time he reached the last stretch to merge with the main road to town, he peered to his right and saw a clump of riders in the distance. They'd never meet up with him. But the medicine hat mustang outrunning all of them just might.

Gaining speed, Brix lay low on the horse's neck, urging him on. Strawberry's grunts of effort and the puffs of wind rang in his ears. Against his body, hoof beats throbbed. Driven by speed and wind, his hat, linked by ties, fell back to his neck, and his breath hurled from his lungs.

Town was in sight up ahead, but he felt, rather than heard, Caldwell Hackett breaking ground, closing the gap behind him.

Frippery waving on the fence posts past the cemetery meant only one thing—the display of bonnets. Brix didn't have much farther to go. Minda's pretty plum-colored thing screamed his name.

The horses were nose to nose. He gave Hackett a sideways glare. Getting there first was one thing. Grabbing Minda's hat was another.

Reaching down, he untied the leather strap that held his lariat to the saddle.

****

"There's two, neck and neck. Too far off to tell just who yet," Nathan, Gracey's brother, yelled from behind an old fashioned spyglass. He was perched high on a structure off-center from the jailhouse that Minda suspected might be a leftover gallows. The crowd in the street below cheered and strained to see.

Some folks lined the road, but Gracey had explained the best fun was watching the snatching of the bonnets. With the race about to conclude, folks made their way toward the gauntlet of old posts past the graveyard.

Minda had hung her bonnet halfway from either end. It seemed the fairest place.

Her heart pounded all the way from the arches of her feet to her eardrums. Was Brixton one of the two?

"Gracey, what if..." she whispered, hardly bearing the thought. "What if Caldwell finds my hat and wins the race?"

Dragging Minda out of the crush of people lining

the street, Gracey faced her, quiet but stern. “Minda, I don’t think there’s but a slim chance Caldwell will win. I admit he’s a fine horseman, but he is a schoolteacher these days while Brix spends his life on a horse.” She reached for Minda’s arm, gently but firmly. “But if Caldwell does succeed, why, you give him a lady-like kiss, and he gets forty dollars. That’s all. Like I once said, it’s all in good fun.”

Fun for whom? Minda wanted to mope, but she hadn’t allowed her heavy heart to ruin even one second of her day. The race would be as it was. Resolute, she followed Gracey to the field past the graveyard. Back home, Minda had never had time for a fair, but today she’d tried to forget yesterday and feel the same glee as Katie and Ned. Paradise was filled to the edges with friendly people, booths for silly games, and long plank tables laden with good things to eat.

She had a bit of freedom, too. Watching a group of boys play mumblety-peg, Ned waved to her with a hearty laugh. Katie and a chum pushed their baby sisters along in a bassinet-perambulator Geraldine Hackett had loaned from the inventory at the mercantile.

All that was missing was Brixton. The thought made Minda’s skin tingle in ways both bad and good. Last night had been the closest to heaven she’d get to in this life. But Brixton wouldn’t be around to give her more of those miracles. She couldn’t see the horsemen yet, but arranged herself on a stack of hay bales to get a good view of the bonnets.

Gracey followed, plumping her skirts delicately. “I can’t wait to get my bonnet back.” She giggled, batting her eyelashes. “Or to share my secret.”

“And what secret’s that?”

“The Lord’s sending us another child,” Gracey whispered.

“Oh, for joy! Have you told Jake?” Minda’s heart

swelled with happiness. At the same time her own distinct emptiness quavered inside. She'd come to Paradise for children of her own. Brixton had made it clear to Ned he wouldn't be getting a baby brother.

But what if, last night? Or the night on Brixton's bedroll? How many times might it take?

Gracey's blonde braids gleamed in the hot sunshine. "We've been suspecting, but Doc Viessman just told me this morning for sure. Jake was already gone, distracted by this race."

Just as they hugged, Nathan yelled from his observation point down the street.

"It's Brix Haynes and Caldwell Hackett! Neck and neck! Nose to nose!"

Taller men in the crowd who could strain to see agreed, setting up shouts and much commotion. "It'll be up to whoever grabs the bonnet he declared," someone shouted.

Minda's heart stopped completely. Both men wanted her hat. Resisting the trembling in her knees, she climbed atop the hay bale to improve her view. Rounding a stand of box elder trees, the riders came into sight, and Minda couldn't hold down her sigh. Brixton was music and magic all at once, racing like he and Strawberry were fused together.

The glance she stole at Caldwell proved him experienced and expert, but he lacked Brixton's poise and grace even at the end of a grueling endeavor. But, she remembered, it didn't matter which man reached the finish line past the graveyard if he hadn't retrieved the right hat beforehand.

Almost as one, the crowd held its breath. They didn't have but thirty feet to go, and a gentleman would slow down to protect the row of hats.

Except Brixton. Mortified, Minda watched Caldwell begin his approach with finesse, forcing his mustang to mincing steps. But something snaked from Strawberry's side as Brixton sailed toward the finish without slowing at all.

He'd roped her lovely bonnet. The crowd went wild. As he reined in Strawberry at the finish line, he drew his prize to his side in a smashed heap, then held it high over his head in victory.

The whoops and applause were deafening.

Minda gasped, but Gracey consoled her. "Now, Minda, it shan't take you long at all to make another beautiful thing."

What was left of Minda's heart fell past her feet and shattered . She needed a place for a private cry.

It wasn't just the hat. Gracey was right. Making hats was what Minda did. Making another one was something else she'd been called to do.

What mattered was that Brixton hadn't won the glorious race because he considered himself her sweetheart.

She sniffed, and Gracey heard her over the throng. "Why, Minda love, he didn't mean it. It was the energy of the race. You can repair it right fine. Let's get back to the parsonage, if you need a place to tidy yourself for the kiss. Jake won't be along for an hour or more."

Merciful heavens. The kiss. The public kiss. Horror wracked Minda's nerves. "No, I'm fine, Gracey," she said dully. "Let's just go get it over with."

Gracey chuckled, but in a comforting way. "Why, Minda, it's just a little thing to tide the winner over. Brix will get the money and Strawberry his wreath of flowers later when all the ribbons and prizes are awarded."

A little thing to tide him over, something that could send her to heaven and back? The money didn't matter anyway. She had cash of her own now, and more to come. A glimpse ahead showed Brixton waiting at the bottom of the tower where Nathan had kept watch. He had never looked more beautiful, hair awry and flushed with triumph. She could either acquiesce or make a scene.

She longed for another encounter with his soft lips, no matter what the reason. If this was expected of the winner's sweetheart, she could bear it. She'd borne far worse.

Their eyes met. The lightning strike that had let Buttermilk escape was but a firefly compared to this. He held out his hand.

For this moment, they were the only people in the world. The crowd parted, like Moses had commanded the Red Sea, and she found her fingers reaching for her husband's. He led her up the steps to the top. The town alderman announced the kiss like Brixton was some king getting his crown.

Brixton bent down to her. For a flash, she remembered their public wedding kiss, the stunning kiss at the riverside before he pushed her away. For the third time, their lips met in front of other people.

The third time compared to no other. Men's jeers and women's coos faded off into another world. Her arms came around her husband for all the world to see. His lips tasted of triumph and the future and everything in between. If this was love, and for her it was, she wanted to proclaim it outright.

"My goodness, Mr. and Mrs. Haynes." The alderman coughed as delicate as an affronted spinster. They pulled apart, Brixton as flushed as her hot face felt.

"Looks like you'll be staying on then, Brix," came a voice from below.

"What man could leave that behind?" someone else goaded.

Brixton didn't look at her now, flexing his shoulders and addressing the throng of admirers below. He thrust his hands deep in his pockets and bowed first to her, then the onlookers.

"Minda, I'm honored to have represented your hat. But don't get me wrong, folks. I'm leaving for Texas soon's I can. Never said anything different."

Skinny Hank called out, "Join me, all you gents. Drinks on the house. Get down here, Brix." Her husband gave her a perfunctory parting peck on the cheek and descended, riding a sea of shoulders down the street.

Bravely, Minda threw a gracious smile to the crowd. After all, she did have the children to think of. Then she slunk down the steps unbeknownst, into Caldwell Hackett's waiting arms.

Although startled, she gathered grace enough to wiggle free and find her tongue. "Congratulations, Caldwell. Why, I hardly recognize you without your spectacles."

He frowned. "They fell off my face jumping a fence at the Boldren place. Thank God I made all those practice runs and knew where to head next."

"Well, spectacles or not, yours was some grand riding."

The throng around them began to disperse, to greet the other returning racers or to enjoy the festivities and displays.

"But not the outcome I wanted." He looked at her with clear brave eyes. "Walk with me?"

"Well," she said, "I suppose you're welcome to come along while I check on the children."

There was no reason to embarrass either of them by snubbing him, although she kept her arms at her side. A chat would keep her mind off her husband. It wasn't Brixton's leaving her side right now for the accolades of his peers that mattered. That was manly and expected.

It was his leaving her at all that did.

"Caldwell, please," she said by the lemonade stand. "It was a race for my hat, not my heart. You do understand that, don't you?" Her voice was serious, but she managed to toss a gay smile at Deborah Kelley, who had ordered a hat not long ago.

"Minda, you deserve a man who'll stay by your side. Yours and the children's. Why, you don't know Brix at all."

She shrugged and smiled, recognizing she knew her husband quite well. "Caldwell, you forget. I *came* to Paradise to marry a man I didn't know. Now, you need to accept your own accolades at Skinny Hank's. Get along now."

"Well, join me for a lemonade first? Racing's a thirsty business." Then he pointed. "And your kids are just over there at the pie table. You can keep an eye out from here."

"I don't see why not." Minda acquiesced, remembering her earlier vow to think only happy thoughts today.

Chapter Fifteen

Brix tossed back one shot of whiskey and downright enjoyed the admiration of his friends, but the noisy saloon with its stink of sweat and spittoon wasn't where he wanted to be. The scent of roses came to mind, but hell and damnation, he'd destroyed his wife's masterful hat. She was bound to be peeved.

Roping it like a maverick calf was the only way he could have won, but he'd better not come upon Minda in any kind of tipsy state just in case.

"Gents." He got up from the scarred square table scattered with half-smoked cheroots and nodded his thanks. "I best be off."

"You best be off for one last congratulatory night in the arms of that wife of yours," someone jeered, "with you leaving for Texas and all..."

"You're some kind of fool to leave her bed," another said.

Anger clung to his shoulders at Minda being the butt of jokes. Likely he should have taken an easier time with that public kiss. But gathering her close to let her and everyone else know she was his and his alone had been an occasion impossible for him to resist.

Hell, he couldn't stay, but he wasn't leaving her. He'd be a husband, in his way. He just wasn't one for walls.

His skin crawled at the recollection of her cash reward, and all those hat orders. She had money now. She'd said she wasn't leaving the kids this minute, but she'd never promised forever.

He'd never promised forever, either, even after yesterday in the barn.

"You keep the subject of my wife out of this saloon. No whiskey mill's any place for a lady." He tossed back another shot to calm his thoughts. "Now if you all will excuse me."

"Where's Caldwell?" someone asked. "He might teach innocent kids, but he ain't no stranger to Hank's."

"Better go find him, Brix," another said. "Maybe your wife gave him a different kind of hat."

Brix's fist clenched. That couldn't be the way of it, could it? Minda couldn't be disappointed that Caldwell lost. Not after yesterday. Likely his childhood rival was disinclined to face masculine insults about his riding and jeers at his loss.

Enough good-hearted insults and jeers met Brix's own back as he left. He had a wife to find.

Around him, Paradise painted a different sort of picture than any of the cow towns he knew so well. Decent-clad women showed off their pies and cakes, and happy kids licked lollipops and played games. Quilts on display might well adorn a museum.

Ned and Katie ran to him, and like it was natural, he knelt, sore leg and all, and drew them to his arms.

"Uncle Brix, you won, you won!" Ned's cheek all but stuck to Brix's own.

"We're so proud of you. Even if you did ruin Mama's hat," Katie said with a hug.

Squeezing her back, he felt a preview of both Minda's delight and dismay. Well, he'd meet up with his wife soon enough. "Now, how's that Dicey of yours? You tend that dog before you left?"

"We left our pup plenty of water and a big bone," Ned said, "and Clem got our heifer here just fine."

"She'll win a ribbon for sure." Katie's braids

bounced across her shoulders. "And blue's the best."

"Well, we're gonna go eat some of Miss Tessie's quince pie now," Ned said. "We don't know what that is."

"And I better go find Minda and Silly," Brix said, casual.

"Oh, Mrs. Hackett's pushing Silly in a special prama-lator," Ned said, then ran off behind Katie.

Hackett. Damn. Just the name set him off. Looking around the herds of folks, Brix noticed Gracey on the parsonage steps. Her hat was big as a cartwheel, blooming with blue flowers. Another of Minda's masterful designs. Jake was practically kneeling at her feet.

Weaving through folks, he ran over to them, untying the knots in his sore leg. He might not be leaving in the morning after all.

"How'd this tenderfoot get back to town so fast?" Brix teased, but Jake didn't even look up at him, acting as moon-eyed as a bridegroom.

"I had good reason to hurry," Jake said, raising Gracey's hand to his mouth.

Gracey's face shone bright like the first sunburst after a blizzard. "I got good news this morning, Brix. We'd been suspecting," she said, glancing shy at Jake, "after all, this isn't our first. But Doc Viessman said it's for sure. I'm with child."

"Then this is a grand day all around." Brix hugged her.

"Children are a great blessing, Brix. You ought to think about it." Jake took his eyes away from his wife to give Brix a meaningful glare.

Brix scowled back. "Got three already, Jake. I think I'll leave you to this private moment of joy. Seen my wife anywhere about?"

But neither of them paid him any further notice, and he set off for Minda. A funny emptiness quivered in his stomach at Jake's words. What might it be like to get a wife with child, and watch a babe grow inside the protection of her warm body? Ned had asked for a brother. Was it possible Brix wanted a son?

Or a daughter? Already it tickled him when folks said how much Silly looked like him. As stuck as he was on his brother's kids, they weren't the fruit of his own loins despite the blood they shared.

At that precise moment, he reached the boardwalk by the mercantile and saw Geraldine Hackett lift Silly out of a push-basket contraption and hold her close. Damn, where was Minda?

He saw her then, sitting on a hay bale next to the barber shop, in eyeshot of Ned and Katie at the pie table.

Sitting next to Caldwell Hackett. His fingers itched.

"Do you love him?" he heard Caldwell ask her, not all that quiet.

She held a glass of lemonade to the lovely mouth he'd drunk from not long ago. "Caldwell, I believe I do."

"Well, believing something doesn't make it a fact," Caldwell said, taking her hand in a way Brix crossly remembered. But he noticed with pleasure that Caldwell Hackett wasn't wearing his spectacles.

Caldwell Hackett lowered his lips, lips that suddenly reminded Brix of a calf's liver, to Minda's beautiful white fingers. Before that mouth defiled his wife, Brix was at her side. He hauled Caldwell Hackett to his feet and cuffed him in the nose with a left hook.

****

"Merciful heavens, Brixton, what on earth?" Minda sputtered, not quite sure of the proper vocabulary. Caldwell Hackett had been all but insolent this time, but perhaps she had encouraged him with the lemonade.

She felt a flash of embarrassment at her own conduct. Besides, he was the children's schoolteacher. They'd be face to face many times during pageants and consultations.

In addition, she was presumably an emerging entrepreneur in this town with her own position as a stepmother to guard as well.

Reputation or not, Caldwell took a lunge at her husband while blood gushed down his chin. His counterpunch was powerful although Brixton sidestepped it nimbly.

As for Minda, she'd had enough of blood.

"Stop at once. I've had enough competition between the two of you today. You may have behaved like this when you were youthful hooligans, but I like to think you're both grown up. Then again, I could be wrong and likely am."

Brixton stopped once he realized a small crowd had gathered, including Katie and Ned. Perhaps realizing his own status, Caldwell stumbled to a halt as well.

"Mr. Hackett, you are this town's schoolteacher with dignity to uphold." Minda went on sternly. "And you, Mr. Haynes, are a family man whether you like it or not!"

"No harm done, folks." Brixton grinned insouciantly to the crowd and bowed. "Merely concluding our competition."

Minda handed Caldwell her handkerchief. "I don't need it back. Now, Mr. Haynes, let's take a walk."

Tossing his head with bravado, Caldwell lurched over to the mercantile, no doubt to clean his face and locate some spare spectacles.

She grabbed Brixton's left hand, feeling more ire this time than explosion. He winced briefly, and she recognized Caldwell's nose bone had done some damage to her husband's knuckles. "Maybe a walk along the river will cool you off."

They headed toward the tree-lined bank.

"Hackett had no right." Brixton moved his fingers through hers in a way that reminded her of them traveling the hills and valleys of her body. It was suddenly hard to concentrate.

But she pressed on along a path of foot-trodden prairie grass. She had things to say and wanted a private place to say them. "I know he had no right, Brixton. I've made it clear that I am a married woman."

"I thought I heard you tell him you love me." Brixton's voice was so soft she barely heard.

Underneath the shade of a cottonwood, she stopped, her heart smacking hard against her ribs. "You shouldn't have eavesdropped. That wasn't for your ears."

"Didn't spy on you at all. Anybody coming upon you would have heard it. So it is true?" He looked away from her.

Minda swallowed hard, knees week. She'd never liked the dishonesty perpetrated upon her by either him or Norman Dale. "Let's sit down here on my shawl," she said, stalling for time, and he obeyed without a word.

For a moment, she watched the river roll peaceably by and heard its song. How different from days ago, downriver several miles, when she was fraught with fear for Ned and her husband, and when a little boy had been terrified by outlaws. Now, Brixton not only sat next to her but lounged on the ground, close by. In a wifely way, she tied the leather string that laced his shirt.

"So is it true?" he asked, watching her eyes this time.

This time, she looked away, figuring she blushed, for she remembered how those eyes watched her face when he slid up inside her.

"Brixton, I came to Paradise to love a man," she said, feeling more heat. "Maybe I would have fallen for your brother had I the chance. I know our wedding was a sham. But I do think I've fallen for you." She quickly glanced at him. "Don't be frightened. I know how you don't want a wife. I know how you feel."

Stretching restlessly, he gave a long sigh. "I don't know that you do, Minda. Not all of it anyway. I don't speak about this to anybody, not even Jake."

He paused for a while, as if deciding whether to go on. "Truth is, I fell in love once. I had no doubt about it. I wasn't fearful for a single second. I spoke the words to her time and time again. English and Spanish." He threw her a bashful look and she remembered the sweet moment when he'd told her of his pinto's name.

Minda wasn't surprised or jealous. It was almost unimaginable that this fine-looking, robust man hadn't inspired another woman's love sometime in his life. What had happened? Had she died?

"Was she someone from here?"

"Nope. Back in Texas. Her pa runs a ranch and I do a lot of work for him. Did, I guess. I should admit things are different now. I fell for her like a bag of rocks tossed in a lake. Built her a house along Butter Creek. Built yours too, have to say."

"What?"

"I helped my brother build that *fine white house* of his." He chuckled.

Minda warmed a little. She had long quashed her disappointment about Norman Dale's lies. The house was cool during the heat of the day and had kept out every drop of rain. Knowing Brixton's own hands had lathed and sawed and nailed filled her with wonder. No doubt he'd continue to surprise her until the end of her days.

She waited for him to discuss the woman he'd

loved, because she would never ask.

"Esperanza was all woman, fire from her Mexican ma and spunk from her rowdy pa. She held my heart in the palm of her hand." His cheekbones reddened and his voice hardened. "Until she stomped on it. I found her in the arms of another man, the day before we were to wed. I come back from round-up early to surprise her. What a hell of a surprise."

Brixton looked away. "I bloodied his nose, too, left and never looked back. Caldwell drooling on your hands reminded me of that bad time. It wasn't all just him and me being rivals in our youth.

"And I know you aren't like Esperanza. You didn't snatch onto Caldwell just to smash whatever heart I got left. But sometimes, she's all I can see and that hurt's all I can feel."

Grimacing as he shifted position, he leaned on his elbows, looking at the bubbling stream.

"Didn't know if I could trust again. And you came here, thinking Norman Dale had money and a big house. I figured you grasping and greedy, never letting what a man could provide, what he was inside, be good enough for you."

His assumption appalled her, particularly when it was Norman Dale who had brought her here under false pretenses. But that seemed like a lifetime ago. She opened her mouth, ready to protest, but he held up his hand. "No, stop. I know that isn't true about you. It took me a while, but I learned the truth watching you with the kids, seeing how you are on the homestead. With me."

"I think Esperanza was a fool for hurting you," she said, even as she remembered her own hurts. But his confidences, his confession touched her deeply. Up to now he'd been a man of few words and even fewer emotions. He was trusting her.

She could confide just as well. "Once Gracey told

me something that stuck. That sometimes we set off for France but the ship goes off course to Holland. The destination is different, but it's still a lovely place to be."

"Not following you," he said.

"What I mean is, I eagerly came to Paradise, but things were different than I expected. And for you, too. You didn't come here to get saddled with a wife and family. But now I can help with Norman Dale's debts. You don't have to leave, at least not until the fall round-up."

She took a breath. "You don't have to ride from ranch to ranch the rest of the summer to earn spare cash. I'll have commissions from my hats. The children need you so much. And don't you start that balderdash about that money being mine, not ours." She finished passionately, though she doubted she'd made a dent in that hard head of his.

His familiar scowl was back. "Well, Miz Haynes, I can't deny that I care something for you. But those words I told Esperanza, well, they won't come easy out of my mouth again. You might never hear me say them. And you do know I need fresh air on my face and stirrups underneath my boot heels."

"I do know that," she said, tingling that he admitted he had feelings, but the desolation crept back, too. Then he moved to place his head in her lap like Jake and Gracey had done for an enviable time on the picnic.

"But I can't deny either that I like a light shining in the window and a woman waiting inside." He smiled crookedly up at her. Then he tensed. "I can't say how long I'll stay, but I reckon I won't be leaving tomorrow." His eyes gleamed with sudden wickedness. "It would mean sharing a bed."

"Mr. Haynes, that was all your doing, sleeping out under the stars," she said primly, swallowing her elation so as not to scare him off. Then he lay down and reached for her, lips brushing across her hair.

"Sorry about your hat, Minda."

She shrugged against his chest. "Yes, well, it was rather impressive."

"Your hat or my roping?"

"Both." She giggled, snuggling tighter. His lips found hers then, and not for the first time, she realized the perfect fit.

"Prettiest you ever looked outside of that wedding veil," he murmured before his tongue teased hers. Her breasts heaved and her body all but cried out.

But reality, and thoughts of the children, intruded. Still, she could hardly speak. "Mercy, that was better than the gallows."

"Gallows?"

"Where we had our victory kiss.

"Gallows." He laughed loudly but not in derision. "Hell—beg pardon, Minda—that's nothing but the scaffold for orations whenever the alderman needs re-electing."

She helped him to his feet just as much as he helped her, already breathless for the night ahead in bed with him.

Like a regular family, they found the children and enjoyed the fair. Geraldine Hackett relinquished Priscilla without a qualm and loaned the pram that Katie and Ned took turns pushing. Minda and her husband held hands just like Jake and Gracey.

"Gracey allow she's expecting another child?" Brixton said in a voice she hadn't heard before.

She nodded against her husband's shoulder but couldn't find words of her own.

"It's time for prizes now," Katie shrieked, saving Minda from mouthing any sort of reply.

Strawberry wore a ring of flowers around his neck, and Brixton went to coddle him affectionately as he accepted his prize money. But Dicey had won, too.

"We got a green ribbon, Uncle Brix," Ned said. "It isn't the blue one we came for, but we love it just as much."

****

Night had fallen soft and warm. It was almost bedtime, and Minda trembled with delight and anticipation. The family had stuffed themselves full at the fair with cakes and fried chicken. Minda had been spared the preparation of another meal.

Now Brixton was washing up outside, getting ready for bed.

"Mama," Neddie said, hanging around her suddenly trembling knees, "our new puppy can sleep with me, can't he?"

It was hard to resist the child. His demeanor all day had been one of cheerful excitement, but he hadn't convinced her that his bad dreams had diminished. The soft warmth of another living creature was sure to keep him good company.

But Clem had warned otherwise, temporarily.

"Sweetheart, Clem says the pup can do his business outside, but we were gone all day and couldn't practice with him. Won't you let him keep Dicey company in the barn for a night or two, just until we're sure? You know what a special day this has been for Dicey. She needs a friend, too."

Ned opened his mouth, but she said, "No. You and Uncle Brix are not sleeping in the barn with them. You can cuddle with your toy dog, all right?"

"All right." He nodded, weariness clouding his big blue eyes. "I love them both." Bending down, he caressed the puppy into a wriggling ball of happy fur.

"Now, clean your teeth and get to bed. Uncle Brix will be in to tuck you both." It had become Brixton's special tradition with the children, and her heart warmed again. He wasn't leaving. It wasn't forever, but at least they had a while. And he would cuddle her each and every night until he went. There'd be no more barn or bedroll sleeping for her husband.

She was already naked under the covers, filled with a tumultuous anticipation greater than any of the other times, when she heard Brixton begin the children's lullabies. Soon, he came in the bedroom bearing a lit candle, and she quivered deliciously at the sight of him.

"This was quite a day." He smiled down at her as he slid from his clothes. In the candle glow, she saw how ready and willing he was. She rose up on one elbow, her right hand extended to caress his turgid flesh.

"No, Minda. It might be time…" He looked away for a second.

Alarm flared. His manhood raged but his voice sounded unsure, somehow. She drew her hand away almost in shame. Did he want to prevent a child?

"Minda, what I mean is, I want you to hold me, there. Like you do. But sometimes a woman pleasures her man. Like I pleasured you, with my mouth."

"You mean?" Her wonder increased. But instead of waiting for further instruction, she moved toward his manhood and he stood as close as he could to the bedside. His manhood angled perfectly toward her mouth. For a second, she looked close up at the length and hardness and the heat, and her womanhood tightened.

She met his eyes with a little nod and bent to blow out the candle.

"No, don't." His hand landed on her hair. "It's a special thing between a man and wife, Minda. I want to watch."

With a maidenly gulp, she took the length of him inside her mouth, her tongue tickling the tip that had taken her virginity with such firm gentleness. Remembering his thrusts, she moved her head back and forth, keeping him from her teeth. At his groans, her nipples ached for his touch, and her emptiness below was almost excruciating. But she wanted to be generous. This moment was for him. For a flash, she let him slip out so her tongue could travel the length of him, and that was when his knees buckled.

"Oh God, Minda." He choked almost desperately.

With no chance to stroke her own magic places, he plunged deep into her core. She gasped, for she was still nearly as tight as a maiden, but she was ready. Already her body knew how to respond to him, this man, her husband. Her thighs wrapped about his waist, and she matched his force and motion. Her blissful spot exploded just as his face shuddered in what she knew was the moment his seed reached the richness of her womb.

He blew out the candle with another of his wicked smiles and climbed in beside her. He fell sleep almost at once, holding her as if he'd never let her go.

For Minda, sleep took a while coming. She was satiated. Brixton had made her a woman all the way, and a wife as well as he knew how. But her happiness had a sprinkle of sadness.

Just after sunup, she woke, hearing the puppy's plaintive whines all the way from the barn. It was nearly time to milk Mabel. She grinned to herself. Brixton was an awfully good teacher in so many ways. As she dressed, she watched the shadows of him sleeping tight in the tussled bedclothes. The memory of their love sport started her breathless and nearly moaning.

The purple gown he liked could last another day of chores, but Minda promised herself she'd head for the mercantile and buy a new length of dress goods as soon as she could. Shafts of dawn from the window above the loft brightened the barn as did the large open door. Even still, she couldn't see the little dog anywhere. But his whimpers touched her heart. He wasn't on the blanket she'd shaped into a bed for him, but no way had he gotten into the horse or cow stalls.

Then, above her, mixed in with the mews of the barn cats that inhabited the loft, she heard agitated whimpers. Why on earth had Brixton put the pup to bed in the loft, chancing that the poor little thing would come tumbling down? She'd definitely have to speak her mind.

"I'm coming, little one," she crooned, as she started up the ladder, wondering if Brixton had built this, as well. It was firm and strong.

"Come right on up, little lady. I'm sitting here awaiting," hissed a terrible voice as she reached the top rung. A strong hand gripped her hair and pulled her into the loft, then let her go. She sank into a heap, heart pounding with indescribable horror. Her lips parted.

"And I suggest you don't scream. 'Less you want this dog skinned alive right in front of you." Hot smelly breath shaped the words as the intruder held a knife to the belly of the squirming dog. He was young, but his smirk was brown with missing teeth.

She hesitated. Her lungs held no air. Her blood had stopped running. Even the hair on her head tensed, although he no longer had his miserable fingers on it.

"Who are you? What is this about?" she finally asked. His filthy eyes roaming her up and down made her feel like she needed a bath.

"Name's Delaware Peavy, ma'am. You can all me Del. That man you just sent on to jail, why, Brentwood and me are cousins. And you're gonna pay."

Her throat tightened like it had a noose around it. Sacrificing the puppy was not as terrible an option as costing her own life, but she couldn't give in without a fight.

"You men are horse thieves. What do you want with a dog?"

"Dog don't matter. A ruse to get you up here. Busted the lock easy and saw you coming out here with your milking pail. I figured then and there your horses aren't enough. I want you."

"But the Perkins gang..."

"Ahab and his cronies don't mean a thing. We just rode with them for a week or two. It's always been Del and Brent. But now I'm alone and it's your fault. And it's been an age since I had a woman." He leered as his knife point nicked the puppy's tender flesh. A stream of blood trickled to the straw, and the animal yelped.

Minda's disgust and fury outweighed any fear. She'd dealt with this man's cowardly cousin not long ago. Her husband had taught her well.

"Oh, Peavy. Put down the dog. At least be a man."

"Don't give me orders, little lady. I am all man." His smirk disgusted rather than terrified her. "I'm gonna have some fun with you. Slice up this dog then slit your throat and nab those horses 'afore your man gets out of bed."

Minda held on to her composure. "If you honestly think that, you're terribly wrong."

Her sitting position was actually a fortunate one. It was easier to lift her skirt and reach for the gun Brixton had suggested she always keep with her.

Her actions were quick. But Peavy was just as quick. He tossed the dog away and grabbed her ankle.

"Ah, no you don't, little lady."

Chapter Sixteen

Brix stretched, missing Minda. Her side of the bed wasn't warm anymore, but he still smelled those roses on the pillow they'd shared. Milking time. His manhood rose in morning joy as he remembered claiming her soft body in the straw, and last night, loving her special heat.

The kids were all asleep. Thrilled at the opportunities ahead, Brix slipped into trousers and boots and set out for the barn. The dawn breeze teased his bare nipples and tightened them, but nothing compared to Minda's fingertips.

From somewhere inside the barn, the pup whined. Probably needed its breakfast. His forehead furrowed a bit. It wasn't like Minda not to tend any needy thing. Stepping through the barn door, he heard scuffles and the loud grunts of struggle coming from the loft.

"Minda? You all right?" He ran for the ladder, unease clawing his back. His lungs breathed more dread than air.

"Brixton, he's got a knife," Minda shrieked. A boot kicked the ladder to the ground.

"And don't you go raising that ladder up, mister." A pocked-face, skinny man rose on his knees and yanked Minda's long hair until she was dragged to the edge of the loft. Her eyes met Brix's with a message he tried hard to read.

Brix lunged on instinct alone.

"Now, now," the man taunted, holding Minda tight with a knife at her neck. "Won't take much to slit this pretty little throat."

Blood trickled down Minda's white skin and turned black on the purple dress. Sweat drenched Brix, and his heart slammed hard against his ribs. A good twenty feet separated them, and for now, he had no way up. Minda would be murdered before he could lift the ladder, much less climb up.

Unless she wore a gun like he'd told her.

"Del Peavy at your service, mister. And damn ready to service your woman. Now, now, missy," the man said to Minda, "seems your man taught you well, that gun on your leg. Too bad you couldn't get past ole Del to reach it." His empty eyes stared down at Brix in a measuring way. "Hmm. Your man came out here unprotected. More's the pity."

Brix's spirits crashed to the soles of his feet. Minda had lost her weapon. Dismay turned to mortal dread. Once again, he might lose something he hadn't known he wanted to keep. Who was this Peavy? Somebody left behind by Ahab Perkins?

Minda had been grabbing for the man's knife, but now she stopped and sank into the straw, lowering Peavy's knife arm along with her. But Peavy still knelt tall, smirking down at him. Minda looked down at Brix with determination.

Truth to tell, her face was full of feistiness, not defeat or fear. And then he knew what her wide eyes and small nods told him. She was remembering the knife he always kept in his boot.

She was getting out of his knife's way as well as she could. "Not much of a man, here, Brixton. Threatening to kill a little dog. And a woman."

Peavy scowled at her insult, eyes off Brix and his guard down as he nodded. "Worked though, didn't it, lady? Don't think your man's gonna like—" His knife blade sliced off her top button. "—what I do next."

Brix's teeth ground with a loud noise, seeing the

man's hands on his wife. But with the knife off her neck, Minda wrenched free and punched Peavy's nose with her fist. Quick as lightning, Brix raised his left knee and slipped his hand into his left boot at the same time. His knife sliced through the air in an upward arc, meeting its aim.

Peavy groaned, breathless, at both impacts and slumped into the straw.

Heart thundering like hoof beats, Brix took deep breaths to calm down as he climbed the ladder. In the few seconds it took him to reach the loft, Minda had taken Peavy's knife to cut strips from her dress.

Smart woman, that wife of his. His pride whirled inside him like a storm. She tied up the scoundrel first, before stopping his bleeding nose with the last strip. Brix pulled his knife roughly from between Peavy's collarbone and shoulder and wiped it on the outlaw's grimy clothes.

Del Peavy moaned, groveling cross-eyed in the hay, and tied firm as any calf before branding.

Although he was too much a gentleman to kick any man when he was down, Brix propped the toe of his boot just at the point of entry. Peavy winced. It was little compensation for what the outlaw had just put Minda through.

Brix knelt next to his wife and held her close, somewhat surprised at her trembling. She'd been so strong and resolute. Relief at her safety and pride in her grit pumped through him, laced with more than a tinge of passion.

"Thought you aimed to kill, Mr. Haynes," she muttered against his bare chest.

"Not with you in the way. Just wanted to disable his arm." He breathed in the scent of her, then teased, "Some left hook, Miz Haynes."

"Oh, I had a good teacher." She grinned along with him, likely remembering Hackett, and waved her bruised knuckles. "I can't say I'll be doing much needlework." Her shivers stopped against his warmth.

"Damn good knots there," he said, looking at the prisoner and feeling not a qualm of pity. "He won't go anywhere 'til we get Sheriff Pelton out here."

"Good knots? Well, Mr. Haynes, how do you think my stitches hold together?" she murmured, so close to a nipple that he tingled. "Should I make him some of that willow bark tea to ease his discomfort?"

He didn't dare scold her. A nurturing woman was who she was, and why he cared. Peavy's right arm wouldn't be much use to him for a long while, but he was in no danger of dying. The bleeding had already stopped. Just in case, though, Brix got some baling wire and hooked Del Peavy up to some bolts supporting the roof beams.

"We're done here, Minda. He's sleeping it off. Stinks like the whole of Hank's alehouse. There's plenty of last night's whiskey running in his veins. Let's get you down." He came to her, where she still knelt in the hay, holding the pup, her gun on one knee.

"Just scratches, thankfully, on my neck and his belly," she said, "but this poor little pup is sleeping in the house tonight for sure."

"None of your stitches for *him* then?" Brix grinned, helping her up.

"Brixton." Her feistiness had left her beautiful eyes. "I remembered to wear my gun. But I couldn't…I didn't… He tossed it into the straw. I just now found it."

Pulling her close against him, he kissed away the sudden dampness on her cheeks. For a flash her mouth parted underneath his. Once again, her taste sparked the new feelings he never thought he wanted. "It makes no mind," he murmured. "You're safe. He's caught. Now, let's get back to the house. And later, I promise you cloth for a new purple dress."

"The children will probably be up by now." She sounded disappointed as she clung to him.

"No doubt about it," he whispered, not keen to let her go. "Truth is, I left them asleep and came to the barn to, well…"

"Teach me something else?" She smiled shy, but the look in her eyes was not demure one single bit.

"Later. There'll always be later." He laid a kiss on her ear. "Now, I'll get the dog and go first, then hold the ladder for you."

He waited at the bottom for her, but when she started down the rungs, her backside at eye level, Brix had no thought at all of the kids. His hands traveled under her skirts, one upon each leg, sliding up and down from thigh to calf, her skin soft as silk, smooth as butter. Memories a man could treasure on the trail.

"Oh, Brixton." She paused at his touch and leaned back against his chest as one hand went higher, the other held her tight.

"No drawers today, Miz Haynes?" he drawled, delighted at her daring. His arousal battled against his tight denims.

She peeked over her shoulder, flirting. "Maybe I wanted another lesson in the barn, too."

But then she stumbled and caught her heel in a downward rung. He moved his searching hands quick so he could break her fall, but her foot stuck awkward as she pitched against him. "Minda?"

"I'm fine," she said, but when she tried to stand, she tottered into his arms.

He bent to knead the swelling flesh. "Not broken."

"How do you know?" Her cheeks paled but she tried to smile.

"Don't doubt me, now, do you?" With a swoop, he picked her up and carried her across the yard into the house.

"No, Brixton. I don't doubt you at all," she murmured against his shoulder.

****

"Time for your bath, Miz Haynes," her husband said, using her married name these days with pure affection as he brought a washtub into the bedroom.

"Now, Brixton, it's been almost a week. I am perfectly capable..."

He leaned down close to her ear. "It's my favorite part of doctoring my wife."

His eyes narrowed with desire, and the furious heat that just a look from him could ignite consumed her. Her sprained ankle had not prevented nights of magic and passion, and she feared her shouts of delight would wake the children.

He set the washtub down, eyes bright. She was still naked under the sheets, and he knew it. "Silly's napping along with the pup. And I got Ned and Katie enrolled today without punching Schoolmaster Hackett one single time." He rubbed a washcloth with soap. "So we are alone."

She giggled in anticipation at his wicked grin. "Brixton, surely it's time for me to be up and about." But she lost her thought as the warm soapy cloth tugged gently across her chest. She shut her eyes for a second, glorying as Brixton's fingers slid up the slippery slopes of her breasts.

"Doc Viessman himself said a week." Brixton breathed out, eyes half-lidded, fingertips tickling her nipples into rosy peaks.

"But I have a ton of things to do." She gasped as one hand slid the cloth down one thigh and the other caressed the opposite.

"No buts. I am keeping house just fine."

He was. How could he look so magnificent and masculine doing women's work?

Even the soles of her feet and her ten toes

turned to fire underneath his touch. She moaned out loud.

"Well, this is day seven." Her breath caught when he flipped her over and kneaded her backside with hands as gentle as the sunbeams coming through the window.

"Good counting." His fingers stroked the muscles of her back firmly but sensuously. "I set a plank on two saw horses, over by the front window. Good light and enough room for those hat makings the mercantile sent over. You can sit up there today." He paused his motions, and said almost shyly. "Might use some of my reward money to get you one of those Singer machines."

Despite her delight at such a possibility, she couldn't allow it. In her heart, she hoped the fifty dollar reward for Delaware Peavy would buy them more time together and keep him away from Texas longer.

"Oh, no, Brixton, no." Her languor at his delicious ministrations halted and she scrambled up to sit on the bed. "The money is for necessary things, like bringing your horse home from Kansas."

"Lay back down," he said, stroking her arm with soap and fervor. "Fara's staying at a real good farm I know well. It isn't the money. I don't want..." He raised the inside of her wrist to his mouth, his tongue taking a quick taste. Her pulse jumped. For a long, sweet moment, his eyes held her gaze, dark and firm. "Don't want to waste any of my days and nights here going off somewhere else."

Disliking the sudden jolt that his time here was temporary, she held out her arms to him. He bent down and slipped his tongue between her lips, then moved to cherish one breast, then the other, enticing her nipples to new enchantment. As she wriggled with delight, his hand reached under the bed sheet again and her lower core parted at his fingertips.

Almost overwhelmed with sensation, she dragged her fingers through the lengths of his hair. For a second, he sparked her center bud to a glimpse of those colors only she could see.

"You're a tease, Mr. Haynes." She breathed against his ear, forcing away her sadness.

He pulled back, his face creased in disappointment. "Damn. Somebody's driving up."

Bereft herself, she didn't chide the curse. He tried hard these days, but now she almost wished she had courage to mouth the word herself. Her emptiness was almost pain.

"I'll go check things. You get dressed." His eyes still held the glaze of desire. "We have plenty of time to finish this up later. I'll come back to carry you out."

Plenty of time. Those words encouraged her in spite of the disruption of their passion. "I'll hobble slow."

Sighing and grimacing both, she managed to climb into a gray dress that had seen better days, but when she heard Gracey's voice at the door, she relaxed, kept her hair down and her feet bare. She found her friend in the big upholstered chair, face aglow with impending motherhood.

"Gracey! You're most welcome, but is everything all right?"

"Oh, I know it's early in the day, but I've gotten the boys to school and couldn't resist some fresh air. I woke up queasy this morning." She patted her belly, then waved an envelope. "So I'm delivering a down payment for Lisa Pelton's new orange hat, and a letter to Brix. He's outside with it. Most of all—" She smiled demurely. "I wanted a chance to wear my new hat. I'm too proud of it to save it just for Sundays."

"Probably his reward money. Mine didn't take long to reach me," Minda said, then teased, "So is postmaster part of the duties of a preacher's wife?"

"No. But when I mailed a letter for my Auntie Faye in Hastings first thing today, Horace at the post office mentioned a post for Brix. I told him I'd deliver it."

"Then let me make you some tea."

"You will do no such thing. You're limping like a granny. I'll get us each a cup."

While Gracey puttered at the stove, Minda leaned on a spindleback chair and walked it over like a crutch to her new worktable. The fabrics, laces and ribbons glimmered like jewels in a treasure chest. She had too many blessings to count.

So sweet, Brixton not wanting to waste their time together. An idea came then. She'd use Lisa's down payment for a higher purpose, as there were many orders ahead of hers.

"Gracey? Do you think your father could handle the livery and smithy all by himself for a while?"

"I suppose. But why?"

"I need to hire your brother." She explained her plan to send the young horseman to Ellsworth to retrieve Fara as a surprise. "Brixton hasn't complained, but I'm sure he'd like his own horse back. Do you think Nathan would accept?"

Gracey laughed out loud. "Indeed. He's at that age where Paradise seems a worse place than Perdition, if you pardon my expression." She blushed in wild apology. "He'll need to wait a bit though, 'til he and Pa finish putting up their new shed."

Since Gracey had been one of her first visitors after Peavy's attack, they found areas of fresh gossip today, Brixton and Caldwell's altercation being news no longer. Indeed, life in Paradise had become somewhat languid with the fair over for another summer, the Perkins gang harassing another state, and the corn not quite ready for harvest. Finally, Gracey rose and stretched. "I'd better get along home and discuss your proposition with Nathan."

"You're absolutely alight with joy," Minda said.

"Yes." Gracey's face stayed soft and bright. "No babe will ever replace our Ruthie, so I don't care a whit if this next one's a boy as well."

"Your sons are all precious," Minda said fondly. "I spent my life raising girls. Not until Ned did I have a chance to hold a little boy close to my heart." Or Brixton either, she reminded herself. Her rough and rowdy husband was every bit the father he claimed he wasn't. Somewhere deep down, her womb reeled with emptiness.

After helping Gracey into her buggy, Brixton came in the back door to stand in front of her at her worktable, tall, tender, and so serious that she knew finishing her bath was the farthest thing from his mind. Even still, her heart lurched with joy at the sight of him.

She swallowed with a loud gulp. "That letter wasn't your reward."

"Nope. Letter was from Buck Hannon, trail boss of my outfit. Wonders where I am."

Minda could hardly hear the words. She'd long known the dream would end. She just hadn't expected it to end today.

As he put his hands on her arms, she felt his pulse run with a sudden chill. "Truth is, Minda, Buck says I got to be back for fall round up. Or he'll hire someone else to ride point. Give somebody else my job."

Clearing her throat kept the melancholy from her voice. She remembered that point riding was what he did. That a point rider was who he was. "Brixton, I do understand, I do. Sit with me."

He hunkered on the big upholstered chair, and she reached to take his hands in hers. "Brixton, you must understand, too. Remember that day you told me things you'd never told anyone?"

"Yep." He nodded.

Her hands tightened. "Well, I have to confess something now. I do not think I have the stamina to raise another family all by myself."

She looked at him, hoping he understood she had none of the anger and threats from those first days left in her. "That night Silly got sick, the load bearing down on me was cut in half when you walked through the door."

He managed a tight smile. "You just called her 'Silly.'"

Her mouth twitched for a second but it wasn't a smile. "Don't sidetrack me. And Ned getting lost, why, without you..." She slowed down with a quiet shiver and a headshake. "And as for our little firefly. Well, it isn't all that far off when boys will be knocking on the door."

"Won't be finding any of them good enough," he grumbled.

"But you won't be here." Minda pulled her hands away.

"Minda." His voice was gentle, but he looked away. "I promised my brother I'd care for the kids. Never promised him I'd stay." He met her eyes then. "Never promised you either."

"I know that." she nodded, laying a hand on his knee now. "I'm just telling you how *I* feel."

"Truth is, Minda, you'd be raising the kids alone even if you had married my brother and not me." He looked away again, face reddening.

"What are you saying, Brixton?" Minda's stomach churned. What other secrets had he and Norman Dale kept from her?

"My brother was dying." His hands started a soothing journey up and down her arms, but he looked mostly in his lap while he talked. "His heart wore out with that scarlet fever that killed Ida Lou and their boy Paul. He even searched out a specialist in Omaha. That's why he picked you so quick. You could raise kids. He was a damn fool for tussying so hard to get ready for you. But truth is, he'd have died on you before long anyway." The eyes watched her now, showing apology for his dreadful secret, but suddenly he turned away. "Likely in your bridal bed."

Minda could hardly absorb the words, overwhelmed that she had been held to such a tremendous responsibility without her knowledge or choice.

And now she was to be alone anyway, despite the fact that her husband was alive and hale.

"But you accused me of contributing to his death," she said, remembering his wrath the day they met.

With a head shake, Brixton sighed deep, his hair tumbling along his shoulders. "I repent of that, I truly do. I was up against a wall and damn angry about it."

Outside, the wind rustled the cornstalks. "I can stick around to bring in the corn," he said, desolate.

"How long is that?"

"Well, middle of September. All I can promise right now, Minda." He stood up and pulled her along with him, holding her like he meant it, tight and strong.

But not forever.

"That's all I can ask then." She gave him a watery smile.

Chapter Seventeen

As August rolled on, Minda prayed that September could stay away forever. Brixton had promised half of that month to her. With the children in school, and unusual rain keeping the crop watered, she and Brixton had daylight hours, while Priscilla napped, to explore their bodies and their hearts, in addition to the dark heavenly nights in each other's arms. Her hat business exploded, and life would have been perfect.

If she hadn't had a husband who was leaving her.

One early September morning, fall tinting the air, Minda displayed her latest wares to Delmar Hackett at the mercantile while Geraldine cooed over Priscilla, and Brixton sought out refreshment at Skinny Hank's. One of his last days of freedom, he'd joked. He'd start the corn harvest in three days.

"Beauties, every single one, Minda. Why, I've had to increase my stock of dress lengths just so we have matching fabrics for your hats." Something sparkled on the older man's left hand, and a plot hatched in Minda's head.

"Mr. Hackett, do you carry men's wedding rings?"

His plump forehead crinkled. "Can't say that I do, not called that anyways. I do keep a few simple bands for the ladies." He winked at her. "And for ladies with prodigious hands as well, if you're thinking of a memento to fit Brixton."

She was, indeed. It might remind him of her

when he was alone on the trail. For a sad second, her heart trembled with bleakness worse than a barren late-winter day. "Then let me see them please. I can visualize his hand and likely select an appropriate size."

"Fact is, my Geraldine gave me this ring upon our betrothal those long years ago," Delmar said. "I'm a businessman, but most menfolk around here wouldn't dare wear such trinkets. Too easy to catch on a barb wire or a tool."

Minda hadn't considered such a danger, but bought the ring anyway. It would make a nice good-bye gift. Her heart fluttered like the wings of a dying bird. But she still had ten more September days.

Priscilla heavy in her arms, she left the mercantile, strongly considering an installment plan on that wonderful perambulator for Priscilla. Nathan Moulton yelled from way down at the livery. He trotted over.

"I just rode in this morning, Miz Haynes. Thanks for the extra job. It was a thrill." His boyish face was sunburned from his ride up from Kansas with Fara. "He's a powerful steed, that one. Does Brix proud. Wish he'd had him for the Bonnet Race. Why, Caldwell would have been a speck"

"Thank you, Nate. I'll go tell Brixton now. He's over at the saloon. I can't wait to see his face when he realizes my great surprise." Her skin prickled with excitement, heart pounding with anticipation.

Nathan reddened even more. "Be doing that for you, ma'am. Skinny Hank's ain't no place for a lady of your caliber. You wait right here." He ran off.

She perched on the Hacketts' pickle barrel. She'd made toys for Ned and hats for the girls, but she'd never concocted a suitable gift for her husband. Fara's return was a surprise, not a present. As it was, a wedding ring wasn't typical, and he might not wear it simply out of safety. A gift for him had been a difficult decision.

Unless. Her hand lowered to her belly. Gracey had mentioned queasiness, and Minda had used the chamber pot for an entirely new reason after Brixton left her side this morning.

Unless she were about to present him with fatherhood. Her heart barely beat. Neddie had insisted he needed a brother because Paul lived with God, and Katie had her own baby sister. In her giddiness, Minda almost felt queasy now. Purchasing that perambulator might make more sense than ever.

She grappled for control in time to watch Brixton's black hair linger on his shoulders as he walked from the saloon with their neighbor, Tom Holden. Seeing her, her husband's face split with a grin that weakened her knees against the cask. He ran to her because with the weight of Priscilla, she couldn't run at all. His wide-spread arms gathered them both close.

Saloon or not, his scent was sunshine and life itself.

"Oh, Minda. My Fara? This can't be real." His words, as well as his lips, kissed her, firm and soft at the same time. "How could you?" His dark eyes accused her affectionately.

"Now, now, Mr. Haynes. I have my own money and can spend it as I will." She glanced down. With all that was between them, how could she still feel shy? "It just didn't seem right, you not having your own horse."

He looked away. "That'll sure save me a trip to Kansas."

Throat tightening with the ache that came more and more often as time sped on, she knew what that meant. He could freight the horse on the same train he took from Columbus to Texas.

"This is a righteous cause for celebration." He

nodded firmly with that insouciant grin of his, but she saw a trace of regret behind the sparkle in his eyes.

"You mean, supper at Miss Lila Jean's?" Minda forced a tease, not wanting anything serious to mar the moment.

"Maybe, but I'm devising how to rejoice with you later on." His voice came out husky, brushing her skin.

"Now, now, Mr. Haynes, Priscilla has ears," she murmured against his kiss, marveling at the passion his lips invoked.

By nightfall, he'd tended and tucked in all three of the children while she stitched eagerly upon a new design for Lorelei Braun. When he came from behind the bed curtain, still humming his lullaby, she dropped the hat at once. Holding out his hand like a true bridegroom, he led her from her worktable. Before they reached the bedroom, he had slipped off his own clothes.

"What's this damn corset for?" he grumbled, trying to divest her of her inexpressibles.

She couldn't help a giggle. "It's essential for the style of this old dress." Kicking away the homely gown, she leaned into his mouth. "You see, someone promised me a new one."

He stiffened, apparently having forgotten, so she comforted him right away, kissing the corner of his mouth. "It makes no matter, Brixton. I've been too busy making hats to think up something for myself."

"I like you far better without dresses anyway," he said into her hair, having successfully untied the corset. He picked her up like any true bride and carried her over her threshold.

His mouth bent to brush her breasts as he headed for their bedroom. Laying her tenderly among the pillows, he knelt on the bed at her side, his hands playing upon her body in the gentle rhythm of a choirmaster. Her breasts became his first area of worship. Heat from his tongue started a slow burn that traveled up to her neck.

His gaze scorched her. She moved almost restlessly, seeing the glory of his raging manhood and wanting to contribute to his pleasure as well.

"Brixton..."

"Not now," he murmured against the coil of her ear, making her quiver deliciously. His tongue briefly parted her lips, then he busied it at her other ear, before taking a long, sinuous sweep under her chin.

Then down to her nipples to drink voraciously. Minda's spine rose up in her delirium, desperate for her breasts to meet the dark soft whorls on his chest.

Her inner legs from hip to toe were next for the travel of his tongue. Once again, his eyes never left her face, and his hair dragged sinuously, tickling her flesh into a spasm of delight. Even at the ankle just healed, his touch caused such combustion that moaned as if with her last breath.

She was empty but satiated at the same time. He was hers and that was enough.

His masterful tongue kissed her senseless at the center of her being. Colors never yet imagined swirled in her head, and sounds never before heard wrenched from her soul.

"Brixton, now. I need you now." She moaned, and reached between the latticework of their legs to find his powerful manhood and grant it entrance. "Now."

He filled her as only he could. As the spiral collapsed into a gentle peace, she simply knew. It would never have been like this with Norman Dale. With any other man.

"Oh God, Minda," He breathed atop her, letting her adore the wonder of his weight upon her. "Minda, this was a sacrament all our own.

Something holy, and I'm no godly man." He rose up on his elbows, searching her eyes. "I will remember this forever. I wish I could find the words I mean."

"I know." She caressed his back, completely overwhelmed. He had already alerted her to the impossibility of giving her, of giving anyone, the declarations he'd spoken to Esperanza.

But at least she had him for a while. Ten more September days.

****

Minda woke up alone and exhausted. From the children's chatter outside the bedroom and the glorious sunshine pouring past the curtains, she knew she'd overslept.

As she sat up, the room swayed and her stomach stirred unhappily. She swallowed hard until it passed. When it did, she rose slowly, her memories of last night overtaking any brief unpleasantness. Lost in her husband's lovemaking, she had known a union that surpassed any other time they'd spent in each other's arms.

As she buttoned her old purple dress—she'd replaced the button Delaware Peavy had cut off and hastily added a ruffle of gray gingham where she'd cut away strips—she reveled in the tenderness of her breasts where Brixton's lips had lingered and feasted, swelling them with so much leftover pleasure the bodice fit tighter. In a moment, she'd likely see him shaving outside, the sinews of his back weaving together in impossible beauty. She quivered like a schoolgirl.

Opening the bedroom door, she swelled with love for the three children who had claimed her heart. Already dressed, his face damp with soapy water, Ned ran to her, and Priscilla called out more of the new words she learned every day. Minda had meant it, telling Brixton she couldn't raise another family alone.

But she'd never leave them. She'd simply hoped her words would inspire a change in his way of thinking, make him reconsider his plans to leave. And after last night, that benediction of love, she had more than a casual notion that he just might stay.

At the stove, Katie turned with her bright smile, her hair unbraided but otherwise ready for school.

"Mama, I lit the stove. I can make grits for you and Silly if you want. Me and Ned had bread and jam." She made a satisfied sound with her lips. Minda beamed. The chokecherry preserves she'd attempted had turned out wonderfully.

Then she frowned. Brixton always lit the stove before his outdoor chores. "Katie, I'm not sure I like you playing with fire." With a smidge of anxiety, her eyes glanced out the window. No one stood at the shaving mirror.

"Oh, it's all right. Papa taught me long ago, when our first mama passed."

"Well, all right them. I am sorry to have slept so late. I don't understand why I'm so tired." Of course she did, and she warmed. Then she smiled. Obviously, Brixton couldn't wait to tend to Fara.

Katie giggled. "Mama, you need a new dress so bad." Then she smiled in her little girl way.

Minda laughed back with a little shove. "I'll see about it soon. You children and those hats keep me too busy. I can hitch the wagon and drive you two to school, if you'd like."

"We can both ride Dobby like always," Ned said.

"Then I'll saddle him up when I'm done with Mabel. Have you seen Uncle Brix yet?"

Katie shook her head, pulling mournfully at her lack of braids.

"Oh, I know, I know." Neddie beamed, waving his arm like she suspected he did all day at school. "It was just past being dark. I went to the privy. He didn't see me so he didn't wave. He rode off on that new horse of his. Do you think he'll let me ride him some day?"

"Of course he will, although soon he'll be busy with the corn harvest, you know."

Her heart lightened. She'd been right. Brixton had merely taken Fara out for a morning ride. If he left at sunup, he'd be back any minute to wish the children a good day at school.

But he didn't come back. She plunked the children on Dobby herself. Missing the noon meal wasn't like him either, and supper was cause for nerves. Even in the first days of their marriage, when anger and resentment had colored his moods, he'd never been knowingly thoughtless or rude.

Still, he was a man, and she'd realized long ago that she had a great deal to learn about living with one. He'd made no secret of his devotion to Skinny Hank's whiskey mill. There might be card games, or contests, or other manly pursuits needing his attention before he consumed his days with harvest.

But that night when he wasn't there to tuck in the children and sing lullabies to them, their eyes were wide with hopelessness.

"Is he G.T.T.?" Katie wept, strangling Ned's toy dog.

"He didn't say good-bye." Ned howled into their puppy's warm thick fur.

Minda didn't know, and she had no real words or reasons, but she gathered them close in comfort, keeping close to her heart the knowledge that Brixton cared for the children, and for her, in his own way.

"Now, Uncle Brix has some good explanation. Don't you fret. He's just been delayed somehow. You sleep tight. Things will be better in the morning bright." She kissed them with fervent belief.

They climbed into bed without a song, although

she prayed their nightly prayers with them, all the while silently adding her own. She had learned his lullabies, but couldn't force them from her ragged throat. Puzzled and heartsick, she dragged herself to their cold, lonely bed.

Before a troubled sleep claimed her, she faced the hard possibilities. Maybe he had left, simply unable to face the children. Maybe last night had been her good-bye. Her heart lodged in her throat. It was all her fault, reuniting him with that horse.

By morning, her attitude had changed. Brixton wasn't neglectful. He wasn't unfeeling. Something important had prevented his return. Waiting for her stomach to settle, she rested on the pillow and put her reasoning power to work.

He and Fara hadn't ridden together in more than two months. Maybe the horse was no longer accustomed to him. Maybe Brixton, skilled horseman though he was, had been tossed off and now lay injured in an irrigation furrow or a field, or along the river.

Terror churned in her stomach. Maybe another Peavy had returned to take vengeance. Soothing the children with half-truths, she got them to school and herself to town, to leave Priscilla with Gracey while she consulted with the sheriff.

And, she admitted, it was time to talk to Gracey. As a spinster, she'd paid little attention to her monthly times, but as a married woman with queasy mornings, she had calculated she hadn't had one since the week before leaving Gleesburg.

Tears fluttered behind her eyelids as she mounted the parsonage steps, and her heart pounded up to her ears. What if Brixton had brought about a child but was now gone?

Or dead?

"Why, Minda, what's wrong?" Jake asked, full of hearty concern as he opened the door and took

Priscilla in his arms.

"Brixton's missing, Jake. I think something's happened to him. Ned saw him ride off on Fara early yesterday morning, and he hasn't been home since." She knotted her fingers together.

Shaking his head sadly, he led her to a tiny settee.

"Minda, I know my words will hurt, but I know Brix better than anyone. I think reuniting with Fara reminded him it was time."

Jake's soft, sweet eyes looked out of Gracey's pretty front window for a long time before he swallowed hard and finished. "For a while, I thought you might have roped him in. But regardless, I know he cares deeply in his own way. He can't stay, but he won't stay away forever."

She wasn't convinced. "But he hasn't been on Fara for quite some time. Maybe he's lying hurt somewhere." Almost with panic she tugged at Jake's shirtsleeve. "Let's go talk to Sheriff Pelton. Maybe there're more outlaws on the loose."

Jake shook his head. "I don't think any of that is likely. I just saw Bob Pelton this morning. And Brix was practically born atop Fara. I think…I just don't think he could bear saying good-bye to you and the children."

"Brixton's not a coward," Minda said with passion, and the truth burgeoned through all of her senses. He'd braved lightning storms and faced down outlaws and most of all, taken on a wife he hadn't wanted, all without excuses and hesitation.

In a fatherly way, Jake took her chin tenderly in his hands. Minda almost smiled, remembering Jake was but three years her senior. "Brix isn't a coward. It took a strange sort of courage, not saying good-bye. You see, he's a man needing to leave. But he wouldn't have been able to, not if he had to look into your eyes."

Jake set Priscilla down to toddle about and drew Minda close in reassurance. "Now, I know Brix well. He'll be back, in his time. His way."

She drank in Jake's wisdom, his compliments, and his hope, then shook away unshed tears. "Now, I'm getting my sniffles all over your tidy white shirt." She reached for Priscilla.

"I'll tend her," Jake said, as he cuddled the baby close with a wry smile, caressing her black curls. "Gracey is convinced she's bearing us another boy. Now, you go find that wife of mine for a good chat. Or a good cry. She plans on having tea with my mother after a check with Doc Viessman. You'll likely find her at the boardinghouse."

Nodding, Minda kissed Priscilla and shook off her melancholy with a smile. It was at the boardinghouse where she'd used a window as a mirror to set right her wedding veil on that hot July afternoon. The hot July afternoon when she'd become reluctant wife to a man who now held her eager heart.

She checked her reflection there now, hair down like her husband liked, topped with a sweet, round-crowned hat Katie teased looked like a plum pudding. Before leaving town, she'd lift her spirits and buy some dress goods to finally make herself something new to wear.

As she opened the door, she didn't find either Gracey or Lila Jean Satterburg chatting over tea. Instead, a lone young woman moved through the dining room toward a table. Black-haired and beautiful, she was obviously expecting, wearing an exquisite Polonaise dress of dark blue silk, the overskirt unbuttoned to accentuate her increasing motherhood.

Jake's mother scurried in from the kitchen with a teapot, aflutter with an emotion Minda couldn't read. Her eyes were like her son's, sweet and soft, but her anxiety was palpable.

"Minda, my dear. Let me introduce to you my new lodger. Arrived last night with a coachman in her own brougham. She's a friend of Brix's, she says, all the way from Texas."

"Esperanza Eames," the woman said, her eyes green as a cat's.

Esperanza. *Esperanza.* The woman who had betrayed her husband with another man was no friend of his.

Minda's eyes narrowed and her mood turned to a blaze of black fire. "I'm Mrs. Brixton Haynes," she said, barely polite.

"Pleased, I'm sure." The visitor laid a hand softly on her belly. "But as you can see, your husband and I are something more than friends. And I'm looking for him."

Chapter Eighteen

"Please, some privacy, Miss Lila Jean. Or should I invite Mrs. Haynes up to my superb accommodation?" Esperanza's voice turned unpleasantly snooty as the innkeeper slipped away, abashed.

But Minda barely heard. No. *No.* This was wrong, all wrong. Brixton had found Esperanza in another man's arms. This woman had broken his heart to such a degree that he believed he could never trust or love a woman again. Each syllable pounded inside her head.

"My husband's not in town," Minda said simply, unable to resist taking a chair. She wanted desperately to leave the boardinghouse, but like a tongue seeking a toothache, she couldn't stay away from whatever calamity was about to descend.

"Let me guess. You have no idea when he'll return. Well, Mrs. Haynes, I've lived that scenario before. Not a word? Not an explanation?" Too casually, Esperanza poured a cup of tea.

Minda's stomach roiled and a sour fear shot up her throat at the familiarity of Esperanza's tale.

Esperanza gave a deep sigh. "But you fared a bit better. There is at least a ring on your finger." She raised her empty left hand to her chin with high drama. "And you weren't left heartbroken at the altar."

Minda turned hot in sudden defense of her husband. "He never found me in the arms of another man."

Esperanza flushed briefly, but her bravado came quickly back. “Oh, pish, Mrs. Haynes. Or may I call you Minda?”

“No.” Now more than ever, Minda needed to hear her married name. “It’s Mrs. Haynes to you.”

“Well, Mrs. Haynes, I explained the truth to Brix then and there.” Esperanza leaned in too close with her startling eyes. “It was just a good-bye kiss from my old friend Rawley. You must know by now what a temper Brix has.”

Sadly, Minda did, but she didn’t dare admit it to this foe. Brix had wanted to smash Caldwell’s face just for that first hand-kiss in the mercantile. A worm of doubt wiggled in her brain. Could his hot temper have led him into overreacting over Rawley’s unassuming good-bye kiss?

Could Esperanza possibly speak even one syllable of truth?

Minda could barely swallow her dread, barely think a thought, barely feel her toes.

“Here’s the thing, Mrs. Haynes.” Esperanza coolly arranged her skirts to display her bump. “I’ve learned the truth of your marriage, how Brix forced you to marry him simply to gain a governess. Well, it won’t take anything at all to dissolve such an artificial marriage.”

Biting her lip hard, Minda halted a shout that it wasn’t an artificial marriage at all. True, it might have started out that way, but memories of authentic, caring passion erupted like crocuses bursting through the snow overnight. Still, the heart Brixton held started to shatter. Esperanza had spoken some truth. Their marriage had begun with lies and tricks.

“My daddy knows powerful barristers who can take care of your divorce in a flash. I’ll make sure you have a nice monetary settlement. Those children will be mine now and off your hands. You’ll have your own life back, and they'll soon be enjoying their new little brother or sister." She pointed both hands insolently out the window. "And in Texas, they'll have a stylish upbringing in a proper town."

The words stabbed. Paradise was good people. Paradise was home. The children were hers.

"I'm Brixton's wife," Minda said.

"Yes, indeed." Esperanza yawned delicately. "Well, if he's *out of town*, my intuition claims he's abandoned you. Just like he abandoned me back in Butter Creek. Buck Hannon told me he was here, but my daddy has the means to find him wherever he's run to. Brix has a very good reason to be with me now."

As Esperanza placed both hands on her burgeoning belly, she examined Minda head to foot. Minda blushed at her homely gray dress, but Esperanza gave a brilliant smile. "So that hat is one of your own creations?"

Minda nodded. "It's the jocket style."

"Well, Miss Lila Jean has been agog about the beauty of your designs. Seeing your craftsmanship up close, I shall order several new styles for myself."

"Sorry. I have plenty of business for the time being." Minda rose from her chair in dismissal.

"Well, Mrs. Haynes, I have nothing to do but wait." Esperanza cast her a spiteful glint.

Minda felt the woman's smirk on her back as she left in a gentle huff, weary of the veiled accusations and insinuations that her husband wasn't here to face.

More than that, she didn't need it spread all over town that Brixton had gone. Priscilla tucked beside her, she fumed all the way home, the wagon wheels squeaking with an annoying and incessant whine.

That afternoon, Minda was far less gentle with Mabel than she should have been, unable to concentrate on the soothing task she'd grown to enjoy. Despite her strength and her resolute nature, doubts and heartbreak had begun to stew, and Brixton wasn't here to assuage them.

Maybe Esperanza's arrival had something to do with his disappearance.

Alone with herself at the homestead, the children busy with studies and play, her demons raged. She'd even avoided confiding in Gracey and Jake, who kindly didn't pry. Brixton had made it clear he didn't have fatherhood in his nature. Esperanza's news could have sent him running.

She remembered seeing him with Tom Holden, the day Fara had arrived, the same Tom Holden who had wanted to enslave little Ned as a field hand. Brixton might have taken it to heart when she revealed that she couldn't raise more children all alone.

He might be parceling them out now to those who wanted them.

That last night of their holy love, she wouldn't have believed such wicked possibilities, but that was before he vanished without the good-bye kiss he'd always promised to give her.

As for the corn harvest, she had sufficient income now to hire Clem and Monty, and he knew it full well. Her gullet rose but she quashed the feeling.

"Mama, are you sick?" Katie had come quietly into the stall. "I can milk Mabel for you."

"I'm fine, Firefly," Calming herself, she tugged at Katie's long braid. "I'm just…" She didn't dare put any of her thoughts and feelings into words.

"It'll be all right. Uncle Brix will be back. I just know it, but Neddie is sad, like you." Katie paused for a while. "He told everybody at school about Uncle Brix not saying good-bye."

Minda's heart sank. Even those folks expecting Brixton to leave someday would not have expected him to be cruel. And now a newcomer had shown up in town, claiming to bear his child. Although Minda would barely be able to hold up her head, the children's well-being was far more important.

"Why, are the other pupils making fun?"

"Oh, no," Katie said with a hug. "Everybody knows Uncle Brix couldn't stay."

Minda sighed with a bit of relief. At least Paradise seemed to accept that Brixton would return in his own way and on his own schedule.

But until then, her mind conjured nightmares at the thought of Esperanza Eames as the children's stepmother.

And as Brixton's wife.

Minda trembled with unimaginable grief. It was all for Brixton to decide. Once again he held her life in his hands. And every time she closed her eyes, she still saw his face.

****

Next morning, she took the children to school after a wakeful night and green-about-the-gills dawn, planning a session of Gracey's confidence and a consultation with Doc Viessman while she was in town.

If her spirits improved, she'd stop at the mercantile for that dress length she'd promised herself.

"Minda." Caldwell Hackett stopped in front of her before she could climb back into the wagon after calling Neddie back for his forgotten lunch bucket. "Walk with me?"

Her chagrin must have shown as she looked wildly around the bustling schoolyard, for he continued, "School won't start for a while yet. Katie and her chums can tend Silly until I need to ring the bell."

She squinted with indecision. She, Brixton, and Caldwell had reached a civilized accord since the fair, but she had definitely seen that solemn look in Caldwell's eyes on a couple of other noteworthy occasions. Nothing in his expression indicated a problem with the children's performance or behavior in his classroom.

She pretended otherwise. "Now, I know Neddie can be a ball of mischief but—"

"No, Minda. This isn't about the children at all. Well, indirectly, I suppose." His eyebrows lowered over his spectacles.

"Caldwell, what is it? You have a schoolhouse to run, and I have errands of my own." Minda was suddenly weary, so weary.

Her instincts told her what this was about. She wanted Brixton, Caldwell wanted her, and Esperanza had tightened all of them into a coil. Only Brixton could do the unraveling.

But he wasn't here.

Caldwell offered her his arm politely, and she took it, too tired to be obstinate. Besides, her husband could be a thousand miles away.

They walked a goodly distance from anyone else's earshot.

"I won't mince words, Minda. I fell for you at my first sight of your daguerreotype." He paused, his throat working behind his collar like he might be struggling what next to say.

He breathed out and plunged ahead. "I would have protested at that farce of a wedding when Jake asked, but my father warned me about making a public scene. He felt it would compromise my position in the community." He grinned boyishly. "Although that punch in the nose has seemed to enhance my manliness."

"Mr. Hackett..."

"Sorry. What I mean is, I've heard that Brix is gone, and well, I've met Miss Eames. That marriage of yours is all but over, Minda. I think you need to accept that Brix now has a child on the way and the children will have a stepmother."

She'd had those very same thoughts, but hearing his words out loud staggered her. Like the day she'd proceeded to her wedding, she stumbled against a clump of blue stem, for this stroll with Caldwell was very like walking up an aisle. All she could do was clear her throat against the pain.

"Minda, I want to make a respectful offer for your hand. The kind you deserve. You know I love the children. If for some unseen reason, they should need someone, I would gladly make them my own. As for you, I will take care of you," Caldwell said in a voice as firm as it was tender. He looked bashfully at his feet, then forced a stare into her eyes. "And I will love you until I die."

Minda was a married woman, but she didn't feel appalled or offended. Indeed, she'd long suspected Caldwell's feelings, and his declaration came as no surprise.

What surprised her, she admitted shamefully, was the possibility that she might accept. She couldn't in good conscience keep Esperanza's baby from its father, and she couldn't go back to Gleesburg.

His mother was a busy-body, but Caldwell was kind, intellectual, and prominent in Paradise. He'd promptly regained his reputation after declaring her bonnet and getting punched in the nose.

More than anything, Minda realized hopelessly, Brixton had already run out on a pregnant bride. She could never let him know about the baby she might be nurturing deep down inside. It needed a father, too, and she was tired of raising children all alone.

Despite the blazing love she had for Brixton, Caldwell just might do. After all, she'd come to Paradise to wed for reasons other than true love. It didn't hurt so much to finally accept that Norman Dale and Brixton had both betrayed her in their in their own ways, just to keep the children together.

True, Caldwell might be promising nothing but the same, but he also promised to love her.

Something Brixton never had.

She nodded, resolute and forlorn both. "Go ring that bell. I never thought I'd say this, and I'll need time. Likely a lot of it. But I promise to think about your offer."

Caldwell took her hand in a gentle squeeze, but she pulled politely away, confusion and a kind of squeamishness pounding with every drop of blood in her veins. The truth couldn't be ignored. It would always be Brixton's touch she'd feel.

****

Around him, the prairie and cornfields and sand hills let Brix know once again he wasn't in Texas, but the sun shined the same, and the bugs bit just as hard. He grinned. Truth was, he'd come to admit those Nebraska roots Norman Dale set down had started to grow up through his own boot heels.

He had every kind of good feeling inside that a man could have. Fara full of beans between his knees, the wind in his face, and Minda waiting back home had him wanting nothing more.

Three days away from her. Damn, it had felt like centuries. That last night of sacred love in her arms had him doubt he could make it until tonight. All he wanted was her. All he needed, too.

But even with his need for a blistering hot welcome home, Brix was man enough to know a polite stop at Tom Holden's farm was the right thing to do before anything else. Tethering Fara, he found his neighbor scrubbing up in a bucket by the front door of his little sod house.

"How do, Tom. Just letting you know it's a deal for sure."

"Now, that's a good thing, giving Ned something else to think about." He shook his head like a wet dog. "Me and the missus got a start on the corn while you was gone."

Brix nodded. "Well, I'll be around to bring in the rest. But don't forget. I got two girls, too."

"That I do. You know, Brix, I don't do with gossiping like an old biddy, but…" Tom's eyes, tight from years in the sun, squinted even more. "My kids've been bringing rumors home from school. About you taking off without saying good-bye to your kin. Me and my missus haven't been to town since church Sunday, so can't say for sure what this next is all about. But our boy claims some fancy Texas woman's showed up, big as a barn, saying she's bearing your child."

Brix's lungs emptied at the wild notions. He'd left Minda a note about his plans fair and square. And while he'd had a few tender affairs in his day, he knew well how to prevent such a thing. With Minda, now, his own true wife who hadn't protested, he hadn't given a thought. As for that faithless bride-to-be in Texas, he'd planned to explore her virginity on the bridal night that had never taken place.

"Pure gossip, all it is," Tom said. "Well, Brix, good luck to you." He extended his hand and Brix shook it. But Brix was uneasy as he mounted Fara, skin cold with dread. Gossip was never a good thing.

Suddenly Fara's hoof beats, once so cheerful, sounded like a leaden death bell. This time around, Minda might find him hard to forgive. She'd been victim of gossip once or twice, their wedding for one, Caldwell for another, and she hadn't liked any of it a single bit.

Ahead of him, perched like a toy behind the windbreak, was home, that magical place where Minda lived. His heart swelled. Whatever had gone wrong since he'd left, he'd fix right up. It was too early for a light on, but it didn't matter. He knew she waited inside. The kids would be home from school by now, and Silly up from her nap.

He tethered Fara at the hitching post at the front door, unwilling to take the time to curry and stable him right now, unable to hold in his joy for another second.

"Minda? Neddie-boy? Katie? I'm home!"

The kids ran screaming from Dicey's side in the pasture, their pup at their heels. He grinned. Ned was still beguiled by that heifer. Damn, he'd make a cattleman of that boy yet. He gathered them close like an armful of flowers.

Then she stood, the reason for every good feeling he felt, and walked toward him from the back porch. Like she had that day at the river, Brix opened his arms wide, ready to hold her to his heart.

She allowed it, a brief stay in his arms, but she was stiff and pale. "You're back," was all she said.

"Minda, what's wrong? Told you I'd be back. Never said I'd be gone for good."

"But you never said you were leaving." She buried her face at the crook of his shoulder. "You never kissed me good-bye."

He chuckled at that, and held her back a bit to see her tragic face. "I most surely did. But you were sleeping so sound—" He leaned into her ear to whisper so the kids couldn't hear. "I think I wore you out that night. Maybe you don't remember."

Nibbling at her mouth now, he attempted to get her to smile. But her kiss in return was short and tight, nothing like he expected after being gone, nothing like either of them deserved. Likely because the kids were so close by.

"All right, if you say so." But still she didn't smile. "I don't remember. But you didn't say anything to the children at all. We've been worried,

Brixton. That was plain rude, and mean." Her voice trembled, but there was nothing coy in her reaction. Her resisting him was real, and it hurt.

"But I left a letter. On your worktable. Said I'd be back." His shoulders slumped in desperation. What had happened?

Coming home to her had spurred him on, mile after mile. Why had his proud arrival turned to failure?

Katie tore from his side and ran to the barn just as Ned shrieked, flapping his hands in excitement. "Company's coming. Look!"

It wasn't everyday visitors. Over the wind, with Minda in his arms as stiff as a board and mad at him, they had neither seen or heard. Right now, turning into Norman Dale's place was something from a story book, a fancy box-like coach pulled by two perfect matched bays. A coachman in a fairy tale suit climbed down and bowed to someone inside.

"Brixton," Minda said softly, looking up bravely into his face like she knew just who it was. His heart stopped before it hammered hard against his lungs. For a flash, he couldn't breathe. Was she leaving him after all?

"Something's happened while you were gone. Someone has come to town."

He recalled Tom Holden's mention of rumors. Swallowing hard, Brix turned back and forth between his wife and the brougham. The newcomer hadn't come into sight yet.

She cleared her throat, but her word still stuck.

"Esperanza."

Brix felt carved from stone.

Helped by her manservant, Esperanza stepped out, gracefully in spite of her burgeoning body. Gorgeous clothes like Brix remembered pulled tight across her belly for greatest effect.

Brix had always wondered what he'd do, what

he'd feel, what he'd say if he ever saw Esperanza again, but he never imagined she'd be large with child, and he'd have a wife at his side to calm. If Tom was correct, she'd be blaming him for her condition, which was physically impossible. But, he almost gagged, Minda certainly believed it.

And why not? She thought he'd left her, too.

"Well, well. Good afternoon, Brix." Esperanza's green eyes were surprised, but sly. "I'm rather stunned to see you here. I heard you were out of town, but don't we all know what that really means? I came by to bring some toys and proper clothes for the children. I found a fairly decent retailer in Omaha."

Brix didn't believe her. She'd come to make trouble, pay Minda to leave him. Threaten something evil.

"If you'll excuse me," Minda said, taking Ned's hand, "I'll leave you two to your privacy. And I'm certain you'll understand, Miss Eames, why I don't welcome you into my house."

"How'd you get here, Esperanza? And why?" Brix stood tall and furious.

"Oh, Brix, you can *see* why." She giggled but looked away. "I didn't hire a Pinkerton if that's what you're thinking. My daddy sent me to my auntie in Council Bluffs so as not to embarrass him." She sent out a bitter little laugh. "When he heard from Buck that you were staying on around here, well, I couldn't resist hiring a coach and seeking you out."

For a moment, her nose crimped with apology, but he knew deep down she wasn't sincere. "I had no idea I'd intruded on a married man. Well, that's easy enough to fix."

"Esperanza, you've lost your mind. That baby's not mine. You come to ruin my reputation?" Anger clenched his fists, but he counted slow and untied them.

"Hmm. Well, Brix, everybody in Butter Creek believes you're the father. And Daddy surely does. He wants me to have a husband. And who do you think people will believe? Him, the richest man in West Texas, or you? The buckaroo who ran out on his daughter?" Her eyelids shuttered closed.

For a vague, polite second, Brix wondered if he should get her some kind of seat. The baby wasn't his, but she *was* a woman with child.

But she stormed along before he could move. "We had something once, Brix. You can't deny it. And we could have that again. The ranch we planned. That little house you started to build me." Her eyes blinked beguilingly.

As he grabbed his hand back, his teeth clenched so tight he gnawed his tongue. "Started to build, Esperanza? I finished it, every square inch. But it wasn't big enough, good enough for you."

"Minda believes me." Esperanza dared him.

Her beauty was still grand and powerful, but he'd recovered just fine from the deep hurts she had caused. It was a good thing after all, their cancelled wedding. For he'd never have been free to marry Minda.

Minda. His eyes closed in frustration. Hell and damnation, he wasn't about to let this cattle baron's spoiled daughter disrupt his future with his wife.

Still, he remembered her pa's money and power and his heart quaked a bit. All he had was his honor.

Esperanza's eyes stared and dared, reminding him of the taunt she'd thrust at him after flinging herself from Rawley Snate's arms. He owed her nothing.

"I'm a man of responsibility, Esperanza," he said, figuring she might have forgot. "Folks hereabouts, far as you can see, know I took on my brother's bride, his kids, and his debts. That baby isn't mine. But if it had been, I would have done right by you, and you know it."

He held her chin tight in his hands and stared her down. "Get your daddy to hire that Pinkerton and chase down Rawley Snate. Remember him? The man who broke up our wedding?"

"Brix?" Her face had turned mostly pale, but the cheekbones had gone purple.

"No, Esperanza. It's over. You can't beguile me again. Likely I ought to have faced you before and said it in person. So I'm doing it now. Right inside there—" He pointed to the little white house he'd helped build. "Inside there's all I ever wanted. It just took me some time to know."

Chapter Nineteen

"Who's that pretty lady, Mama?" Neddie asked in his voice that was somewhere between baby and boy.

Pretty lady? Minda turned cold from head to foot as she quietly shut the back door, wishing she could slam it instead. But Priscilla was still napping. That pretty lady was someone who had the potential to destroy their home and family.

"Someone who knows Uncle Brix from Texas," she said as mildly as she could, holding off a shiver.

"But she said she brought toys."

Minda knelt to hold the little boy against her heart, praying their world wasn't ending. "Well, let's wait and see about that. Don't you still love your toy doggie from me best of all?" She hid her tearful gulp with a little cough.

Neddie grappled her neck. "Oh, I do, I do. But I love Schatzi, too." He wiggled away and grappled his puppy next. "Me and Katie thought that's a good name. Miss Marylaura told us it means *sweetheart* in the German language. That's what you like to call me sometimes."

The love shining in his eyes warmed her through, and she hugged him again. "Ned, you will always be my sweetheart. No matter what happens. Now, why don't you go outside and play with Schatzi for a while? But leave Uncle Brix alone, you hear? He and that lady have things to sort out."

Lady! She snorted.

After the little boy left for the pasture, Minda

sat weakly at her worktable, looking out the front window at her husband and their visitor like she watched a sad play on a stage.

How could she feel hot and cold at the same time? Brixton's arrival should have filled her with tumultuous joy, but there he stood, bearing blame. To hold down her trembles, she picked up her Bonnet Race hat and half-heartedly continued her repairs, recalling Brixton's glorious kiss after he'd won the race.

But she couldn't keep her eyes away. As she peeked out the window, her innermost heart rejoiced that Brixton didn't appear to behold Esperanza with any kind of affection. His actions and presence weren't those of a man learning the tender news of fatherhood, or of a man rendering forgiveness and renewing a promise.

Or of a man caught in a trap. He had the stance of a determined man who knew he was in the right. Like it burned him, he dropped Esperanza's hand, said something with a firm nod of his head and looked straight at the house.

Through the window, their eyes met, and she read gratitude and hope. For Minda, it was like they saw each other for the first time, making up for their initial meeting of secrets and anger.

Her heart tumbled in a new way. He claimed he'd left a note on her worktable, that awful day when he'd ridden off without a word, breaking her heart, but he hadn't. She kept the house tidy as a pin, and the house was small. Had he told another convenient untruth to save himself from a predicament?

After all, he'd kept truth from her before—painful raging truth that had changed her life forever.

No. Changed her life for the better. Something blossomed inside that had been ripening all along.

Brixton wasn't a man who ran out on his responsibilities. He'd taken on a wife he didn't want. He'd ridden in a race even though his little niece had secretly entered his name. He'd harvested crops he despised. He'd stayed on through illness, stayed on through danger, and stayed on despite all his threats to leave because downright affection had overtaken his heart. She knew it, and she knew him.

Despite his hard edge, Brixton was a man who cared deeply and fondly for those in his charge.

If he'd chanced to give Esperanza a child, he'd never have left her.

Now he had come back. Back to her. Despite the anxiety of the past few days, she had to let him know she believed in him, and always would.

And that she loved him. It was time to say it out loud.

Katie ran in from outside, a bundle in her arms, and her face flushed with what could only be guilt. Minda felt a trill of alarm and hugged the child close.

"Firefly, what is it? What's the matter? And what do you have there?"

Moving free from Minda's arms, Katie tore away the brown paper and held out a glorious bolt of violet gossamer silk. Minda gasped at the beauty.

"Why, Firefly? What is this? Where did you get it?"

"It's a surprise from Uncle Brix. For you. One day I came out to get Schatzi and he was hiding it in the barn and I saw. He told me to keep it secret. It's for a new dress."

"Then why now?"

Katie wiped her nose on her sleeve. "You're mad at Uncle Brix, and sad, too. I knew if you saw this, you wouldn't be angry anymore. I don't want you to go, Mama. That lady's outside. At school Emma said Uncle Brix used to love her back in Texas. So I thought, maybe, Uncle Brix's surprise will make you feel better. I can help you make the dress if you stay with us."

"Oh, Firefly. I'll never leave. Whether I have a new dress or not." The depth of Minda's love overcame any doubts, and she cast another look at her husband outside. Head shaking firmly, he remained a pillar of resolve. It was time for Minda to stand by his side.

Katie giggled. "It's been hard to keep this a surprise. Why do you think I always talked about you needing a new dress?"

After kissing Katie's cheek, Minda rose, took a little package from her worktable, and said, "You tend Priscilla if she wakes. I've got something to say."

As she joined her husband and Esperanza outside, Minda wondered at the woman's fortitude. Even in her delicate condition, Esperanza's shoulders were steady, her body tall. For a frenzied moment, Minda wondered if the motherhood might be nothing but a stuffed pillow. Either way, she had no qualms about interrupting their discussion.

"Sorry to interrupt, Brixton. Miss Eames." Resolute, she walked across the dusty yard to her husband's side and with an emphatic nod, took his hand in hers. Like always, she felt the heat from him that started her own delicious warmth down inside. "I am sorry about your predicament, but don't cast blame on my husband in your desperation. He does not run away from responsibility. I am living proof of that."

Brixton looked down at her with eyes so meltingly dark that she knew he could see into her heart, into her very soul. She knew he believed her.

For a moment, she returned his gaze until Esperanza's feet shifted. Minda gestured at the coachman to come assist. "Now I wish you health and I wish you well, but please, Miss Eames, leave our home."

****

Our home? Brixton's heart twinged with doubt. Had she grown so attached? Was his plan bound for failure?

Her hand clamped in his, she stayed so close to him their bodies touched, starting all kinds of heated thoughts as the carriage drove Esperanza away, and hopefully out of his life for all time. But no hatred bloomed. Desperation drove people to unimaginable plans.

Look at Norman Dale.

The babe was sure to be Rawley Snate's. The cattle trail was long, but its world wasn't wide. If Esperanza could be honest with trail boss Buck Hannon, he could find her lover in a flash and calm down her old man.

Brix had a home and family of his own now, and a wife to soothe.

"Minda, I never…there was never a chance, me and Esperanza never, I mean, we didn't…"

She smiled up at him, glowing in a way he hadn't seen before. "I know, Brixton. I believe you about that. I don't think she expected to see you here today. I'm sure she came here today to buy me off and enchant the children with gifts." She glanced away for a moment, but then looked at him with a tease in her eye. "She found out the truth about our wedding fast enough and figured I'd enjoy a way out."

Brix hated to think the words, much less mouth them. "What would you say to something like that?" He gave a quick glare at Esperanza's departing dust.

She spit fire. "What? I haven't proven myself yet that I want to stay? You're the one who took off, Brixton, without a word. And you can say all you want about leaving a note. But you didn't."

"Can we go sit somewhere, Minda? I left a note, truth as I live. On your worktable with your hat fixins." He kept her hand tight in his and led her to the porch steps, and she sank down in seeming appreciation.

"I'm there every day, Brixton. There wasn't a note." She nodded as vigorous as a schoolmarm.

"You say I'm lying about that?" Brix wasn't lying at all. How could he convince her he spoke true?

Minda's eyelids closed. "I hope not, Brixton. But you've had some difficulty with the truth in the past. Thing is, you always said I'd know when you left for good, because you'd kiss me good-bye. That didn't happen either."

At least she didn't mind leaning against him. Her shoulders pressing into his made him want to tuck her underneath his arm and keep her always by his side. But there were things to say.

"Well, for one thing, I didn't leave," he said. "Had an important errand to run for this family that took me away from home. Like I said previous, I did kiss you, but you were sleeping sound. However, I can sure make up for it now."

When she didn't frown at him or pull away, he drew her against his chest for an embrace he hoped would prove he wasn't lying. Or leaving again. Leastways not for the reasons she thought. His lips brushed the top of her hair, then traveled down her ear like he knew she liked, swooping across her cheek to her mouth. For a moment, she let him linger like two butterflies mating on a breeze, then she sat up again.

"Oh, no, you don't, Mr. Haynes. You can't charm me without some good explanation." But her eyes sparkled a bit. "I had some pretty bad days there."

"I believe I am in trouble, you using my formal name again," he teased back. "Thing is, maybe my note blew out the window on a draft."

"Not good enough, Mr. Haynes." Once again she looked at him in that schoolteacher way, but by no means did her stern lips prevent his craving another kiss. Her eyebrows rose. "Since our adventures with the Peavy boys, I shut up tight at night."

"Well, Miz Haynes, likely a good explanation will come to life." He took his chance with another kiss, and she allowed it, closing her eyes promptly. Even better, her lips danced across his like Fara's hoofs minced through a flower garden. Her tongue teased. Down below, his manhood came to the new life only she could give it. For a flash, he remembered that last night in her arms when all the stars in the heavens had melted together at the same time.

She pulled away, and her eyes dropped shyly to her lap. "I hope so, Brixton. I've got things to say, too."

At her words, his heart skipped a half-dozen beats, but she no longer wore the somber expressions from the days the kids got sick or lost, when she said she couldn't do it alone. She wasn't going to have to, now.

He had to let her know, and drew her close. "Well, Minda, if you can forgive me for my lapses, I can explain the nature of my errand. But most of all, I need to apologize for those bad days you had. Never was my intent."

"Why, I don't believe you've ever apologized for anything." She settled against him and gave him her teasing smile, but her voice turned serious.

"All I know is what happened, Brixton. Like this. I tell you I can't raise the children alone. Fara comes back into your life on a day I see you consulting over something with Tom Holden. The next morning, Neddie sees you ride off without a look back. Esperanza shows up. I think maybe you learned her news and ran off. I think you're planning to parcel off the children—I remember Tom wanting Neddie. You've left like you promised. But without a word.

"I seek out Jake and he tells me you'd never have left if you'd had to face me. Every little puzzle piece seemed to fit."

At her words, he felt her pain straight into his gut. How could he know her so well already? How could his plan have gone so far out of kilter?

"Minda, none of your sad thoughts bear fruit." He spoke fast and fervent, not wanting her hurts to fester. "Tom, now, he did me a service. He mentioned at Skinny Hank's that day some news he got from a cousin in the Sand Hills."

"Sand Hills?"

"Yep. Cattle country. Not so very far from Paradise. His neighbor woke up and died two weeks past. Widow's selling the ranch fast to get back home to St. Louis. I've been thinking thoughts that came to me slow, about giving up the trail and starting my own herd. My Bonnet Race prize can get me five healthy beeves for sure, maybe six or seven if I haggle right. After all, we already got two cows.

"I took off for that rancher's widow next day, to offer my Peavy reward as down payment on her place. After leaving that note." He stared at her, wishing he could read her thoughts.

Her eyes were bright as the sky, with no unhappiness showing. "But the farm?"

"Tom'll lease it from us these next ten, twelve years 'til Ned's grown up some. See if he wants to farm. But I'm growing high hopes our boy'll be a cattleman like I am. What with that heifer, he's showing the signs."

"But..."

"I know what you're thinking. We got girls, too. Maybe by then we'll sell the farm, divide in thirds. But in the meantime, Tom's woman is delighted to get out of their soddie and into that fine wooden house."

Minda smiled when he mentioned the fine wooden house she'd come to Paradise for, but her eyes were on guard.

"But none of this is gonna happen if you don't want it to," Brix said. "I thought it a righteous surprise, but I recall just now that you aren't much one for me keeping secrets. All bargains are off with him and the widow if you don't want to go along with any of this. I know…I know your hatmaking's bound for success and you made friends here."

"More than friends, to be sure," Minda said. "Caldwell made a formal offer for my hand the other day."

He growled, feeling his finger bones up against Caldwell's face one last time. But those days were gone. He had a family now.

"Well, what'd you say?" Brix had to ask, had to know.

Minda looked down again and was so quiet for so long that he wished he hadn't asked.

"I said I'd think about it. But his question came in my darkest hour. I've told him no for certain." Her face brightened with a laugh. "He promises he will not hold my refusal against the children at report card time."

Brix growled again, not feeling like laughter at all, but Minda went on, "But more important than any of that was Priscilla climbing halfway up the loft ladder this morning while my back was turned, milking Mabel. You should see her, Brixton, how much she learns every single day."

"Well, Minda, what do you say to these possibilities?" Brix took a deep breath. She hadn't said. Likely it wasn't something she could decide all at once. "Take your time. It'll be all right."

"Let's go inside, Brixton. Priscilla must be

awake from her nap by now. She knows more words each and every day."

****

A ranch of their own? He was giving up the trail? She placed her hand on her belly. Doc Viessman had confirmed it yesterday. Dreams were coming true faster than she could count.

Her news was so special she couldn't blurt it out on a rough hewn porch with Esperanza's dust still blowing.

Inside the house, Priscilla slept soundly in her little trundle. No doubt her sojourn partway up the ladder had tuckered her out.

"Now, Brixton, don't wake her up," Minda said, wanting a proper quiet moment to share her joy.

Guiltily, Katie looked up from Minda's worktable, where she sat with the Bonnet Race hat on her head and the purple cloth in her lap.

"Firefly, what you got there?" Brixton said almost sternly.

"Don't be upset with her, Brixton. She gave it to me just now. She figured if I saw it, I couldn't stay mad at you."

His hand on Katie's shoulder was as gentle as a father's. "Was a pretty hard secret to keep. Looks like your mama's fixing up her hat. Think she forgives me for wrecking it?"

Katie threw herself into his arms, starting a flood of tears. "Oh, Uncle Brix, it's all my fault. All mine."

"What's gone wrong, Firefly?" He knelt in front of her, eye level, and gave her braids a kiss. "Looks like you're braiding up your hair just fine."

"But nobody does it like you," Katie said.

"Nobody else has got to. I'm home, Firefly. To stay. Wherever it might be." He got to his feet, eyes on Minda. She still hadn't agreed to his wonderful plans, and she saw hope deep in his glance. "Now what's this fault of yours?"

"I didn't know 'til now. Mama slept late that day. She was so tired."

Minda caught Brixton's hot glance then, but it was more than likely the little load she carried that had exhausted her. Katie was clearly distraught.

"Silly woke up and I went to get some clean britches. She was toddling all over, chewing on a scrap of paper. I pulled it from her mouth. It was all crumpled up. I thought it must be trash, so I used it to kindle the stove. But Uncle Brix, I think now it was your note!"

He held tight to the sobbing child, but managed a wink at Minda. She smiled back in defeat and victory both. He had left a note like he'd said. In her heart, she had wanted to believe.

"Now listen, Firefly. You couldn't know, not 'til just now, what that was. You dry up those tears. Looks like your new mama has something to say to me. So how about you find Ned outside and do some playing before suppertime?"

Katie kissed him on the cheek and ran out like any happy healthy child, and Minda's heart surged at Brixton's acknowledgement of her as the children's new mama. She'd never replace Ida Lou, nor would Brixton ever become more important than Norman Dale, but between the two of them, they would be all the parents the children would ever need, and more.

"Brixton, the dress fabric. It's beyond beautiful. I'm sorry Firefly ruined your surprise, but she was something like desperate."

He grinned boyishly, but his eyes let her know he was all man. The tiny cracks in her heart had already healed, and she knew she'd go anywhere with him, and back again.

"Well," he said, "I got it to match your lovely hat. And I am pleased it isn't beyond repair. That hat, well, Miz Haynes, I may have said it before. Other than that wedding veil of yours, nothing has ever made you look more beautiful."

Her healing heart melted at his words, and her skin tingled from his touch.

"Thing is, Minda. I got gifts for the kids on my travels. Oglalla dolls for the girls and a drum for Ned. But that..." He pointed ruefully at the fabric. "That dress bolt was your surprise."

"And indeed it was, Brixton. But I have a little something for you, too."

His eyes lightened like a child's but he shook his head. "Now, Fara was more than enough."

"I don't think so. Not when you hear. Remember you mentioned someday selling the farm and dividing the profits into thirds?"

He nodded.

"I think you'll want to try fourths." She took his hand and laid it on her belly. As his eyes widened with wonder, she watched the realization bloom.

"Sweet Lord. Minda," His voice and hands trembled in the same rhythm. "You sure?"

"Yes. Doc Viessman is, too."

Tight against his chest, she heard his heart beat, arms holding him as close as they could be without the ultimate loving that she knew would keep them both awake all night long.

"Can hardly believe it," he murmured.

She looked away with sudden anxiety. "Brixton, after Esperanza, I have no wish to have you think you're trapped."

"Minda, this is a natural result of our love. I can't even bring my joy to words." He gazed into her eyes. "Each time Neddie-boy yapped about needing a brother, I kept thinking about how it would be, our babe nurturing deep inside you."

Our love? Our babe? Minda's heart soared. "Brixton, that ranch sounds like a grand place for a cattleman to raise his family. I'll be there every step of the way. And I can bring in a load of hats to sell every time we come visit Jake and Gracey."

He squeezed her harder. "I have made my intentions known, Miz Haynes. I intend to be there every step of the way myself."

Minda believed him, and knew he meant it as well as he could. He'd long stated he wasn't a hearth and home man, and she knew that didn't preclude his love for any of them. But she remembered her discussions with Gracey, and with Jake who knew Brixton best of all.

"Brixton, I love you. I truly do, and I've known practically forever. I've accepted you as who you are. It wouldn't be fair to do differently. You need open space, and no roof or walls. Since that's who you are, well, I won't mind if you need to take off sometimes. Just don't leave a note. Let me know for real."

"Oh, Minda. That won't happen."

"Tut, tut, don't make promises," she said. "I'm just laying down some basic rules."

"I mean it, Minda. When you're not at my side, it feels like, well, I can only describe what my old pal Timmy Jacobson said. Truth is, I doctored his leg one time on the trail but he lost it to the gangrene anyway. He said ever after that it felt like he still had his leg attached at the hip, even though it was all the way gone."

"So, Mr. Haynes, you are comparing me to a gangrenous leg?"

His glorious face flushed just for a moment. Then he took her in his arms. "Not at all. What I mean is, wherever you might be, wherever you might go, Minda, my home is you. And I love you. Time was I never thought I'd say the words again, much less feel them. But I do love you, Miz Haynes. With all my heart."

With one hand, Minda brushed tears from her

lashes, love and hope covering each inch of her body with a warmth she knew would comfort her all the days of her life.

"Then, Mr. Haynes, I think it's time for this," she said, nearly breathless. She reached into her pocket for the wedding band she'd bought at the mercantile and gently took Brixton's left hand.

It fit perfectly.

About the author...

A native Californian, Tanya Hanson loves life near the Pacific coast with a real-life hero—her firefighter husband—and two very spoiled black Labs. Her son and daughter survived the college-prep classes she taught as a high school English teacher and went on to obtain their own degrees. These days she just can't get enough of her toddler grandson, but she does take time to snorkel in Hawaii and work on her rose bushes when she's not writing or reading. New England in the fall is just about her favorite place to visit, although New York City and Nebraska run close behind.

Visit her at www.tanyahanson.com

Thank you for purchasing
this Wild Rose Press publication.
For other wonderful stories of romance,
please visit our on-line bookstore at
www.thewildrosepress.com.

For questions or more information,
contact us at info@thewildrosepress.com.

The Wild Rose Press
www.TheWildRosePress.com

Other Cactus Rose titles to enjoy:

OUTLAW IN PETTICOATS by Paty Jager:

Maeve Loman has had her heart crushed before; she isn't about to have it happen again. Zeke Halsey has wanted Maeve Loman since he first set eyes on the prickly schoolteacher. Offering to help her find her father, he hopes to prove he's not going anywhere. Neither one knows the extent to which they will stoop to get the answers they crave.

SECRETS IN THE SHADOWS by Sheridon Smythe:
The lovely widow Lacy had taken in two young children—and the rambunctious little angels wasted no time getting her into trouble with Shadow City's new sheriff...

STANDOFF AT THE WATERIN' HORSE SALOON (Rosette) by Stacy Dawn:

Bridget Schneider has a few things to say to the cowboy who stole her heart over a year ago and never came back—but she's not about to let her anger be hog-tied by sudden...distractions. Jonas might've stolen her heart, but she's sure as shootin' gonna get her pride back.

A LAW OF HER OWN (Miniature Rose) by Linda LaRoque:

When Charity Dawson resigns her father's corporate law firm to pursue a career as a trial lawyer, she gets more of a change than she wanted. She finds herself transported to 1888 Texas in the middle of a murder trial.

Printed in the United States
218975BV00004B/3/P

9 781601 544698